MW00626567

PULSE

JUDY G. WALTERS

64

PULSE

JUDY G. WALTERS

64

Pulse
Copyright © 2021 64 Squares Publishing, LLC

Cover Design by C.S. Fritz
Formatting by Albatross Design Co.
All rights reserved under the Pan-American and International
Copyright Convention. This book may not be reproduced in
whole or in part, except for the brief quotations embodied
in critical articles or reviews, in any form or by any means,
electronic or mechanical, including photocopying, recording, or
by any information storage and retrieval system now known or
hereinafter invented, without permission of the publisher.

*This is a work of fiction. All the names, characters, businesses, places,
events and incidents in this book are either the product of the author's
imagination or used in a fictitious manner. Any resemblance to actual
persons, living or dead, or actual events is purely coincidental.*

ISBN: 978-1-7363342-0-1

This book is dedicated to all the healthcare providers who gave so selflessly of their time, their talents, and often their own lives to serve in the 2020 Covid-19 tour of duty.

PROLOGUE

"Looks like we've got a drowning coming in. Child, ten years old," said Barbara, the nurse on staff at Methodist Hospital. Her blonde wavy hair was exceptionally messy that day, swirling around her blandly pretty face like she'd been swept up in a hurricane, which was totally out of character for her usual tidy self. Even her scrubs were wrinkled, something I meant to give her a hard time about but never ended up having the chance. Barbara and I had a relationship like that. Actually, all of the emergency room staff were pretty tight with one another, and practical jokes were an everyday occurrence. Like the time Dr. Johnson hired a drag queen to show up dressed as a drug rep—conservative little pantsuit and all—to detail me on Nodrah, a new erectile dysfunction drug guaranteed to work in three to five minutes. It wasn't until she broke out in song that I realized that Nodrah was 'hard on' spelled backwards.

I'd practiced at Methodist for the past five years and had the best team a doctor could ask for. We all were well-versed on each other's aspirations, family issues, and personal struggles. We were one large, happy dysfunctional family, and it was that bond that made us one of the best trauma teams in all of Texas.

That day the emergency room was steadily busy. I remember fixing my gaze on a sweet little old lady who was sitting patiently in the waiting room, clenching her shiny, black patent leather purse in her lap. She was thin as a rail, and her tiny feet barely touched the floor. There was an angelic, mysterious look in her hazy blue eyes, filmy with cataracts. She nodded at me, her face almost expressionless, as if to somehow give me a vote of confidence and reassurance until I finally broke away and looked back over at Barbara replying, "Another drowning? That's the third one this week, right? It's the worst part of summer."

Just then the doors to the emergency department opened and in came a stretcher with paramedics flanking it on either side.

"Age ten." One of them barked, wheeling the gurney in. "Mom said he was under for a while, not sure how long, but speculate seven to ten minutes. Where's Dr. Morrison?" He asked impatiently, looking past me. I've encountered many paramedics before, but none that seemed as nervous as this one. No matter how hard I tried, he refused to make eye contact. Instead, he was stoic, blank-faced and clearly going through the motions as if this were some sort of training drill. In hindsight, I was oblivious to the awkwardness that was rapidly filling the room like a poisonous gas, and on top of that, I was annoyed. Why was this guy asking for Morrison when I was standing right in front of him, ready to take charge?

"He's in another bay, why?" I asked, still trying to get a glimpse of the patient. my clipped tone betraying my irritation. Usually the paramedics get out of our way and let us take over, but these two were hovering over the body, rendering it completely impossible for me to make an assessment of the patient's condition.

"The mother is insisting that Dr. Morrison handle this one," mumbled one of the paramedics who was delivering breaths to patient while the other continued chest compressions. Still, neither one of them acknowledged my existence. This particular patient had rolled in with three paramedics, not two, and the third was starting to piss me off. It was as if he'd somehow been appointed the patient's bodyguard, always seeming to stand between me and the gurney. He was a big guy too, well over six feet and at least two hundred and fifty pounds.

I was so put off that I finally looked over at Barbara and said, "Fine. Go tell Dr. Morrison. I'll tag team with him. Where's the Mom?" I asked, scanning the ER for the hysterical parent I knew would be awaiting me.

"She insisted on bringing her own car," said the paramedic in a stoic, low tone. "Should be pulling up any—"

But before he could finish, I saw the frantic face of the mother as she walked into the ER. Her eyes were wide and her pupils so dilated that the color of her eyes was almost nonexistent. She was dressed in a bathrobe and tennis shoes, no socks, her hair twisted up behind her head with a large plastic clip. I felt my heart sink in my chest, and my blood ran cold with fear. It was a face I knew all too well, and a chill went up my spine as I stared at her uncomprehendingly. "No!" I yelled, as turned back toward the paramedics, literally pushing them out of the way, all of them, except the bagger. Even the large one was no match for my adrenaline. I straddled the gurney and put everything I had into the chest compressions I began to administer to the lifeless body beneath my hands, counting out loud each one, as if louder was better.

"Come on, Jeremy," I yelled through my clenched jaw.

The little boy beneath me had no signs of life. His limp, pale body was cold. His wet blonde hair pointing in every direction. His deep summer tan had been replaced with a grey hue, the color of wet cement. As I straddled his blue, Hawaiian print swimsuit, my inner thighs and the seat of my scrub bottoms dampened. The wetness was so cold against my legs. While he had no pulse, mine was racing in stark contrast, the blood thudding through my veins, mocking me with its insistence.

"Bobby," Dr. Morrison said in a soft, comforting tone. Somehow, he'd materialized beside me, and reached up to touch my arm, but the minute he made contact I shoved him away.

"I'm busy!" I snapped, my eyes locked on the boy's face. His lips, I noticed, were the palest shade of blue, like the summer sky. The same sky I remember from our family vacation to Maui the previous year. It was, perhaps, my favorite memory of that trip, watching both kids as they played up and down the beach each night until the big, orange sun was inevitably swallowed by the deep blue of the ocean.

I couldn't take my eyes off him, that face I knew so well, now so still, but I could sense that the room was filling with people, that more and more bodies were starting to surround us.

"Dr. Jackson," Barbara said quietly. "Let us help you."

I didn't stop the compressions, but I did take a moment to look and up noticed the mother, my wife, standing there silently, not even a tear streaking her passive, beautiful face. By this time, tears were not only streaming down my cheeks, but watering Jeremy's chest. I was soaked with tears and sweat, and Jeremy was drenched from the pool of my grief, but my wife, Jaqueline was completely dry, silent, and staring at Jeremy. Like the paramedics, she never made eye contact with me in those moments that seemed to stretch on forever, elongating time.

"You want to help me," I said a bit flustered. "Grab the defibrillator, we're not giving up." To my surprise, nobody moved. They all just stood there as if I were in a nightmare and crying for help on the deaf years of those around me. "Damn it, grab the paddles!" I yelled, my eyes wide with frustration. It was the first and last time they ever heard me yell at them like that.

"Bobby," Dr. Morrison said in a slow, careful voice. "He was already gone when he got here. There's nothing any of us can do. You know that. It's time to stop." His voice was so calm that it stirred a deep well on anger from somewhere inside of me, a fury that rose to the surface quickly, manifesting itself in a growl.

"What's wrong with you?" I yelled as I looked around the room. "All of you. How can you just stand there?" My heart was pounding against my rib cage as if it were trying to break free from the cage of my chest. It was as if I were watching the scene unfold from somewhere high up and far away, hovering somewhere above it all like a specter. I could see it all, hear it all, even myself, but it was as unreal as a movie playing out before me. My whole body felt numb and tingly. I could feel each hair individually as they lifted from my scalp. I had heard about this phenomenon before, when physicians were unable to wear their doctor hat and civilian hat at the same time. I'd never thought that person would be me, but suddenly it was. I couldn't think, I could hardly breathe. There had been no warning. Not even a strange feeling beforehand. Nothing. One minute I was standing at the nurses' station updating charts, a dad of two, and the next minute I was a dad of one. Without warning, my son had been ripped from my life, and there wasn't a damn thing I could do about it.

That knowledge came crashing down on me in a wave, and I collapsed over Jeremy. My warm tears washed over his cold body like a second drowning, or some sort of baptism, which had come far too late. Deep howls came from within my body. *Who's that?* I wondered as I sobbed, unaware that the wailing sounds were coming from the depths of my being. It was as if my soul itself was crying out to God.

Visions of Jeremy played through my head like an old home movie, flickering from one clip to another. The day I held him in my arms for the first time and he grasped my finger with his tiny newborn hand. When he took his first step on his first birthday. I thought of him on the baseball fields, that first hit off the tee when he just stood there cheering in excitement for his accomplishment, and the time he cried all the way home from the championship tournament because he'd struck out as the last batter of the game. I even remembered saying goodbye that morning before I'd left for work. He was asleep and I didn't stop to kiss his forehead in fear that it would wake him. Why didn't I wake him? I howled louder at the thought of the missed opportunity. Oh God, why didn't I give him that last kiss while he could still feel it?

I don't even know how long I was there, but at some point, Dr. Morrison and Barbara pulled me off the gurney. I hung head my head low, forgetting to look back for one last glance. I don't even remember how I got there, but eventually I went home to a house that was silent as a tomb without his presence, his little feet hitting the wood floors as he ran excitedly from room to room. At some point there was a funeral. Then a few years later,

I realized that I'd stopped holding my breath every time the emergency room doors opened. I'd gotten past it all, I told myself, and come out on the other side.

But you never really do. I know that now.

ONE

As I opened my eyes to the darkness of the early dawn, I could almost visualize the tiers of the recessed ceiling. Although I couldn't see the expansive wooden fan blades spinning lazily above, I could feel the breeze they created as it swept across my face and shoulders. I laid there thinking about how much effort had gone into the details of that bedroom, a room I rarely saw. The inner ridge of the drop ceiling was gold leaf, broken only by eight inches of trim. The innermost section, also gold leaf, soared at thirteen feet, creating a vortex. The gold wasn't my idea, but the fan was. I gave into my wife's desire for opulence as a bargaining chip to buy me some much needed comfort. The ceiling fan may not have looked as good as the fancy chandelier she'd planned, but I've always slept with a ceiling fan whirring away above me.

I'm not sure if it was the subtle breeze, the quiet hum, or familiarity that did the trick, nonetheless, it was one of the only times in our marriage where I refused to budge.

A cold, wet nose nudged my cheek until I pulled my arms out from under the covers. It was definitely time to rock-n-roll. Timing was an important part of my job, but as one of my attending physicians taught me back in my residency days, the most important hour to remember was when your shift started. Never, ever be late. During those years, I stopped setting an alarm, not because I'd developed that keen sense of time most doctors were known for, but because I'd already received the perfect alarm clock as a gift. I'm almost certain that when my mother gave it to me, she had no idea it was going to serve as my bugle call. Honeysuckle. Pure white, with golden eyes, and over the years, the once small and delicate Maine Coon kitten had morphed seemingly overnight into twenty-five pounds of pure muscle.

Honeysuckle had my routine down pat, and at exactly 5:00 a.m. each morning, she would pounce on my chest, touch her cold, wet nose against mine and nudge me ever so slightly until I ran my hand over her long, silky fur. She was my refuge throughout residency, even when I lost my mother, who kept her breast cancer a secret so as not to distract from my studies—something I never quite got over. After all, what shot did I have at becoming any kind of a decent doctor if even my own mother wouldn't share her health problems with me? Maybe giving me that little kitten was my mother's way of reminding me that she would always be around.

This particular Tuesday morning, there she was, nudging my nose as usual at exactly 5 a.m. on the dot. I sat up on the edge of the bed, glancing back at Jacqueline as she slept. Jacqueline had never liked Honeysuckle, or my mother for that matter. In fact, Jackie was the only person I ever met who absolutely hated my mother. It should have been a red flag, but my brain was overruled by the fact that Jacqueline was beautiful and that she was the answer to my raging hormones. I couldn't imagine getting through residency without the bouts of daily, passionate lovemaking that took my mind off the cases of the day. I imagined, incorrectly I might add, that every day of our marriage would follow suit.

Everyone had always loved my mother. She stood up straight with her shoulders back and was always punctual, probably because her father was a career Army veteran. At five foot ten, she was the tallest of all her friends. She dyed her blonde hair to keep the grey from showing, and the short cut matched her athletic frame. Some people said she had more energy than most twenty-five-year old's. She was president of her Rotary Club, even receiving Rotarian of the Year more than once. When she died, the Catholic parish I grew up in had people lined up clear out the door. We may not have had much money, but our family had always been rich in friends.

I remember the first Christmas after Jacqueline and I moved into our new house, my mom had spent at least three months sewing a needlepoint tapestry of our new home. She even added our names, along with the names of our children. She had custom framed in an ornately carved golden frame. The day we opened it, Jacqueline looked at it, and back at me, saying just loud enough for mom to hear, "Are you kidding, what is this, 1960? I am not hanging that up, it will ruin the look I'm trying to achieve. Didn't you tell her? Old *World*, Bobby, not old *lady*."

I turned to her, my mouth opening in surprise. I didn't even know what to say. But Mom, true to form, blew it off without saying another word.

I ran my hand over Honeysuckle as she arched her back. Jaqueline lay there so peacefully, her long blonde hair fanned out across the ivory 800 thread count pillowcase, the only thread count that was acceptable to her, even when I was a struggling resident. As broke as we were back then, the sheets always seemed to matter more to her than the grocery budget. The daughter of a highly successful personal injury attorney, she'd grown up on fancy sheets. I grew up on whatever was on sale at Walmart or Target. Now, I was just happy to sleep anywhere, on anything.

As for the sleep thing, being an emergency room physician meant there was not much of that to go around, as sleep was considered a luxury for the privileged few— podiatrists, radiologists, dermatologists, and the like. Let's face it, acne wasn't an emergency unless you were seventeen and it was the day before prom. The world of radiology has changed over the years and x-rays could basically be read from anywhere, including a beach house in the Bahamas. Podiatrists seemed to have it easy, but you couldn't pay me enough to deal with other people's feet all day.

In medical school I remember thinking those types of doctors were sissies or copouts. Doctors who wanted the title but didn't want to get their hands dirty with blood and guts—the test of a real physician. Now that I was older and wiser, a nine-to-five gig sounded pretty good, especially after long nights of endless, mind-bending, adrenaline-rushing cases. Nonetheless, emergency medicine was in my blood, perhaps my DNA, and as my senior colleagues had taught me over the years, once you lived this lifestyle, there was no turning back. When a doctor chooses emergency medicine, it was a choice that lead to addiction, not to drugs or alcohol, but to one's own adrenaline. Unlike the shame of most addictions, this one came with rewards like income and at least some prestige.

Looking back at Jacqueline, I knew all too well that her peaceful, calm self was just an illusion. I watched her as she slept, her long, golden, tanned leg with neatly manicured pink toes peeking out from under the side of the blanket. This sight would have teased most men right back into bed, but not me; I understood clearly what was attached to the other side of that leg. I treaded lightly across the dark, wide-planked walnut floors, careful not to wake her.

The bathroom was oversized, but for good reason. We each had our own side, with plenty of storage and counter space. The stainless steel digital scale bumped up against the end of the sink, probably because I was the one who used it every morning. That morning, Honeysuckle was perched upon the white Carrara marble countertop. She looked down at the lit up number on the scale and back up at me with her ears slightly turned back, as if to show her disapproval. "Don't look at me like that," I whispered. "Ok, so I need to lay off the donuts." Just then I realized that I was whispering to my cat, and I knew they made medication for that. As crazy as it seemed, talking to my cat was like talking to my mom. She even looked at me with my mom's expressions. Like the look of disappointment when she saw the scale read 199. It was as if I could hear my mom saying, "Nothing over 200 looks good unless you're over 6' 3." And at 6' 1, I knew that 198 was seriously pushing it.

I caught a glimpse of my aging face in the bathroom mirror. It wasn't that I was really old, but something happened to a person's features after forty. That something was happening to me. My blue eyes, the ones that I attributed my high school dating success, had lost their sparkle. They looked much better when they were surrounded by solid white, not the blood shot streaks of a busy life. Those dimples I used to have had faded into the lines across each side of my mouth. As I looked a little closer, I noticed that my disheveled blonde hair and the two days' worth of stubble on my face made me look like nothing short of homeless.

Nothing could've been further from the truth. Not only was I standing in a 200-square foot master bathroom, the bathroom was inside of our 8,700-square foot home. Jacqueline once said that anything under 6,000 square feet would make her feel claustrophobic, so when we built the house, it was at the top, the very top, of our agreed upon budget. Then, of course, the pool and landscaping blew that budget completely to smithereens. So, like any good husband, I took on extra shifts to pay for it all. It wasn't so much about keeping her happy, I needed to keep her calm and keep the peace. I would do anything to keep the peace, and staying out of the house was a win-win for both of us, or so it seemed.

I hit the button on the wall so that the shower would come on when the temperature reached exactly 102 degrees, then climbed in, pulling the hinged glass door behind me. The warm water beat down from the rainfall shower head and swept across my body. I could feel it hit my broad shoulders and then split apart, covering both my front and back almost evenly. As I rinsed the shampoo from my hair, I saw Honeysuckle batting at the shower door, chasing the water droplets as they zig-zagged down the glass.

Walking toward the kitchen, I passed the large wall of windows just off the living room. It was the perfect frame for the sparkling turquoise pool and lush greenery of the backyard, especially in the spring and summer months. I never really wanted the pool, but Jackie did, she insisted that our children grow up with a pool out back, just as she had. She said it was for the kids, but I knew the truth. She couldn't be the only house on the block without one. Besides, where would she spend all her time? I stopped for a moment and glanced out the window. It was dark and quiet, but the longer I looked, the more I could see the memories, the kids laughing and splashing in the summer sun, the golden rays dancing on the water, making it sparkle like diamonds. "Marco," BJ, would say. Bobbie Joe, or BJ as we called her, was the oldest. Echoed by "Polo" from Jeremy, our feisty little seven-year-old. I could see myself flipping burgers on the oversized stainless steel Viking grill and Jackie doing what she did best: baking her own tanned flesh, poolside, in her little yellow bikini.

The smile on my freshly shaven face faded away almost as fast as it had materialized. Suddenly, I could see Jeremy's face so clearly, bubbles rising up, as his eyes grew wide with panic. It was a sight I'd never actually seen, but one I'd imagined time and time again. What if I had been home that afternoon? I was almost certain it would never have happened. This was a burden I could never seem to let go of. We had an agreement that the kids could only swim if one of us was out there, I trusted Jacqueline to be there, and to be watching. She never could explain how he'd been underwater for more than ten minutes before she called 911. The day they rolled Jeremy into my emergency room was the worst day of my life. Out of all the patients I'd saved over the years, why couldn't I save my own son? I tried to focus in the months that followed, but all I could see was his lifeless body on that stretcher. After that day, I instructed the staff to only use the room he had been in if it was absolutely necessary. Eventually, I couldn't do it anymore. I had to leave Methodist Hospital and the position I had worked so diligently to obtain.

I shook my head, as if to snap out of it. I'd let my mind travel down this path countless times, a path that led to a very dark place. I knew better than to do it again, so I shut it down, buried my thoughts, and continued on to the kitchen, turning my attention to a case I'd had a few weeks back. It was a forty-five-year-old male who showed up in the ER with a curious blue tint to his skin. Usually when people come in blue, they're completely unresponsive, if not outright dead. This patient was not only conscious, he was a bit of a know-it-all. Not only was he rude to the nursing staff, but he sat there with his arms folded, rolling his eyes at every question I asked, looking like a belligerent Smurf. After much back and forth, I had the answer. Argyria—a condition caused by continued use of colloidal silver. Brainy Smurf, apparently turned to Dr. Google to treat his recurrent sinus infections. Now, he had an irreversible skin condition. Karma really was a bitch.

My body was up and moving, but my brain couldn't fully function without my drug of choice—Barista Prima Italian Roast. In medical school I'd lived on Dunkin Donuts coffee, but somewhere along the way, I'd become some kind of a coffee connoisseur. Or maybe an idiot savant—I still wasn't sure. After all, I couldn't afford to be a wine connoisseur, not with my mortgage. There was also the thought in the back of my head that if I ever started drinking, I might never stop. I knew full well that I could easily become an alcoholic, just to escape the pressures and disappointment of my own bad marriage, behavior I'd witnessed in my own patients more times than I could count.

Unlike Jacqueline, I didn't need fancy, expensive things. Well, except for my car. I always told myself that my reward for graduating medical school would be a sports car. One marriage, two kids, and five years later I finally drove my metallic blue, BMW Z-4 off the lot. It was a bit extravagant, but the little boy in me, the one that had ridden around in my parent's ten-year-old tan station wagon, the one they passed down to me at age sixteen, had always dreamed of being a superhero. And superheroes drove sports cars.

That morning, I slid into the black leather seat, I was already in full uniform, blue scrubs that tied at the waist with the logo for St. Mary's Emergency Department stamped across the chest pocket. As the garage door opened, the light poured out onto the driveway, a reminder of just how early it was. The other houses on my street, the ones owned by lawyers, bankers, and business owners, all remained dark, with the exception of the lights that glowed from behind the front shrubs and onto the brick and stone facades. Each house standing two stories tall, just high enough to be seen from behind the fortress-like brick wall and iron gate designed to keep out any sort of unwanted trouble.

I could feel the java penetrating my brain, and after the usual fifteen-minute drive to the hospital. I parked in one of the spots marked "Doctors Only," and walked toward the sliding glass doors of the emergency department. The bright lights inside were a reminder that no matter what time of day or night it was outside, the inside of an emergency room is where the sense of time is lost against the backdrop of more important matters, like life and death. The expansive overhead lights seemed to hum quietly in the background. With the addition of various beeping machines, the opening and closing of automatic doors, and the howls of pain or despair, any emergency department has an almost orchestral sound, one that illustrates whatever drama, thriller, or horror story that's playing out. To most people this was just cacophony, but to a trained conductor, each sound is heard and deciphered in its own context.

"Here's the list," Dr. Roberts said, shoving a piece of paper into my hands before I'd even so much as had the chance to look around and assess the situation. "Let's get through it as fast as we can, I have a honey-do list a mile long waiting for me when I get home," he added rolling his eyes a bit. John Roberts was a good doctor, one I never minded coming in behind. He graduated top of his class, albeit thirty years ago, and his education and experience made up for his matter-of-fact bedside manner. I also admired his dedication to his family, especially his wife, who kept him plenty busy. His brown hair was thinning around the crown of his head and his green eyes were surrounded by slightly drooping eyelids. The wrinkles on his face, especially those across his forehead looked as though he carried the weight of the world, or at least the weight of working the night shift, for decades.

The patient list was filled with the usual: gastroenteritis, cardiac observation, domestic dispute injury, and pelvic pain. All of which Dr. Roberts pretty much had under control.

"Cardiac enzymes are back," said Mary, an older nurse I had worked with for the last few years. Her perfect posture made her 5' 2" frame seem much taller, and her neatly pressed scrubs and brown shoulder-length bob matched her conservative and professional demeanor. "They're normal. Do you want me to start the admission paperwork for twenty-three-hour observation?" Mary was always respectful, not to mention almost weirdly intuitive, which made my job a hell of a lot easier.

"Yes, and get a cardiac consult ordered so he can have a stress echo first thing in the morning," I replied.

"Oh, and room four, the older lady with pelvic pain, she has a list of her own for you. She pulled it out after Dr. Roberts left. Sorry," she added almost sheepishly.

She knew how much I hated lists. They're great for primary doctors, but emergency room docs don't have time for lists. Being that this patient was 67, I was hoping her list wasn't derived from an exhaustive internet search.

About fifteen minutes passed and I stepped out of room four, giving a thumbs up to Mary. She knew that I had successfully convinced Mrs. Johnson that she didn't have cancer, some rare disease of the intestinal tract, or Parkinson's. She simply should avoid eating things like popcorn, nuts and seeds for a while until her lower intestinal tract had time to heal from diverticulitis. Mary looked back with a smile and a return thumbs up, a sign that she was starting the discharge papers.

Just then, the flashing lights of the ambulance filled the entrance and the front doors swooshed open. Atop a stretcher was a teenage boy, blood dripping from his forehead. His right pant leg had been cut open, exposing a white flash of bone, the tibia sticking out from the side of his lower leg. "17-year-old male, MVA. Compound fracture to the right leg. Vitals stable, but he was unconscious when we arrived. Single vehicle accident," chanted the paramedic as I walked beside the gurney towards an open bay.

"Single vehicle?" I wanted to clarify, since a single vehicle accident potentially added a whole new dimension to his care.

"Yes. According to some witnesses, his car drifted off the side of the highway, right down the embankment." On the count of three he lifted his side of the sheet, transferring the patient from his gurney to ours.

"Did it roll? I need to try and understand if he passed out before or during the accident."

"It didn't roll, but we're not sure. Since he hit his head on the windshield, it's hard to say?" He replied.

"No airbag?"

"Not in a 1978 Ford Mustang," he replied as if he were a little annoyed. "Another classic headed to the junk yard. Pretty much totaled." His head shook in disappointment. "Not sure why kids are allowed to have that much power to begin with."

I shined the ophthalmoscope in the patient's eyes to check his pupils, "Kids?" I said with a chuckle, looking back up at the paramedic with a grin, "Isn't that the pot calling the kettle black? What are you, early 20's?" The paramedic shrugged his shoulders a bit. "That's a significant amount of power and responsibility you drove up in today. Complete with sirens and lights, too," I added with a wink.

The dispatcher on his shoulder-clipped radio called out to him. He smiled, shook his head, and waved good-bye as he grabbed hold of his gurney, taking it back with him. "We're on our way," he replied back to dispatch picking up his pace as he ran down the hall.

"So, hot-rod, do you have a name?" I asked.

His face was peppered with acne and he smelled of sweat. That teenage, hormonal sweat that worsens with nerves. "Michael," he replied, wincing his bloodshot blue eyes in pain.

"Ok Michael, I will give you something for pain in a minute, but first I have to ask you a few questions. How you answer will help me better understand how to treat you. Ok?" I looked at him and tried to offer a comforting smile.

He didn't speak but attempted to nod his head yes as he grimaced.

"Do you remember going off the road?"

"No. Not really." He managed to push the words from between his clenched teeth.

"What's the last thing you remember? Any weird symptoms?" I looked up at Mary who was standing bedside and ready to type anything pertinent into his medical record. "Any history of seizures?"

"No," he said, wincing again. There was a pause and then he added, "I did have a funny feeling in my chest, like a flip flop, and then I felt like I needed to . . . to cough."

I looked at Mary and nodded. She typed, knowing exactly what I was thinking.

Just then the curtain pulled back and a tall blonde woman, roughly forty years old stood with one hand on the curtain and the other holding a brown, monogram, Louis Vuitton shoulder- bag, the same one my wife owned. "What happened? Are you ok? Oh my gosh! I have to call your Dad," she said reaching in her bag for her cell phone. "Is he going to be ok?" she asked looking at me with wide, frightened eyes.

"He'll be ok, but I need to ask you to wait outside for just a moment." I looked and nodded at Jennifer, another nurse who had followed in behind her. The two of them almost looked like twins, both blonde and relatively tall. Taking the mother's arm, Jennifer steered her back toward the emergency waiting area.

"Ford Mustang, huh?" I said, looking at Michael. "I bet it was a King Cobra."

"How did you know?" he said with a smile that followed with a grimace of pain.

"The paramedics told me it was a 1978. They changed the body style after that. It was a great year for the Mustang."

"He knows a little about everything, Michael. That's what makes him a great doctor," Mary said with a smile and a wink.

"So, how many energy drinks did you have today?" I asked.

"Three . . . or four," he said closing his eyes for just a moment to escape the pain. "Why?"

"I think you had a heart arrhythmia—an irregular heartbeat. That's what made you feel the urge to cough. We're going to get some tests going, Hot-Rod. And I'm gonna go chat with your mom. Mary, here—they call her Nurse Feel Good—she's gonna get you something for your pain. Oh, and stay away from those drinks in the future," I said, placing my hand on his shoulder, looking him right in his blue eyes to make sure he heard me.

"Michael is going to be fine," I told his mother who relayed that message almost simultaneously to his father. "This is what keeps orthopedic surgeons in business. He'll need surgery."

"How did this happen?" She asked. "What about the other driver?"

"It was just his car. Luckily, he didn't hit anyone else. I think he may have passed out from an arrhythmia caused by the energy drinks, but its standard protocol to rule out any congenital heart issues. Besides, he took a pretty nasty hit to that noggin of his, so I'll need to get a CT of his head. He'll probably be here for a couple of days."

As I walked back to the station to call the orthopedic surgeon, I heard Jennifer quietly ask the others, "Has anyone told him?"

"Told me what?" I asked looking at a sea of guilty expressions that stood around the desk. Each one of them avoiding eye contact.

Then Sergei, the janitor, whose olive skin and dark hair matched his Russian accent, got a big smile across his face. He stood up tall, as tall as he could with his short stature, and said with pride, "You won. It's official."

"Won what?" I said holding the phone to my ear. As I looked around people were giving Sergei dirty looks as if he ruined some sort of surprise "Sorry," I added as I held up my first finger. "This is Bobby over at St. Mary's. I have a 17-year-old male with a compound fracture to the right tibia . . . yep . . . yep . . . thanks, Bruce."

Sergei still had the big grin on his face and by then the others were grinning too. Jennifer said, "Ok, cat's out of the bag. We really wanted to tell you this in a quiet moment, but—"

They all chimed in, "Emergency Medicine Physician of the Year!" As they clapped, raised their hands and let out the sounds of whooping and hollering.

I must have looked shocked by the way my eyebrows raised and my eyes widened. I didn't even know they knew about that award. "Thank you. I know you guys all had something to do with this. Besides, a doctor is only as good as the team he works with, and I have the best team in the entire country," I said, my voice rough with emotion, looking over at Mary and back at Jennifer. "Maybe this should be the Emergency Team of the Year award." I patted each of them on the back, trying not to get too emotional, but I could feel my face flushing in spite of my efforts to stay calm and collected.

Mary leaned in and said, "Well, it's quite the event, black tie and all. So, will we finally get to meet her?" She held out her hand and dangled it as if to show off a wedding band, "Mrs. Jackson." All the attention suddenly turned from the award to my love life, or lack thereof.

Suddenly, all the joy I was feeling dissipated. My stomach felt sour almost instantly, and I could feel my blood pressure rise with dread. I wanted to yell NO, but all I could muster was a weak, "Probably. We'll see. She's very busy." I couldn't believe I just said that. Busy? Doing what? Shopping? "This isn't really her thing, but maybe," I said quickly, trying to brush it off and hoping it would end the conversation.

Jennifer looked at me with wide eyes and with a bit of sarcasm said, "Not her thing? Seriously? I don't care if it's her thing or not, it's *your* thing. Doesn't that count at all?"

I opened my mouth to speak but closed it again in a weak smile. Just then, Dr. Bruce Ortega, the orthopedic surgeon, walked up. "I heard the good news," he said. He'd made it over to the emergency room in what seemed like record time.

"Bruce, who are you, The Flash?" I asked, grateful that he saved me from that dreaded conversation. Bruce was the quintessential orthopedist, muscular, cocky, and a chick magnet. His thick sandy hair rippled across the top of this head, and his scrubs looked a size too small, at least for his biceps, but I am pretty sure that was intentional. My stubble just made me look old, but his stubble made him look like one of the handsome doctors on *Grey's Anatomy*. I often noticed the nurses and other hospital staff checking him out in the cafeteria.

"I was actually rounding on another patient upstairs when you called. Mrs. Jackson, huh. Yeah, I'd like to meet her. If you don't produce her this time, we're all going to think that beautiful tall blonde in the photo on your locker is someone you Photoshopped off the internet." His words were met with a community chuckle from the group. I wanted Bruce to meet her all right—sweep her right off her feet and take her away . . .

I'd felt my phone buzzing in my pocket for the last half-hour or so. I'd tried to ignore it, but I knew that if I didn't answer it, it would only make things worse. "Hang on. I have to take this," I said putting my hand up as I slipped away from the desk and into an empty exam room.

"I am really busy," I said sternly as I closed the exam room door behind me.

"Busy? You don't know busy," she started screaming. "Do you think I have nothing better to do than clean up after you? I am not going to tell you again, stop leaving your pods in the Keurig. I don't have time for this! What the hell's wrong with you?"

I stood there thinking that she must have been equipped with some kind of radar. Anytime I have a moment of happiness, she finds a way to take it away. "Look, I really need to get back to patients," I said, trying to end the conversation as soon as possible.

Then, in a mocking tone she said, "Patients. *Oh, your precious patients.*" She paused, then went off on tangent that ended in, "I bet you just want to get back to breasts and vaginas. Why do I have to be married to the guy who looks at other women all day?" She yelled, her voice screeching through the phone.

"Stop. Just stop it!" I said in with my jaw clenched and my lips tightened. There was a long pause, during which I thought of all the horrible things I really wanted to respond with, but instead I simply said in a commanding voice, "I'm hanging up now. Don't call back. I'll see you tonight."

As I walked back by the nurse's station, they were all there. Everyone was still smiling and laughing. I was only gone for a moment, but it was as if I had traveled miles away in my head. My body was present, but my brain was numb. It was like living a double life, one for my body and one for my brain. My body was strong and able to go through the motions as if on autopilot. My brain, on the other hand was short circuiting, flickering between Jaqueline's words and what was being said right there in the emergency room. "Ok, let's break up the party," I said with a forced, fake smile. "Everyone back to work." A few seconds went by and nobody had moved. I raised a hand to shoo them away and with my best try at a Hispanic accent I yelled "Andale!"

The rest of the shift was spent conducting a symphony of cases, none of which stuck out as unusual or particularly interesting. It was hard to be present in the moment when my head was swimming with what-ifs. What if everyone learns the truth about Jacqueline? These people didn't even know about Jeremy. I came to this hospital for a fresh start. The plan was to fly under the radar. Now, I was glowing like an unidentified flying object about to be discovered and dissected.

TWO

The last few nights had been nothing but a storm of arguments with Jaqueline. Her glares were lightning bolts and the words that followed were claps of thunder. "I hate you," she would scream, holding a margarita in one hand. "You're stupid and I don't know why everyone thinks you're so great." She even went as far as to criticize my physical appearance. "Too bad you don't look as strong and handsome as the man I married," she said with a look of contempt, poking me in the stomach with one long, pointed, red fingernail. Her shiny hair, perfect nails, and well-sculpted body was result of a woman with too much time on her hands.

Her time and my hard-earned money, to be exact.

I tried to ignore her, but she just wouldn't let up. Her tantrums always brought out the worst in me. I found myself slamming the door with a few expletives and then going for a drive with no real destination in mind. Even though I was driving down the same streets I'd navigated many times before, I felt lost. Hopeless. Most people couldn't wait to get home, but I usually couldn't wait to get *away from* home. I found myself wondering if all the other homes with their neatly manicured lawns were filled with couples entangled in complicated and messy relationships like mine. Were they all chasing each other around the house giggling like teenagers, or exchanging heated words over seemingly irrelevant topics?

It was good that I had never taken to drinking, but if I had, this would have been a great time to tie one on. I remembered a patient of mine, Jerry, a large, friendly African American man who'd frequented the last emergency room where I worked, who'd been injured working in the backyard, drunk. When I asked him why he was doing yard work while drinking, he dropped his head down, raised one eyebrow and replied, "Doc, are you married?" Before I could answer his question, he added, "I am and you know that if you're married, you *gotta* drink." Over the past few years, Jerry's advice had actually started to make sense to me.

My shoulders and back were stiff from sleeping on the living room sofa, but it was a small price to pay if it meant I didn't have to sleep with the enemy. I entered St. Mary's still a bit drowsy from the night before, which had been perhaps the worst night of them all. Jaqueline was screaming about our teenage daughter, BJ for most of the evening, and how she didn't have time to be her personal chauffeur. Of course, a volcanic eruption occurred when

I asked her what exactly she did all day. I felt it was a fair question given that we had a housekeeper come three times a week and Jacqueline long ago decided that she no longer liked to cook. Besides, driving a child to school and then seven hours later home again didn't exactly qualify for chauffeur status.

Nonetheless, my question caused Jaqueline's face to turn beet red as she growled at me, ripping the sheets from the sofa. Then she grabbed my pillow and stomped off, her silky red nightgown billowing behind her. As she turned to me and sneered, I couldn't help but think that the devil might actually be female. She slammed the bedroom door and then I heard the click of the lock, a sound I was all too familiar with. If it wasn't for the warmth of Honeysuckle, who curled up next to me, the night would have been unbearable. I even had to shower upstairs, and my hair smelled of BJ's herbal scented shampoo. The slightly medicinal scent of rosemary was a sharp reminder of why I've stayed all these years.

"Jackson, my man," said Jarrod his big smile and wide eyes, both in stark contrast to his deep skin tone. "Are you ready to save some lives today?" Before I could say *not really,* he grasped my hand and pulled me in close, giving me one of his famous bro-hugs. He leaned in and sniffed again. "Flowers?" He said joking, "I think you grabbed your pretty little mamma's shampoo this morning."

Pretty little mamma? I thought darkly. *Not exactly.* Jarrod was an emergency room technician whose two hundred and fifty pounds and six-foot something stature would be intimidating if it weren't for his warm heart, something that was evident the moment you met him. He was the first one to push the wheelchair of an elderly patient or give a brightly colored sticker to a child soaked in tears. Jarrod was somehow always aware of the needs of others, always living in the moment. He was the master of mindfulness before it was even a catch phrase.

I met him on my first shift at St. Mary's. He took me under his wing, showing me the ropes. Whenever I couldn't find a piece of equipment, an instrument, or even the basics, he would be right there, handing it to me before I even had a chance to ask. Later I found out that he was clocking out and then staying by my side, just so someone would, "have my back." He did this for about two months. HR told me that he donated at least twenty hours of his own time to my cause.

It also didn't hurt having Jarrod around when the drunk and disorderly cases came in. One night after he broke up a fight between two drunks who had been arguing over a Dallas Cowboys vs Washington Red Skins game, I told him to add resident bouncer to his resume. He looked up at me with a big smile and a bloody lip and said with a wink, "You know Doc, even if it wasn't my job, no Cowboy's fan is going to get his butt kicked on my shift." A few days later I gave him some tickets to the next game. Anyone who's willing to take a punch to defend the honor of the home team deserved it.

"Hey Jarrod, I missed you. Looks like you had a few days off lately. What's up with that? This is the ER. We don't keep banker's hours around here. Besides, HR has strict instructions to always schedule you on my shift," I said half-jokingly.

"I know. I'm the one that told them to schedule me that way," he replied with a head tilt and a smile that faded to a more serious look. "No man, I had some serious studying to do. School is kickin' my . . ." He took his hand and smacked his behind, mouthing the word boo-tay, but not saying it out loud. He looked me in the eye and added, "But I'm back. Promise."

I took a boxer's stance and delivered a soft punch to his huge bicep and said, "Good, I can't work without my muscle wing man." As my fist hit his arm, it was a reminder that I needed to work out more, way more. His bicep was the size of my quad and hard as a rock. Luckily, he didn't hit me back. "Besides, we can't work the ER without our first line of defense against the crazies."

Jennifer came around the corner, her curly blonde hair was pulled back in a scrunchy that matched her hot pink scrubs. She grabbed the stethoscope from around her neck and placed it on the nurse's station, "Oh, don't worry, Jarrod, looks like someone else took over security around here. She may not be a big brother like you, but trust me, I wouldn't want to cross her." Jennifer's eyes looked over at Elizabeth, the new nurse, and she nodded for Jarrod's eyes to follow hers across the room. Soon, we were all gazing at the new girl. She was petite, but strong, like a gymnast and looked to be in her mid-thirties. Her thick, curly hair was tied back in a ponytail. We were gawking at her as if she were on display at the zoo. Actually, there was some truth in that. She was on display, and the emergency room, well, on most days it was a zoo.

"Ooh, a red head." Jarrod shivered a bit. "No ma'am, I wouldn't mess with her either," he continued shaking his head and then started looking down as to not make eye contact with Elizabeth.

"You are both overreacting. Tough is good, and we could use a bit of that around here. You can't all be sucking up to the boss, just to get dibs on the first break," I replied, clearing my throat and making sure I made eye contact with both Mary and Jennifer.

Mary had just walked into the conversation, but ended it with, "Flattery will get you—"

Just then the emergency doors opened and in walked a tall, thin young man in jeans and a T-shirt that read "Who's Your Daddy?" holding on to a women with long dark hair, which hung in snarls around her face, and dripping with sweat. She was hugely pregnant, looking as if she were about to explode, and on top of this, she was pale and weak, her face drained of color. Just as she made eye contact with me, I saw her eyes roll back in her head as she collapsed in her husband's arms. His thin frame wasn't strong enough to hold her limp, and very pregnant body up. But before she could hit the floor, Jarrod was right there, single handedly scooping her up and carrying her to the first open room. This was one of those times when Jarrod reminded me of the Hulk, only a blacker, friendlier version.

Jarrod placed her on the bed and pulled his arms out from under her slowly as her knees dropped down. I noticed that Jared's right arm was covered in blood. The man noticed it too. Nobody had to tell him something was wrong, he knew. His pupils were large, the way the eyes of animals were when they're on high alert. "You ok?" I asked, glancing over at the man, who now looked almost as pale as his pregnant wife. The last thing we needed was for him to faint. Husbands of pregnant women were notorious for fainting when things get real.

"Yeah," he muttered shakily. "I'm her husband. Please don't make me leave," he said as he grabbed the foot of the bed in an attempt to stay upright.

"You're not going anywhere." I said calmly, but firmly. "I need you to stay here and answer some questions." I looked right into his frightened blue eyes. "Can you do that? Can you stay calm and help me? I'm counting on you."

"Yes," he said swallowing hard and tightening his grip on the footboard. "I can do that."

"Good," I replied as I looked across her lifeless body. She was about 5'6" and looked fairly fit. She was breathing and had a pulse, both good signs. "What's her date of birth? And what's the expected due date of this baby?" We were all scurrying around the bed working quickly as each second counts in a situation like this. Jennifer had already started the IV, taking a vial of blood for type and cross match.

I looked at Jennifer and said sharply, "We don't have time for cross match. Get me six units of o negative. STAT!" Everyone on my team knew what that meant. They knew that time was not on our side and that there was a good chance this patient could die.

The husband looked at his wife and back at me matching his answers to the speed of my voice, "June 8, 1993. Our boy, he's due in just three more weeks. I don't know what happened. She was fine this morning. She even had a checkup yesterday and everything seemed to be on schedule."

Mary moved to the other side of the bed to get the blood pressure. "80/60,"she said, looking at me to be sure I had heard.

"Who's her doctor? Michaels? Farrin?" I asked, hoping it was someone on staff.

"It's O'Brian. This isn't the hospital we were going to deliver at, but this was the closest one. Will he come here?" He asked, looking a little confused.

"I'll call him," said Elizabeth.

"No," Mary snapped. He was not on staff here. "Jennifer, call Farrin, STAT, he may actually be upstairs rounding."

The IV was wide bore, open with the hopes of getting fluids in as fast as they were leaving. The oxygen was flowing and the bed was tilted head down. The woman, although lucid, was alive. The baby, well, that was to be determined.

The woman opened her eyes slightly and the husband came right up next to me, almost pushing me aside to get to her, "Abigail, I'm here. Everything's going to be fine. Don't worry," he said in tone that was shaky and unconvincing.

"Abigail, huh?" I said, as I gently pushed the husband out of the way. "Ok, Abigail, I have to ask your husband to move back, but I promise, he'll be right here in the room with us."

I looked over at her husband, whose face was now streaming with tears, and asked, "Drug allergies?"

"No. None that we know of. Is she going to make it? Is my son?" I could see the panic across his ashen face, his lip quivering.

Elizabeth came back into the room. To my surprise she had found a handheld Doppler. My guess was that Jarrod had found it for her. She lifted the bloodied gown and squirted clear gel on Abigail's abdomen. The woman's lifeless body didn't flinch, even though I knew from experience that the gel was cold. She placed the Doppler over the gel, looking for the heartbeat. The room seemed to get a little quitter as if we were all holding our breath in hopes for a miracle. She moved it to the left, then to the right. Then, cutting through the tension of the room the sound of a very fast beat was heard. Elizabeth looked that the doppler and back up with a smile, "170."

"That's good. We have a heartbeat. It's a little higher than I'd like," I said, trying to mask the concern I felt.

"Probably due to the loss of blood," Elizabeth said. "I have labor and delivery sending down a fetal heart monitor so we can check for contractions. She feels tight."

Almost as fast as she said that, the monitor arrived. "Great job, Elizabeth," I said as she pulled the straps across the abdomen, hooking everything up.

"Ten years in L&D," she said crisply as she finished strapping on the monitor. "How about I focus on the baby while you take care of mom?" Wow, I thought, I never had a nurse dictate the roles before, but I rather enjoyed it. From the surprised look on Mary's face, followed by the roll of her eyes I think I was alone in that sentiment.

I wanted to tell the husband everything was going to be fine, but in cases like this one, that's not always true. I was pretty sure Abigail had placenta previa, which is when the placenta grows over or near the cervical opening. Often times these patients can bleed to death, and the babies were still born. The fact that she'd made it into the hospital so fast might have been her saving grace.

"Was she bleeding before you came in?" I asked, looking over at the husband.

Before I could answer, Jennifer came in with the six pints of blood I'd asked for. "We need a consenting signature," she said, looking at me and then over at the husband.

I asked quickly, "Can we get your permission to give your wife blood?" His face went blank, and he opened his mouth as if to speak, then closed it quickly. I could sense his hesitation, so my voice got a little louder and much sterner. "She really needs it. It'll help her and your baby boy. The sooner Abigail gets this blood, the better off both she and the baby will be." I motioned Jennifer to have him sign. Every minute was starting to feel like an eternity.

The husband nodded his head, then realized he hadn't actually said anything out loud, "Sorry. Yes. Yes, whatever she needs. Just do it." He scribbled his name and then added. "She said she felt something warm. I guess she thought maybe her water had broken, but when she put her hand down there to check, it was blood, not water. That must have been when it started, in the car. I brought her here because you were so close. We were just a couple blocks away, heading to her sister's house for breakfast."

"Jennifer, go check on O'Brian." I looked back at the husband, "So, she hasn't eaten anything yet?" I asked in hopes he would say she hadn't.

"No, nothing yet. Why?"

I made an audible sigh of relief. "That's good, because—"

Jennifer came back in the room, "O'Brian said send her up to O.R. number two. He just wrapped up a C-section in O.R. one and is scrubbing back in for this one."

"95/70," said Mary, smiling at me because things were moving in the right direction. The blood had already made a difference and the increased blood pressure would improve her chances of surviving the surgery.

"O.R.? Isn't that operating room? Wait, is she having surgery?" asked the husband in a panicked voice. I wanted to say *Of course she is, otherwise she'll be dead and so will your son.* He suddenly looked as if it were all becoming real to him, his eyes darting back and forth between us, as if he was trying to catch up with the conversation and make sense of it all. Things were moving so fast.

The dialogue in my head was more like: *Move it buddy, I don't have the time to deal with you,* but I quickly shut that off. Knowing what it was like to be a dad, I knew that what he needed at that moment was both hope and reassurance. After all, he was part of that parenting equation, too. I came down to the end of the bed, pulled off my gloves, and then put my left hand on his shoulder, "That due date you gave me," I said, reaching out with my right and shaking his hand. "Well, change that to today. O'Brian's good. Real good." His eyes looked down at the blood soaked floor and his shoulders drooped a bit. "Hey," I said as I lowered my head to make eye contact. "You did the right thing. Stopping here, that was the smartest thing you could have done. Jarrod's going to take her up. You can go with him, but you'll need to wait in the O.R. waiting room."

Jarrod gripped the head of the bed, his arms spread wide, and sprinted down the hall toward the anesthesiologist who had come down from surgery and was holding the elevator door open. Mary was at the foot of the bed, keeping a careful eye on Abigail. The husband followed right behind Jarrod and soon all four were crowded in the elevator. As for the rest of us, we stood there in the aftermath of the storm. The room, once a tornado of excitement was now eerily calm. The floor was littered with empty packaging, IV supplies, and towels soaked in the blood that was also smeared across the floor. Elizabeth and I looked at each other, her lips pressed firmly together as she nodded her head as if to say, "We did all we could." Instead of returning the nod, I simply looked down and slowly walked out. As I left, I heard her ask Jennifer, "Is he all right?"

"He'll be fine," she said solemnly. "But, if you need him in the next ten minutes or so, you'll have to page him." Jennifer knew precisely where I was headed, and it wasn't upstairs to the O.R.

Whoever built St. Mary's knew exactly what they were doing because they put the chapel just down the hall from the emergency room. As I sat in the front row pew, a place I frequented quite often, I thought back to the woman lying still on the gurney, imagining her prostrate body on the operating table as they sliced into her. I prayed that I'd done everything I could. I thought about how young and naive they both seemed. Either way, their lives were about to change forever, but I hoped it would be because they were parents to a healthy, new baby boy.

I sat there a few more moments, thinking back to the day BJ was born. She was so perfect, even Jaqueline was close to normal back then. We were fortunate not to have any emergencies like Abigail's, or other countless pregnant women who come through my emergency room. For a moment, I envisioned Jaqueline in the bed, holding BJ.

She was probably the only new mother on the ward that refused to wear a hospital gown, but needless to say, she looked beautiful in her baby blue silk kimono. We wanted the gender to be a surprise, but the fact that she'd brought a blue gown to the hospital was a dead giveaway for her preference.

Jaqueline had always said she would name the first child after me. I guess that's why I always assumed it was going to be a boy. Although it was a girl, she still kept her word, and we named her Bobby Joe. The second I laid eyes on my baby girl, the desire for a boy evaporated. She was so perfect, so small, and so fragile. For a split second, I was pulled back into the happiest day of my life. It was that memory that had allowed me to hang in there through the years, but the more distance that grew between that day and the present, the more I could begin to visualize a life without Jaqueline. But how could I let my little girl, my namesake, down? BJ was my pride and joy. How do you look at a child and tell them you hate their mother and that life would be so much more enjoyable if you'd never married her in the first place?

Before I knew it fifteen minutes had passed. As I rounded the last corner back into the emergency department I ran smack into Elizabeth. With an almost expressionless face, her eyes met mine. It was the first time I had looked at her, really looked at her close up, and I couldn't help noticing her green eyes that seemed to shine like emeralds. I dropped my gaze quickly, feeling guilty for even noticing. "Oh good," she said authoritatively. "Just the person I was looking for." She put her hands on her hips, just like an old grade school teacher of mine used to do and planted her feet shoulder width apart. "I'd like a list of all the specialists on staff here at St. Mary's. Put a star next to the ones you prefer. If you get it to me by the end of the shift, I'll have it memorized by tomorrow." Then, without even waiting for me to agree, she turned around and marched straight into an exam room. With her back to me, she missed the fact that I clicked my heels and saluted her as if to say, "Aye, Aye Captain!"

Much to my embarrassment, I turned and there was Sergei. He had one hand on his mop and he was fighting back a smile. When I gave him a sheepish grin, he allowed the rest of the smile to spread slowly across his face, and I had to break eye contact. Sergei and I had always had a great working relationship, but it was one where he seemed to always show respect towards me, deference I guess you could say. As I stood there cringing inside, I hoped that I hadn't diminished his vision of me as a stoic leader. He was always observing, as if he were a student in class trying to learn something, or maybe it was just that he wanted to be seen as a part of the team in some small way. No matter what the emergency might be, he was always right there to clean it up.

After a very messy motor vehicle accident about two years ago, Sergei pulled me aside and quietly said, "You. You're good. Very impressive." He continued with his heavy accent, "I'll be your cleanup crew any day of the week. You're like an Indy racecar driver and those nurses, they're your pit crew. It takes a team to finish the race." Those were profound words and a uniquely American sounding analogy. After that, I surprised him with a Saturday at the Texas Motor Speedway. I thought we would talk cars the whole time, but interestingly enough, he wanted to talk about past patient cases. He was very interested and asked a lot of great questions. Who knew a janitor could absorb so much from the sidelines?

The bay where the all the excitement had been with the pregnant patient was now spotless. The beige curtains had been pulled back toward the wall and the laminate floor was clean enough that you could eat off it. Not a single drop of blood or bit of trash anywhere. "Sergei," I called out. "Nice job. Clean as a whistle." I gave him a thumbs up and big smile. He smiled back, said something in Russian that I didn't quite comprehend, but nodded his head as if to say *I've got your back, Doc . . .*

THREE

The next few weeks in the emergency room were exhausting. For some reason, there was a run on gastroenteritis, apparently a stomach virus that even the Center for Disease Control was reporting. The number of cases were up by at least twenty-five percent and it looked more like an outpatient clinic than a true emergency department. People were littered everywhere, most holding buckets or bowls from home close to their faces as they wretched into them with uncontrollable force. Others were lined up at the restroom, with looks of distress across their face. This was one time that I wish the ER had larger restrooms with stalls, rather than single-seaters.

Many of the patients were dripping in sweat from the fever that accompanied the illness. I knew from just looking at their miserable expressions that most of them thought that it would never end. I had to admit that watching them, it was hard to imagine that in

24-48 hours, they'd all be back to normal again. Then again, these things did seem to go in spurts. I remember another time, years ago when there was a run on strep throat, every visit was no longer than fifteen minutes, but it was the sheer number of cases that seemed almost unbelievable. People were lining the halls, some actually waiting in their cars because the waiting room was too full, packed to the gills with bodies that coughed and hacked violently, as though they were trying to expel the very illness from their throats through sheer effort. It was winter, which made things considerably worse. The doors were constantly opening and closing, letting in the cold, crisp air and making it impossible to keep the department comfortable. It was like working in a meat locker.

I was fortunate enough not to catch strep then, and I was fortunate enough not to catch the stomach virus this time around either. Like most healthcare workers who had spent their time in the trenches, I had built one heck of an immune system over the years. I just wished I could've also built up a tolerance for the incessant stream of desperation. It was hard to get used to seeing sick people everywhere. Working with little to no break moving from one to another was exhausting, both mentally and physically.

It was just after seven in the evening and my twelve-hour shift had finally ended. I walked out into the parking lot, dragging one foot after another with exhaustion. The quietness of the parking lot was a stark contrast to the hours of chaos inside the hospital. The sun was just starting to set, giving the sky had a warm, orange glow. Jarrod jogged toward me, calling out, "Jackson, hey, wait up, man." I couldn't believe he still had enough energy to move so quickly. His blue scrubs still looked clean and ironed, as if he were starting his shift, not ending it. I saw how hard he worked all night, so expected him to look a bit more like me—wrinkled and disheveled. He touched my shoulder and smiled. "If memory serves me right, tomorrow's your birthday."

"Don't remind me," I replied. I clicked my car fob, which let off a faint beep as the doors unlocked and the lights flashed.

"Forty-five, huh? Hey, let's grab Sushi tomorrow night right after—" He paused, and his energy faded a bit. "Oh hey, you probably have plans or something," he said, looking momentarily downcast, his usually open and jovial face falling slightly.

"Nope, no plans." I said, exhaling loudly, thinking about how sad it was that I had nowhere to be for my birthday. As a matter of fact, I'd totally forgotten about it. "Sushi? You're seriously down for sushi?" I never took Jarrod for the sushi type, not sure why. Could have been his size or the fact that I've never seen him eat much else but meat and potatoes in the cafeteria. "Ok. I'll take you up on that."

His smile grew big and his bubbly energy was back. "Yes, man, it's a date." He gave me a funny look and added, "Not that kind of date." We both chuckled.

"You know you're medical freaks when you can deal with crap and vomit for twelve hours and then discuss what you want to eat tomorrow." I gave him a sideways grin, shaking my head, and then reached out for a fist-bump.

He smiled and said, "Yep, nothing makes me want to eat raw fish more than spewed chunks of other people's dinner." Then he made a look of disgust, turning his head to the left and shaking his right hand back and forth in front of him as if to rub his words out of the air.

Jarrod didn't know it but his comment about dating made me reflect upon how long it had been since I'd been on a date. When you're married to someone so hateful, it a catch-22. I found myself longing for attention from Jacqueline and wishing she would magically change somehow overnight. Like some fairy could tap her on the head with a wand and turn her bitter, angry self, into a sweet and fun-loving woman. The kind of woman a man would like to spend time with.

Yet, even the simplest dates, the ones that couldn't possibly go wrong, somehow ended in an argument. Like the time I took Jacqueline to see *Les Misérables* and she went on a twenty minute rant about how stupid it was for the priest to give John Valjean the additional silver. I couldn't possibly make her understand the gesture. Jaqueline was more into holding grudges and setting expectations that nobody could possibly live up to. Even the Christmas I suggested that we spend an hour at the homeless shelter serving meals, she proceeded to spend the day lecturing the kids on how people choose to be homeless because they'd simply stopped trying to earn a living.

As I drove into my neighborhood, I noticed cars lining the streets. BMWs, Mercedes, Lexus, and an occasional Jaguar. I barely missed the cars crowding on either side of my driveway as I pulled in. As soon as I opened the door, I could hear the sound of cackling coming from the kitchen. It looked as though Jacqueline had at least thirty women or so over for bunco, a game that more closely resembled the name 'drunco'. I never understood why they had to mask a drinking party around some game of dice. Why not just say they want to get together to drink and gossip? I guess that wouldn't be very ladylike. Almost all the women in this particular group of friends tended to focus more on appearances and brand names rather than their own character and manners. I once overheard one of them whisper, "Who cares if he divorces me, it's Texas and everything's community property. Divorce just means I get to shop, go to the spa, and my social groups without having to worry about dinner or explanations. It's kind of a sweet deal, but you have to time it right. Never divorce when the stocks are down."

"Hi, Bobby," said a tall woman with long, straight brown hair, green eyes, and large hoop earrings. She was wearing a light blue sleeveless jumpsuit and heels that had to be at least four inches tall. As my eyes looked up from her shoes to her face, I smiled and nodded in an effort to be polite. Walking across my kitchen was nearly impossible. They were all gathered around the large, granite covered island as if it were an altar. Bottles of wine were lined up across the middle of the island, but most were empty. Their glasses had those little annoying charms dangling from the stems, trinkets that help discern one's own glass from someone else's. But this crew was so loud and inebriated that I doubted they paid any attention to them at all.

Just then, Jacqueline entered the room. She must have spent hours on her hair, which was loosely curled and draped over her shoulders. She looked like what Texans refer to as a Dallas Dolly. I guessed the term derived from Dolly Parton, because Dallas Dollies always have cleavage, a big smile and big hair. The diamond studs glinting in her ears were a present from me, as was the teardrop necklace that graced her tanned chest. A chest that revealed a bit too much cleavage, considering it was just a night with the girls.

She pushed past me as if she hadn't seen me at all. But, before I could get to her, she did an about face and grabbed my arm. Cutting through the crowd, she led me into the side hall. "I guess you forgot. This is *my* night." Her eyes filled with anger as she clenched her jaw. She took a moment to get her composure, letting go of my arm, she pushed her hair back and slid her hands down the sides of her black, silky dress as if to iron out her composure. "If you want to make yourself useful, be sure to pick up BJ from basketball practice at 8:30," she said, in a much nicer voice, the kind she used when she wanted something.

Without another word, she turned and started walking back to the kitchen in her red high heels that clipped against the tile like a series of gunshots. She turned back and without any emotion at all added, "Oh, and you might want to take her out to eat, too. Husbands and daughters don't really mix with friends, you know?" She gave me a tight smile, one as tight as the dress that was molded to every curve of her figure. "We should be done around 11:00. You can come back at around 11:30 just to be sure."

I stood there, still in my scrubs, my feet aching. All I really wanted was a hot shower, to sit down and flip on the television to some mind-numbing show in order to decompress. But unfortunately, that wasn't my life. Whomever said, "The quality of your life is determined by your wife," was so very right.

I went to the bedroom and quickly changed my clothes. As I pulled a T-shirt over my head, the bedroom door opened, and a woman entered, no doubt a friend of Jacqueline's. She looked like some kind of red-head floozy standing there with her twenty-thousand-dollar front end alignment bursting from the buttons on her green silk blouse. Instead of quickly shutting the door, she stared at me just long enough to make it awkward. "Excuse me," I said in an irritated tone as I grabbed a pair of khaki shorts from the drawer. She just stood there, one arm stretched up into the door frame while the other held a half-empty glass of merlot. She lowered her head, looking at me with a faint, seductive smile. I walked right past her, shaking my head in disgust. I was pretty sure they lived about four doors down and I had seen her husband before. He was fairly good looking, tall, muscular, and from the convertible Porsche 911 Turbo he drove, it was safe to assume he was also highly successful.

I grabbed the door handle to leave, but then noticed our neighbor, Carol, sitting by herself at the kitchen table. Her husband, Frank and I, got to know each other over the years. While we weren't bosom buddies, we'd had the occasional chat about sports, the weather and such. I walked over and placed one hand on the chair next to her. "Carol, so I guess you and Jeanie come to all these things, huh?" I said with a wry smile. Jeanie was one of Jaqueline's long-time friends, the only one I ever really liked. She was kind and warm, not like the others at all. While they were always talking about themselves and their first world problems, Jeanie was busy putting others first. Over the years she had brought over a meal or two when anyone in our house was sick. She even stepped in and helped plan the funeral for Jeremy because we were in too much pain and shock from the whole ordeal. She picked out the clothes he would be buried in, remembering how much he loved that T-Rex shirt and his light up sneakers. It was much better than some stuffy designer suit Jacqueline would have probably chosen.

Carol looked at me oddly. "Not Jeanie. She hasn't been to one in over a year." She looked down at her glass of chardonnay and back at me again, motioning for me to sit down. "I guess Jaqueline hasn't told you."

I sat on the edge of the chair and leaned in to hear her. "Told me what?" Little did Carol know, but Jaqueline didn't really tell me anything.

"Jeanie has Stage 4 breast cancer. It's not looking good at all." Her lips pressed together, grabbing her mouth and wiggling it across her face. She was shifting her footing as if she were a bit nervous to tell me.

"No. No she didn't tell me," I said. I shook my head and she could tell I was angry. Not at her, but at the news. I sprung up from the chair and pushed my way through the kitchen, swinging the door leading to the garage open as I left. I'm sure the squealing of my tires didn't even penetrate the raucous noise of the house. I was so angry about Jeanie that I hit my steering wheel with the palm of my hand until a few tears escaped my eyes. If God wanted to take someone, why her? Why did it always seem that the good ones died and the bad ones lived forever? Doctors said this all the time. If anyone struggled with this concept, it was people in medicine. The meaner people were, the longer they stayed. The angry, non-compliant smoker hangs in there costing the system thousands, while the innocent nice person got some stupid, rare disease. It sucked but it was true.

I never had a crush on Jeanie or anything like that, it was just that she reminded me so much of my own mother. There was a gentle kindness about her. Although she was always the first one to help, she was the last to take credit for it. When she and the other girls were together, she seemed to stand out of that crowd. Kind of like that old Sesame Street song, *"One of these things doesn't belong."*

I pulled up and waved to BJ though my car door window. She walked out into the school parking lot that was now lit by soaring flood lights. Her light brown hair bounced off her shoulders with each step. She moved like a star player, not because I'm biased, but because she had the build for it, strong and lean. She wasn't the tallest girl on the team, but she could hold her own. I didn't usually pick her up, but I could tell by the beaming smile on her face and the way she picked up her pace, running toward the car, that she was pleasantly surprised. When she waved back, she almost dropped all her gear. Between her gym bag, backpack, and water bottle, she was completely weighed down.

"Dad!" she said with a smile as she climbed in the car, tossing one thing after another into the backseat. "Awesome!" she added as she reached for her seatbelt and gave me a big cheesy grin. "Thanks for picking me up. So . . . what's the occasion?"

"Just wanted to spend some time with my favorite daughter, that's all," I said with a smile.

She rolled her eyes and said, "I'm your *only* daughter, Dad." Then added, "But, I'll take it."

"What's your fancy?" I said, pulling back out onto the street. "Burgers? Hey, we can stay out as late as you want, so it's your choice." I didn't have the heart to tell her we weren't welcome back home, so I let her think the whole night was my idea, and what we did with it was up to her.

Easier that way. Also, what was the harm in making her feel good? Special? Her mother certainly didn't make her feel that way, that was for sure.

After laughing through an hour of pizza, it was still only 9:45 pm, so I suggested ice cream and a stop at the bookstore after. Luckily, she took me up on it.

Taking a bite of the double scoop of rocky road tucked inside my waffle cone, I mustered up the courage to ask her, "Did Mom tell you," I began tentatively. "I mean, did you know that Jeanie has cancer?"

BJ looked at me with her blue eyes glistening with the tears that were forming and said, "I know. But, not because of Mom. Actually, we had an argument over it. Maybe more than one, or three, or five, actually."

I looked at BJ, so grown-up looking and civilized. She sat up straight, her legs crossed as if she were wearing a dress and not gym clothes. She ate her ice cream one tiny spoonful at a time out of her cup. She hadn't used a cone since that time when she was six, and she licked the scoop so hard it fell right out of the cup and into the grass. While I had to hold back my laughter, she didn't find it funny at all. Instead, she cried for at least an hour and vowed never to get a lousy cone again. "Argument?" I asked, resting the hand that held my cone on my knee, focusing all of my attention on her.

"Yeah. I found out from someone at school. When I told mom she said she already knew. First, I was really pissed that she didn't tell me about it. Jeanie was always my favorite. She was the only one who could keep mom halfway calm and rational," she said drily, a bit too drily for someone so young. And I wondered for maybe the first time how much her mother's presence was affecting her, shaping the person she was becoming and making her grow up way too quickly in the process. There was a sudden pain in my chest at the thought, and I swallowed hard. The ice cream that had been so sweet just moments before now tasted as bitter as poison.

"I'm sorry she didn't tell you. She didn't tell me either. I found out from Carol." I looked at her a bit puzzled, "Why did you argue about it the other times?" I felt drops of ice cream land on my calf and run down, sticking to the hairs on my leg.

She took another bite of her strawberry ice cream, turning the spoon upside down and pressing her lips together as she pulled it out of her mouth. She paused and looked down, "Because Mom refuses to go see her. She says they no longer have anything in common and she can't imagine how bad she must look."

Part of me wanted to pretend that couldn't be true. How could I be married to someone so horrible, so self-ish? But, the other part of me knew that this sounded *exactly* like Jaqueline. A wave of sadness overcame me, and my stomach dipped as though I suddenly had the flu. I reached out for BJ's hand. She placed the spoon back in her cup and held my hand tightly, scooting a little closer and resting her head on my shoulder. A single tear ran down her cheek, "She said she just wants to remember her how she was. I guess she doesn't plan on seeing her ever again. It's awful. They were friends for as long as I could remember, since I was little." She let go of my hand, wiped away the tear and stared forward. "Dad," she said quietly. "I don't ever want to be—"

I knew what was coming. It wasn't the first time I've had to reassure her. "BJ, honey, you're *nothing* like her," I said in a quiet, firm voice. "Nothing at all."

When we arrived back home, closer to midnight, BJ could see for herself exactly why we'd stayed out so late. The kitchen was strewn with glasses and the whole house smelled of wine and cigarette smoke and stale hors d'oeuvres. BJ, tossed her backpack to the floor and shook her head in disgust. She started picking up glasses and scraping leftovers into the trash. As I grabbed a few glasses from the other rooms and came back into the kitchen, she looked at me with compassion and said, "I got it, Dad. Go get some sleep." Then she came over, gave me a tightly held hug, resting her head on my chest for a minute. She leaned back, looked at me and said, "Really. No sweat. Go get the bedroom before she wakes up and takes it."

Jaqueline was sound asleep on the couch, still in her slinky wrap dress and heels. I went to the bedroom as quietly as possible, closing and locking the door behind me. I figured her drunken state was good for at least six hours, the exact amount of time before I had to get in my car and go back to work.

The next morning, the kitchen was spotless and BJ was sitting at the kitchen table doing some last minute homework. I walked toward the Keurig, but BJ jumped up and grabbed my hand, placing one finger over her lips with a "Shhh." She was absolutely right, even my favorite java wasn't worth waking the sleeping monster in the next room. I blew her a kiss goodbye, a smile plastered on my face, and quietly exited, closing the door behind me.

FOUR

Blood-stained scrubs didn't go too well with sushi, so the next morning, I stopped in the doctor's lounge to toss a change of clothes into my locker. Even though I was tired from the night before, I was really looking forward to having dinner with Jarrod. A change of pace was always a good thing, and there was nothing like boats of salmon rolls and sashimi to make me forget about my troubles at home.

As I stood in the lounge, a room filled with recliners that were never used, I noticed how quiet it was. Perhaps the lounge seemed foreign to the rest of the hospital because it was quiet. The grey and black carpet always seemed a bit out of place since the entire hospital was filled with practical linoleum floors that could be easily sterilized. The kitchenette counter was loaded with pastries and fresh fruit, compliments of some drug rep that had stopped in most likely hoping to sell Dr. Roberts on some new medication.

I took an extra moment to clear my head from the night before, resting my right hand on the grey laminate locker door. Inhaling, I smiled a faint smile as I glanced at the photo of Jeremy and BJ taped to the back of my locker. It seemed as though it were taken yesterday, not years ago. They were standing on the sandy beach in Maui, the sky so perfectly blue, not a cloud in the sky, just the outline of Kahoolawe, the smallest of the eight main islands, above Jeremy's right shoulder. I remember him saying how he wanted to be an Olympic swimmer so he could one day swim to that island.

Just as I closed the door and turned the key, I heard a low voice call out. "You can tell a lot about someone from their locker."

I was so deep in thought that the voice was startling. I turned around quickly to find a familiar face looking right back at me. "Sergei, are you trying to give me a heart attack?"

"Sorry," he said in that unmistakable Russian accent of his. A few grey hairs I had never noticed before were peppered throughout his jet black hair. "I thought you saw me." He had a sheepish grin, one that proved he knew certainly well that he had taken me by surprise. His head shook from side to side as he chuckled a bit under his breath, as if to say, "Gotcha." He was always smiling. He even smiled for the photo on his hospital name badge. Most people's badge photos look like mugshots, but not

Sergei—his looked like he was having the best day of his life with a smile that went from ear to ear, like a dental commercial.

"No, it's ok. I guess I'm a little jumpy this morning. Didn't get much sleep." I wasn't going to tell him, but I had tossed and turned all night over what to do about the awards ceremony, Jacqueline, BJ, everything. I reached over and patted Sergei on the back and headed for the door. Just before leaving, I turned back to face him, cocking my head a bit, I asked, "What did you mean by that?"

"By what?" He asked.

"That comment about my locker. You said you can tell a lot about a person by their locker. What can you tell about me, for instance?" I asked with one hand on the door handle. I wasn't sure if my tight grip was in anticipation of me opening the door, or holding it closed to secure anyone from entering as Sergei explained his comment.

He walked toward me, stopped parallel with my locker which was about five feet away and said, "People put what they want the world to see on the outside, but what's really important is always on the inside. That blonde," he said pointing over at a picture on the outside of my locker. "She's your wife?" The photo was of Jaqueline and me, five years ago, back when I called her Jackie. Things were good then, not great, but better than now. That photo was probably the last time we stood next to each other smiling. It was the summer before Jeremy died. I guess Sergei was right, that's what I wanted the world to think my life was like.

"Yep, that's my wife," I said quietly without a smile. I think he sensed the lack of enthusiasm in my voice. I looked at him, looked away, and then back again. I took my hand off the door and placed it on my hip. Our eyes met, but I couldn't bring myself to offer an explain.

There was this moment of silence. This moment of unspoken truth. I felt as though I didn't need to elaborate. On some level Sergei could feel my pain. He shook his head, then looked down at his feet. After a long pause he said, "Inside the locker. The two children. The boy and the girl. Those are your real treasures," he said softly with a wink of the eye.

I could feel the corners of my lips raising slightly to make a faint smile. Then I nodded in agreement. "You're pretty smart, Sergei." I didn't quite know what to say after that and I could feel my eyes starting to tear up. He was right, those two children were the best thing that ever happened to me. I reached back to grab the handle of the door again, breaking eye contact with Sergei and focusing on the door in an effort to snap out of the emotional trance I was feeling. I added, "Hey, um, let's just keep this conversation between us. Ok?"

Sergei simply replied. "You can trust me. I see a lot of things around here, but I never say a word. Besides, it's not a crime to love your children. It's honorable. All I see here is a man who loves his children." While I didn't look back as I left, I could tell he was sincere, I could feel it.

I walked swiftly towards Dr. Roberts at the nurse's station for morning run down. "Hey, hey, don't sit down," he said as he quickly got up to greet me. "Let's go in here to talk." He put one arm on my shoulder and walked be toward an empty dark patient room. I couldn't imagine what he had to tell me that couldn't be said in front of the staff. Besides, none of them were at the station anyway. As he grabbed the door handle, he turned and said, "Bobby, it's been a hell of a night. I hope your morning goes better." Then he leaned into the door as it opened, and he flipped on the light.

"Surprise!" they all yelled. Then Mary reached over and patted a rather large rectangular box that was sitting on the gurney in the middle of the room. "Open it, it's from all of us."

I couldn't believe so many people had crammed into the same exam room. I peeled the paper away and was thrilled to see a vertical chessboard, complete with hand carved wooden pieces. The squares on the board were stained different colors and clear slats held the pieces in place. Dr. Roberts said, "We thought you could hang it the doctor's lounge. That is if you're fine with being crushed on a regular basis." I knew exactly what he meant by that. Dr. Roberts and I had bonded over chess when I first started. We'd talk about our favorite players, best moves, which country had the most legends, and on and on.

Before I could answer, we heard the sirens of an ambulance. Just like that, we all went into emergency mode piling out of the exam room like clowns emerging from a Volkswagen Bug. Only, we weren't clowns, we were just normal people having a good time. It was a funny thing the way medical people did this. No matter what we were doing moments before an emergency, some part of the brain takes over without even thinking about it and we're transformed. We can go from laughing and joking to making life or death decisions in an instant.

"Drowning. Six-year-old male. Mother started CPR. Unresponsive," said the paramedic. He was bagging the patient through the endotracheal tube, this allowed the air to go directly from the bag to the windpipe.

"How long was he under?" I asked as I swallowed hard.

"Estimated four to six minutes."

I felt my heart pounding in my chest. *Why did I have to relive this on my birthday?* I looked up at the ceiling as if to ask God, "Why? Why today?"

Elizabeth was right on it, she didn't miss a beat, and never seemed to tire from the chest compressions she took over to give the paramedics a break.

Mary was typing notes into the EMR and a respiratory therapist who happened to be in the emergency room took over the bagging. I held the paddles in my hands, squeezing them tightly as if that somehow that would make them work better. "All clear," I yelled. Each time I delivered a shock I saw his body lift off the table and fall back again. Nothing. Flat line. Repeat. Nothing again. Repeat.

I knew, the moment I saw this little boy, it wasn't going to end well. Still, I tried. I tried and tried. I couldn't give up. Not this one. Not this time. Ten minutes went by, then twenty.

"Call it," said Mary sternly. "Dr. Jackson, you need to call it."

Elizabeth looked at Mary and over at me. She had never heard Mary talk to me like that. I don't think I had ever heard Mary talk to me like that either. I wanted to tell her, "No," but I knew she was right. I knew it was an exercise in futility.

I leaned up, wiping the drips from my forehead with my forearm. I could feel the blood going to my face, like a rush of heat. "Time of death, 7:45 a.m." Then I put my head down and left. I didn't want to make eye contact with anyone.

As Mary started to follow me out, Elizabeth touched her arm to pull her back. "Don't."

Mary jerked her harm away and replied in a rude tone, loud enough for me to hear, "Don't tell me don't. You haven't worked with him as long as I have."

I heard Elizabeth's response faintly as I walked down the hall. "Maybe that's why I can see it. I know that look. Give him time. Let him go wherever it is he goes." I was grateful for Elizabeth's insight. She was right. I wanted to be left alone.

I needed time, even if it was only ten minutes. I was angry. Angry at God, angry that I couldn't save that little boy. There was certainly a bit of irony that I found solace in the chapel. Every time I was mad at God, at work, or at life in general, I would go to the chapel and sit on the hard, wooden pew. The chapel wasn't very ornate. There was a simple alter with a cloth across it, and a cross centered in the middle. It didn't matter that there wasn't much to look at since all I could see what his little lifeless body. I sat there and sobbed. I could hear the echoes of my cries, but it sounded like someone else. It was as if I was sitting there, watching myself fall apart as I relived that fateful summer day, the lifeless body of my son as he was on the gurney, his dark hair plastered to his forehead.

They say that when you're stricken with grief your heart hurts. It was true. At that moment my heart hurt. It was a deep seeded pain that took my breath away. The kind of pain that came when current circumstances collided with your worst memories.

Just then I remembered that I had two very anxious people waiting to hear the outcome. It was a long walk to the waiting room, one that I preferred someone else take. As I approached the room, the parents weren't hard to spot. The mother's face was red and blotchy from crying and the long brown hair around her face was wet with tears. Her husband was trying to console her, but his face was ashen white. You could tell that he had been holding her in a long embrace before I arrived, because his blue suit had a rather large dark wet mark on his right shoulder.

My eyes met the dad's eyes first. Before I said a word, he knew. He reached for her hand and clasped it tight. She then turned, and she too saw my face. No matter how we doctors tried not to wear the bad news across our face, it was inevitable that answer came from our eyes long before it ever passed through our lips.

"I—" I started to say, but the mother cut me off.

"We know. You're going to say I'm sorry," she said as black mascara streaks ran down her face. "Just—" She paused, waving her delicate hand frantically between her face and mine. "Just don't say it." Then she reached forward and grabbed the lapels of her husband's suit and buried her head in his chest. Her knees grew weak as she sobbed, and her husband led her to the seat behind them.

"Nothing I can say will help ease this pain. I know," I offered.

"Oh, you know," the mother said sarcastically through the tears. "How could you possibly know?"

I didn't answer her. I could've and perhaps I should've, but I didn't.

"Well," she continued with an angry voice. "Did you know that little boy was it? He was our everything. The only child we ever had. The only child we will *ever* have."

She was right, that was one thing I couldn't understand. When Jeremy died, I felt as though I had to stay strong for BJ. Perhaps BJ is what kept me out of a strait jacket. I had to stay strong because I was still a parent. I was a grieving parent who had to bury my pain, so I could find a way to still be a dad, a husband, and a doctor.

I stood there a little longer. It was an awkward moment. I knew if I left too soon I would appear uncaring. But, if I stayed too long, I myself might break down all over again.

I walked back up towards the nurse's station. Mary and Elizabeth both gave me an understanding smile, but no words. The rest of the shift I went into doctor autopilot and nobody brought the drowning case up again. Even if they wanted to, there wasn't any time. The emergencies came one after another—big stuff, like heart attacks, car accidents, even someone falling off their roof, fracturing both their legs. It was a welcome distraction though, I couldn't think about the drowning because I had to stay focused on the next case, and then the next. I was exhausted from the adrenaline of the day and vowed never to complain about gastritis cases again. This was a day that made those gastric days seem like a walk in the park.

I saw Jarrod all day long, but no small talk, just business. It had been one of those shifts that felt like three days in the span of twelve hours; 7:00 p.m. couldn't have gotten there fast enough.

As two long bamboo boats arrived filled with all types of sushi and sashimi, I looked over at Jarrod and shook my head in disbelieve. The boat in front of him was completely full. His eyes widened and with a big smile he said, "What? You don't think I can eat all this?"

"Oh, I think you can eat that much all right. I've seen the way you devour those pastries that I bring out from the lounge."

The meal was mostly silent except for the occasional moans from Jarrod as he ate . . . and ate. Just as he anticipated, we finished off every last piece.

"Ok," he said dabbing the napkin across his lips. "I have a question for you. You're a smart guy."

"If this is about that microbiology class, forget it. I have long forgotten that stuff." I leaned back in my chair. "Man, I ate too much," I said as I rubbed my belly and arched my back. "Hey, I bet you'll be glad when you graduate. Isn't that coming up?"

"Last semester, baby!" He said with a big grin that suddenly went flat. He was now in serious mode. He leaned across the table and asked, "How do you know when it's the right one?"

I sat there for a moment thinking how ironic it was that he was asking me this question. "Jarrod, that's a question for Dr. Roberts, not me."

"Come on man, you're married. From what Dr. Roberts says about that photo on your locker, she's hot." He raised his eyebrows, and his dark eyes seemed to pop with the word "hot."

I could feel myself wiggling in my chair a bit, not really knowing what to say. "Jarrod, no offense, but if I knew the answer to your question, I wouldn't be sitting here eating sushi with you on my 45th birthday."

He looked at me, took a sip of his water. "None taken." Then he looked at me again as if he understood what I was trying to say. "Fair enough. I won't ask. That is unless you—"

"Nope," I said quickly.

The rest of the time I sat there thinking about what a fraud I must be. To the world I have this perfect life, this perfect wife. Jarrod had his whole life ahead of him. I wished I'd given him some sort of special life-changing wisdom, but I sat there in full knowledge of the fact that I should've been seeking, not giving, relationship advice.

As we walked to our cars after dinner Jarrod said, "I know what I forgot to tell you, man." He stopped, looked me right in the eyes, "they came back to thank you."

"They? Who?"

"That couple. The pregnant one. They brought by Johnathan. 6 lbs. and a full head of hair," he said, tilting his head to one side and offering a right-handed shake and left-handed pat to my shoulder. "Doc, sometimes there's nothing you can do to make a difference. Other times, it's everything you do that makes the difference."

Jarod was right. Those words of advice rang true in more ways than one.

FIVE

A few days came and went with no mention of my birthday. It wasn't like it really mattered since spending time with Jaqueline wasn't exactly on my list of favorite things to do. I'd much rather spend my evenings snuggled up on the sofa with Honeysuckle and BJ watching reruns of *The Big Bang Theory*, a favorite past-time of ours.

I was lucky enough to have a Saturday off and there we were on the couch, laughing over some ridiculous comment Sheldon Cooper had made, when BJ suddenly blurted out, "Oh, crap! What's today?" Her eyes widened as her hand went to the top of her head, grabbing at her hair. As her fingers ran through her shiny brown hair, the scent of that herbal shampoo floated in the air like a whisper meant for the nose not the ears. "Dad, I can't believe it. I forgot your birthday." Her wide eyes started to fade as they welled up with tears and her hand moved from the top of her head to over her mouth. Then she pulled both hands into her oversized sweatshirt and curled her legs up to her chest to form a seated fetal position.

"Don't worry about it," I said, brushing off her concern. "It's no big deal."

She cocked her head sideways as if she didn't believe me.

"No, really," I protested, picking up the remote and muting the sound. "When you get this close to fifty, you stop counting."

She smiled and was quick to set the record straight. "You are not that close to fifty. You are only forty-five. That's halfway between forty and fifty."

"Correction," I said as I raised my first finger and looked out of the tops of my eyes like a school teacher. "The day after my birthday, I was closer to fifty and growing closer with each moment. Hear that?" I looked around at the clock on the wall and added, "Tick tock."

BJ, snuggled up close and said, "Whatever, Dad," in her best dismissive teenage voice, and without missing a beat I unmuted the sound. Three episodes later, we said good night and retreated to our rooms for the night.

A few minutes later, I heard Jacqueline arrive home and the rustling sounds coming from downstairs as she put her purse and keys down in the kitchen. Quickly jumping into bed, I closed my eyes and pretended to sleep. I didn't want anything to ruin my perfect day off. Besides, she got her perfect day, and I deserved mine. According to a call BJ had overheard the day before, Jaqueline had treated herself to a full day at the spa. If it wasn't for the beauty of not having to be around her, I would have complained about her $1,500 outing. *Some things*, as my dad used to say, *are just worth the price you have to pay.* While I'm positive he wasn't talking about paying good money to get a break from your wife, as far as I was concerned, the old adage still applied.

The next morning, the doors of the emergency department glided open with a whisper, and I re-entered the world of organized chaos. "Every room's full," Dr. Roberts said as he quickly passed me, sterile dressings in hand. His scrubs had streaks of betadine across the abdomen, which was a tell-tale sign of a car accident or some other trauma. Since betadine stains can often be mistaken for blood by civilians, dirty scrubs were usually changed right away. But the overcrowded waiting area teeming with bodies told me he simply hadn't had the time to change into a clean pair yet.

I caught a glimpse of Mary and true to form, she was early to work, her dark brown hair pulled back, makeup on, looking as if she had been engrossed in work for hours, not minutes. Nobody ever officially announced it, but we all knew Mary played a maternal role in the emergency room. She was organized, studied all the cases so the transition to our shift was easier, and for the most part, she made me look good. *That's it!* I thought, the realization dawning on me. *Elizabeth probably was the one making the doctors at her old hospital look good. Hmmm . . . a little competition . . . that could be a good thing.*

I walked toward Mary. When I got there, I asked like a soldier reporting for duty, "Where should I start?"

Without even looking up from her clip board, she replied, "Take room three. Unexplained fever, unrelieved with Tylenol. Just triaged, so no workup yet."

"On it," I said. I didn't mind that the roles seemed reversed. I was happy to dive in and take orders so we could get the emergency room under control. I walked quickly down the hall and as I pushed through the door of room three, I found a pale, sweaty male, age thirty, give or take a few. He had sandy brown hair and a day's growth around his chin. His wife was in the chair beside the bed with one hand on her husband's leg and the other holding their little girl on her knee. The little girl was fair like her mother with frizzy blonde curls that touched her shoulders. Her legs were swinging back and forth and each time they hit the edge of the bed her shoes would light up.

I looked at the wife, so sweetly tending to both her husband and her child as best she could. Her hair was straight, the kind of straight you get with a flat iron. I had to wonder if she straightened it because it was naturally curly like her little girl's. Her voice quivered a bit as she asked me, "Can you please figure out what's wrong? He's never sick. Like never . . . ever. He's been a bit tired lately, but that's it until last night when I noticed how hot his side of the bed was. He rolled over and when I rolled closer I realized the bottom sheet was wet and his body was hot."

"What time was that?" I asked looking over at the little girl and smiling. She smiled back so innocently as her little blue eyes peaked from behind a curl that had fallen to the middle of her little round face.

"About 3 a.m.," the wife replied. "I got up and gave him something for the fever. Uh—I only had Children's Tylenol in the house."

I looked at her with my head cocked to one side. "Well, that's—"

She quickly cut me off, as if she knew exactly what I was thinking. "But I gave him enough for an adult dose."

I nodded and then examined his lungs, carefully listening for any rattles. "Well, your lungs are clear," I said looking at the man's tired, half-mast eyes. His heart-beat was rapid, about 90 beats per minute, but that's par for course with a fever. "Any unusual rashes? Nausea? Anything besides being tired?" I said as I flung my stethoscope back around my neck.

"No," she said shaking her head from side to side. "Not really anything I can think of."

The husband was dozing off, exhausted from the fever. I shook him awake, looking him directly in the eyes and said, "Ok, Papa Bear, we need to get to the bottom of this."

The little girl looked at her mom with a smile and giggled, "Papa Bear."

The man, pale and weak, just looked at me with droopy eyes and whispered, "Ok."

I have always found the complex cases to be interesting. The bigger the mystery, the better. The wife's pale skin had turned slightly pinkish as her eyes filled with tears. She raised her little girl's hand to her lips and kissed it softly. It was a tender moment and I could sense the uncertainty in the mother's eyes. I could only imagine how she feared for her husband, her future, and the future of her daughter. While I didn't know much about the family, I could feel that he was their rock, their provider, and their world. I wondered if this was their first real emergency as a young couple. The first one always seems to be the hardest.

I knelt down next to the mom and the little girl, holding the end of the bed to keep my balance. "What's your name?" I asked the little girl.

"Mary," she whispered burying her face in her mom's chest as if she were suddenly shy.

"Mary," I replied with wide eyes and a big smile. "That's the same name as one of my nurses. You know what?"

"What?" she asked as she peeled herself off her mom and turned toward me.

I pointed at the door and said, "I am going to go and get my Mary right now. Since she has your name, I think she is just the right nurse to take care of your dad." I gave her a big smile and patted her softly on her small, plump arm.

Mary looked at her mom and smiled, her first real smile since I'd entered the room. I stood up and my attention turned to the mom, my voice growing a bit more serious. "First things first. We're going to get an IV started, take some blood and urine, and see where that gets us." I stood up and headed to the other side of the bed. Touching the patient on the shoulder I said, "Hey, Papa Bear, did you hear all that?"

He blinked his eyes open and nodded his head as if to agree. Then he looked at his wife and pointed at his neck.

The wife glanced over at him and then at me and said, "Oh, I don't know if this matters, but yesterday when he woke up he said he must have slept wrong. I guess his neck was stiff. He complained pretty much the whole day about it. Probably silly and not related at all, but I think that's what he wants me to tell you."

"Silly?" I said, raising my eyebrows. "No, that's exactly the kind of information I need, and it may explain what's going on. There's a chance that you have a bacterial infection, one that's best identified through spinal fluid. That means we need to numb a portion of your back and place a small needle into the epidural space to drain some fluid. It will only take a few minutes for the procedure, but a bit longer for the results."

He looked up with tired eyes but didn't seem to object one bit. I could always tell how sick a patient is by their reaction to needles. The more ambivalent they are, the sicker they are. As I turned to leave the room, I added, "We use the anesthesiologist for this test. Don't worry, they put needles in backs all day long up in labor and delivery."

Elizabeth had been hovering just outside the door. "Can I get you something in there?" She asked rather eagerly as she poked her red curly head through the door, batting her green eyes, while she smiled and waved at the little girl.

I was a little annoyed that she popped in unannounced. Most nurses wait patiently for orders, but not this one. "No. I need Mary," I replied, ready to walk off and find her.

"I can help you," she insisted.

I took in a deep breath and held it, then almost dismissively, I replied, "Is your name Mary?"

She nodded wordlessly.

"I rest my case," I shrugged and kept walking.

About thirty minutes later, Mary came out of that patient's room, and as she approached the nurse's station where I had been typing in my notes, she said, "Anesthesia just finished the spinal tap. Looks like you're right on target. Guess where he works?"

"Where?" I asked, looking up from the computer.

"Southern Methodist University. He's the maintenance man for the SMU dorms. Oh and Mr. Never Gets Sick refused the free vaccine they offered about a year ago." She shook her head in disbelief and then looked over at Elizabeth. "Yep, colleges are breeding grounds for meningococcal."

Elizabeth rolled her green eyes, grabbed a clipboard, and as she walked away, said in a snippy voice, "I am well aware of the connection between universities and meningitis."

The entire shift was filled with one case after another. It was a good thing we were busy because you could cut the tension between Elizabeth and Mary with a scalpel—even a dull one. *I swear that as long as I live, I will never understand women. Anyone who says men are competitive has never worked with women.*

My phone had been buzzing all day, but I assumed it was Jaqueline, so I just ignored it. It wasn't until an hour before the end of the shift that I finally took my phone out to look at it. It was BJ. She'd called me at least five or six times, and it wasn't like her to call me at work. I heard from her during work hours maybe once a month, at most. I felt the blood rush to my head and the adrenaline made my heart skip a beat or two. Something must've been really wrong. "What is it honey?" I said the moment she picked up. "I'm sorry for not answering sooner. It's been crazy busy, and I didn't realize it was you."

She was crying, sobbing actually, taking deep shaky breaths in between sobs. She blurted through the tears, "Mom said I'm fat. Do you think I'm fat?"

I could feel my blood boil. It was one thing for Jaqueline to insult me night after night, but our daughter? Now she had finally gone too far. "No," I said firmly. "You are not fat. I'm a doctor, you have to believe me when I say that if anything you could gain another five pounds and still be an ideal weight."

It was true, I wasn't just saying that to make her feel better. BJ was so athletic, she burned more calories in a day than most grown men could ingest. Because of her age and dedication to sports, she could eat whatever she wanted, whenever, and she never gained so much as an ounce.

"I was just trying to be nice, offering to go to the mall with her. She was in a really good mood, so I thought—" She started crying harder, and I could hear her trying to catch her breath. The sound infuriated me. I wanted to crawl through the phone and take her in my arms, rock her back and forth the way I'd done when she was just a little girl and she'd woken up in the middle of the night after a bad dream. But this wasn't a dream and I couldn't make it go away. This was BJ's life—and mine.

"I thought she was going to be normal." BJ continued. "But then she started saying how she wasn't going to spend any money on me, just on herself. She said if I wanted new clothes, I needed to drop at least twenty pounds." There was a pause and then she added, "She said I embarrass her. I'm fat and I'm a slob. Oh, and she said I wear boy's clothes."

BJ only weighed, at most, a hundred and twenty-five pounds soaking wet. *This is exactly how girls get eating disorders*, I thought. *The kind I see people die from all the time.* "BJ, don't listen to her. This is how girls get body dysmorphia—a condition that leaves you thinking you're overweight when you're not. Eating disorders are dangerous, they can kill you. Don't let her get in your head." I implored her, worried that my words were falling on deaf ears. The damage had been done. I knew that in some small way that BJ would probably always think of herself as fat, no matter what I did in damage control. I honestly wanted to leave work, drive home, and throw Jaqueline out of the house with my own two hands. "And I don't think you dress like a boy. You're athletic and you dress like an athlete. There is nothing, you hear me," my voice growing a little stronger, "nothing wrong with you."

"She'd like that, you know. She'd like me to start throwing up or working out too much. She said it," BJ said bitterly. I hated that note of bitterness in her voice. It reminded me of Jacqueline.

"She said she wanted you to have an eating disorder?" I asked as I cleared my throat. This was even a bit much for Jaqueline.

"No, she asked me why I had to be the one to . . . live." BJ forced the words out, as if they hurt leaving her throat. "She said she never wanted a girl anyway."

My heart sank into my chest and I immediately felt as though someone punched me in the gut. I couldn't believe she'd told BJ that. It was true, but I still couldn't believe she had actually said it. "I hope it's not a girl. I only want boys," Jaqueline said over and over when she was pregnant. When I asked why she didn't want a girl, she wouldn't give me a straight answer. But, I overheard her once talking to a friend on the phone. She explained that two girls under one roof was just too much. "Besides," she'd said. "I don't want anyone getting more attention than me." At the time I thought she was joking around, but after BJ became a Daddy's girl, Jaqueline became distant, cutting her off emotionally.

The distance between Jaqueline and BJ was unnatural. Girls weren't supposed to get the period talk from their dad, but BJ had. She also came to me in middle school when she went through her own version of *Mean Girls* and lost her best friend. It wasn't my intention to play favorites, it happened out of necessity.

As early as two months of age, I could see that BJ and Jaqueline weren't bonding the way a mother and child should've. Jaqueline refused to breastfeed, telling me it was inconvenient and that she had read somewhere that breastfeeding would make her breasts sag later in life. Four months after that, she insisted on getting a nanny because she had better things to do. She rationalized it by saying that it would make her less depressed. Although I gave in, the whole nanny phase didn't last long because she hated someone being in "her space."

But once Jeremy came along, Jaqueline smothered him with attention as if she were trying to make both BJ and me jealous. We weren't, of course, but I found it a bit weird. If anything, it made me give BJ more attention, the exact opposite of what Jaqueline would have wanted. It all started a vicious cycle. A cycle of who could out do who in building a stronger parent/child bond. *Stupid*, I thought. *How could I have fallen into that ridiculous trap?* When Jeremy died, I missed the chance to prove that I loved him just as much. I figured that sports would eventually bond us together and then BJ and Jeremy would both see I was the better, more genuine parent. Thoughts that seemed all too ridiculous now.

Remembering that I had a broken-hearted daughter on the other end of the line, I said, "Hey, I'm going to have a word with your mom tonight. I'm sure it's not something you want to be party to, so can you stay over with one of the girls from the team?"

"I already asked," she replied. At this point her hysteria had been downgraded to the occasional sniffle. "Brittany and her mom are coming over to pick me up."

"Good. We'll talk later. I love you, Sweet Pea."

I was glad the shift was finally coming to an end, but I knew my evening was just beginning. It was going to be a long night with Jaqueline. My jaw was already stiff from clenching it in anticipation. I stopped in the doctor's lounge to grab a quick bite and a cup of coffee. *Fuel for the fight,* I thought.

As I turned to walk out, I noticed that the chess game had been hung and that Dr. Roberts had made his opening move. A chessboard was organized using a system of letters and numbers. the letters a-h ran horizontally and numbers 1-8 ran vertically. One light colored pawn had been moved from e2 to e4. The pawns in a chess game were almost always the first to move. Each side had eight pawns and they stood at the front lines. Chess was a game of war, but much like life, it was also a game of strategy. Each player had to be defensive and offensive at the same time, all while anticipating their opponent's next move. A single move in the wrong direction could cost the whole game, ultimately losing the war. I picked up the dark wooden pawn from e7. I rolled it around in my hand for a moment, noticing how smooth it was, then I placed it at e5 before heading out the door.

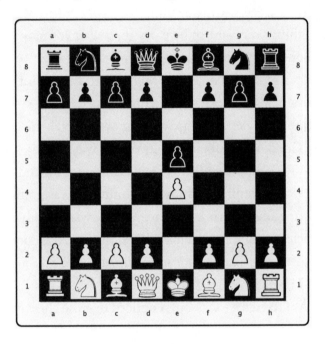

No sooner had I exited the lounge that Mary and Elizabeth walked up to me together, almost cornering me in the hall. Simultaneously, they blurted out, "Can we talk to you?" Mary had her hands on her hips and Elizabeth was taking a wide stance as if to cement herself to the floor.

"No!" I snapped, scrubbing a hand over my tired face as I rolled my eyes. I honestly couldn't take anymore drama.

They stood there, wide eyed, looking at each other and then back at me. They were obviously shocked by my unusually stern response. I had always been approachable, but not at that moment. I had more drama than I could handle, and I needed to get home to deal with Jacqueline.

As I was walking toward my car, I heard the scurry of footsteps on the pavement behind me. It was Elizabeth and she just couldn't leave well enough alone. "Look, about that meningitis case." She cleared her throat and added, "I am fully capable—"

"Stop," I said, raising a palm to her face, as if to say *talk to the hand*. "It had nothing to do with you." I put my hand down and looked Elizabeth square in the eye. If she couldn't tell I was fed up by my pursed lips and strong tone, then she obviously wasn't as bright as I'd given her credit for. I paused for a moment, softening a bit before adding, "Look, the little girl's name was Mary, so I told her I'd bring her a nurse with the same name to take care of her father."

She let out an audible sigh, one of obvious relief. She gave me a small smile, and then began again. "Ok. I feel pretty stupid right now. I'm sorry. I—"

"Look, forget about it." I said, cutting her off. "Elizabeth, I can't have cat fights in my emergency room. You're smart, real smart. I see that." Her eyes started to glisten a bit as if she appreciated the praise. Then I pointed toward the emergency room doors and said, "Please go and make this right with Mary. Emotional intelligence is just as important as book smarts and experience."

"You're right," she said firmly with a nod, squaring her shoulders and walking away.

Jaqueline's usually well-kept hair was messy and the redness of her face showed through the layers of foundation she had applied hours before. There was yelling, cursing, and the slamming of doors for hours. I'd love to say that Jaqueline was the only one, but I was just as guilty. She tended to bring out the worst in me, time and time again. During the height of the argument, Jaqueline got up in my face and with the most demeaning and critical voice she could muster she hissed, "I hate you. You're stupid and ugly. I don't understand why on earth people respect you." Her face was squished together in disgust. "It makes me want to vomit." She spun around to walk away, her silky blue skirt spinning quickly as if to catch up with her movement. No sooner had it met her legs again, that she did an immediate about face. She leaned in, taking her first finger and pressing it into my chest she said in a low menacing voice and nonetheless rang with the truth, "You're no doctor—you couldn't even save your own son."

At some point I must have left, because I woke up the next morning on the sofa in the doctor's lounge in the same rumpled clothes, messy hair and swollen eyes. Sergei was standing over me holding out a cup of coffee. I rubbed my eyes and sat up, nodding in appreciation as I took the cup.

"You like?" he said, pointing toward the board on the wall.

I squinted a bit, noticing that Dr. Roberts had made another move. His knight was moved from g1 to f3. Each side has two valiant knights to protect the King and Queen. They're the only pieces that can jump over other pieces as they move in an L pattern. "It's great. Did you put it up?"

"Sure did. And it's steady, not going anywhere. It looks like your game of war is now well underway," he said with a wink and a smile. Then he turned and grabbed his large trash can, wheeling it out through the lounge doors as he hollered back toward me, "Good luck to you, my friend." And then he walked out the door.

I hollered back, "Thanks, I'll need it." He had no idea how right he was. The war was well underway and I was going to need more than just luck to win it. I reached over and moved the black knight from b8 to c6.

SIX

"I didn't even see you come in," Dr. Roberts said matter-of-factly without even looking up from the computer at the nurse's station where he was making notes. He must have been sitting there for a while because his reading glasses had slid down his nose a bit. As he looked up and pushed his glasses back up the bridge of his nose with one finger he added, "I hate to tell you this, my friend, but you're about two hours early for your shift. In my mind that means I can put you to work." The corner of his face lifted as if he were deciding whether to smile or not. "Nobody stands idle in the middle of a war zone."

There was that word again: war. It was as if everyone knew on some transcendental level that my life was anything but peaceful. Dr. Roberts was a veteran of Desert Storm. He never talked about it, but HR told me when I was hired. They said he was tough on new recruits so be sure to be punctual and pay close attention, because he didn't like slackers and he didn't like idiots. From day one I was out to prove I was neither.

"Happy to pitch in," I said as I straightened up and pulled my shoulder's back.

"Not like *that*," Jennifer said as she looked me up and down and shook her head in disapproval hard enough that her blonde ponytail wagged.

That comment got Dr. Roberts's attention. He stood up and peered over the edge of the nurse's station, taking in my unshaven face, bloodshot eyes, and wrinkled scrubs. He handed his badge to Jennifer, motioning toward the doctor's lounge door. "Get him a clean pair of scrubs," he said authoritatively

Looking down, I realized that I was still wearing the same pair of scrubs I'd left in the day before. The yellow mustard stain from the sub sandwich I'd eaten for lunch the previous afternoon was a dead giveaway. There was an awkward pause and I was hoping that he wouldn't ask too many questions. I could feel a slight twitch in the corner of my right eye, the kind that's subtle, but that you feel like the whole world notices. I wasn't sure if it was from the nerves of the awkward situation, the leftover adrenaline from the fight with Jacqueline, a lack of sleep, or all three.

He looked at me with compassion and tilted his head to one side, considering something. It was as if he was as much concerned as he was confused. He took off his glasses and leaned forward, resting his arms atop the nurse's station that separated us. "Have you been drinking?" He asked in a low voice. "No judgement," he said evenly as he looked me over, his eyes sweeping across my face as if they were searching for clues. "But I have to know."

"No," I blurted out with a faint chuckle as I shook my head from side to side to drive the point home. "I can assure you I am not impaired in any way." Then, looking him in the eye, I confessed, "Well, unless you include a lack of sleep."

He leaned back and let out a small sign of relief. "Not worried about a lack of sleep. That comes with the territory." He nodded to Jennifer as she plopped a pair of freshly ironed scrubs on the ledge of the desk. "Well, you couldn't have come at a better time." Then he pointed toward the lounge door and with a drill sergeant tone ordered me to go get changed.

I looked at Jennifer and took the scrubs, pressing them against my chest. I gave her a slight bow as if to say thank you. Then it hit me, *what was Jennifer doing here in the middle of the night?* I glanced at my watch and back up at her, my expression radiating the confusion I felt.

"A double. I pulled a double," she said by way of explanation as she smiled and puffed out her chest as if she were proud of her contribution. "Turns out they were short staffed, so I pitched in," she said as she waived her long, slender first finger between Dr. Roberts and me and said, "It worked out. Besides, now I get to work with both of you at the same time." Her smile turned into a sarcastic smirk. "Wait, is that a blessing or a curse?" She paused and then asked, "By the way, who's white?"

"White? Last I looked we both were," Roberts said, raising one eyebrow, seemingly confused by the question.

"Seriously?" Jennifer replied as she rolled her hazel eyes. "I'm talking about the *game*. You know, the chess-board! I saw it when I grabbed the scrubs. Now that you're both here, you can get some moves in. Otherwise, this game may take all year," she said with a laugh.

As much as I didn't want to admit it, she had a point. One move each shift *would* make the game go on forever. "Well, people used to play postal chess and some moves would take days if not weeks. At least this isn't that bad," I said with a shrug as I walked away.

No sooner had I slid into those clean scrubs that the emergency room doors swooshed open and the sounds of moaning and crying filled the air. There were two gurneys. "They're all teens. Skittles party. Parents came home a day early and found their living room filled with these kids. We sent some to Methodist and some to Parkland, but trust me, there's enough of them to go around."

"Skittles?" asked the frantic mother who seemed to appear out of nowhere. She looked as if she had just woken up and rushed in. Her clothes were wrinkled prob-ably because they were yesterday's outfit that she just threw back on. She didn't even have time to brush her sandy brown hair, but like most mothers, hair, clothes and makeup become a nonissue when their baby was in trouble. One thing I had learned in the ER was that no matter how old a person gets, they were always their mother's baby. "I don't understand," said the mother a bit dazed and confused.

"Not the candy. Your little girl, along with the others, have ingested God knows what. The more colorful the prescription meds, the more excited they are to *taste the rainbow*," I replied to the mom whose mascara was running down her panic-stricken face. "Alert radiology, respiratory therapy, everyone. This is either a race against time, or a sit and wait." I said, looking at Jennifer and a nurse form Dr. Roberts shift.

One of the girls was unconscious but had a clear airway. Since she'd be at risk for choking on her own vomit, we had no choice but to intubate her. Her pulse rate was low at 48. She was wearing jean shorts and a pink shirt that was unbuttoned exposing the lacey edges of her hot pink and black bra. A bra that was a bit inappropriate for a fifteen-year-old. The kind you wear because you're planning on showing it to someone.

The other girl, the woman's daughter, was conscious but talking nonsense. She was wearing ripped jeans and a white T-shirt. Her eyes were brown, just like her mother's but they couldn't track my finger. It was hard to tell if it was due alcohol or the combination of alcohol and medication. The only clue we got out of her was the phrase, "Breakfast in a Glass," when she held her arm in the air as if to toast all of us. Then we watched as her body contorted, one shoulder raising to her head and her hand forming a claw-like position. Now we knew we were dealing with both. Probably an extrapyramidal reaction to an antipsychotic medication, like Thorazine. This happens when the nerves that control motor skills were affected.

Jennifer looked at me with wide eyes. Normally she would be moving quickly, but this time she seemed to stammer a bit, shifting from foot to foot as if she didn't know which way to turn. "Are we going to get toxicology? If so, I will pull off some blood and get an IV going," she said, her voice sounding shaky and unsure. I could tell this was her first Skittles experience.

The other nurse and I shook our heads as if on cue and I replied, "No. Won't do us any good. These aren't street drugs. You can't test for the things they most likely ingested. Experience tells me we more than likely have a chemistry project on our hands – one that's made up of prescription medications."

Both girls were, what we called in medicine, a train wreck. I knew we needed to just dive in and gather as much information as we possibly could. "Alcohol levels, O2 sats, stat blood sugars," I ordered. "Saline 200cc per hour. Oh, and be sure to get pregnancy tests on both, along with the usuals." The usuals referred to a CBC and CMP—hardly anyone escapes an ER visit without a blood count and a chemistry panel.

I looked back at the mom who stood there glancing around as if she were searching for answers. Her arms were crossed so tightly that the fingers from her right arm were nearly white as they clenched her upper arm. I knew she wanted an explanation, so I tried to explain. "They call it Skittles because of the colors of the pills. The kids bring everything they find at home or at grandma's and dump it all in a bowl. Then they scoop and swallow," I said in a rush, unable to keep the anger from creeping into my voice. All I could think of at that moment was my own daughter, BJ. *What if this had been her?* Everyone always thought it couldn't happen to their kid, but the truth was that no one was immune, it could happen to anyone's child at any time. Good parents, bad parents, anyone. Period. "Do you know this one?" I asked pointing at the girl in the gurney next to her daughter.

The mother, with a look of horror on her face said, "Yes, that's Nicole, Bethany's best friend." Her voice grew loud and panicked and as she shook her head back and forth. "Oh my gosh, tell me this is NOT happening!" she muttered, mostly to herself I suspected, as this was indeed every parent's worst nightmare. By this time, her brown, tear-soaked hair was sticking to one side of her face.

I looked her straight in her dark brown eyes and said, "Call her mother. I need the parents here. Call all the parents of all the friends you think may have been at that party. They need to track down which hospitals their kids are at and get there." She nodded her head as she fumbled through her tan leather bag in search of her phone. "That's your job. You hear me? Now go out there and do that," I ordered as I pointed toward the waiting room.

I wasn't trying to be mean or dismissive of the fact that her daughter might be dying. It was just that I found relatives needed to do something, anything, to help, and getting in our way wasn't going to help anyone, least of all her daughter. And standing alone in the waiting room with nothing to do but worry wasn't going to help much either.

Dr. Roberts came to Nicole's bedside. "Stimulants, barbiturates, opiate, or all three. Hell, it could be blood pressure or depression meds too." He took a deep break and exhaled heavily. His hand went to the top of his head, as if he was running it through hair he didn't have. "We don't even know what we've got. Damn these kids!" he said as he slapped his hand against the bed rail. He was right. The main reasons these pharmaceutical parties were so dangerous was because first you didn't know what they took, then it was hard to decide if the symptoms were an overdose or a drug interaction. To make matters worse, the patient could be allergic to any one of the meds they swallowed. It was crap shoot, and every emergency room physician's worst nightmare.

Dr. Roberts nodded toward the wall, and his nurse peeled off the toxidrome chart that was Velcroed to the wall and brought it to the bedside. Since doctors couldn't possibly memorize the tell-tale signs of different drug overdoses by class, these pictograms helped us make decisions quickly and accurately, listing symptoms by categories like heart rate, blood pressure, temperature, and pupil dilation. The only problem was that toxidromes don't list all the drug classes, just the most common. "Get the Regional Poison Control Center on the line. I don't want to miss something."

"I did get one clue out of this one," I said pointing at Nicole. "She said, *Breakfast in a Glass* which if I was a bettin' man, sounds like alcohol, coffee, and one of those flavored energy drinks. It explains the 140," I said pointing to her heart rate on the monitor.

Roberts had pretty much taken over Nicole's care, while I tended to Bethany. Luckily, both girls were in a large trauma room where we could all work together, switching off between nurses if need be. "Look at this," Roberts said pointing to the side of Bethany's head. A rather large bruise had started to seep from her temple to her forehead. He came over and separated her hair to see how far up the scalp it went. "No bump. Yet." He then undressed her completely looking for any other clues. The patient I thought was just here to sleep it off, looked to be the most serious.

I felt pain in my jaw, especially on the right side. It was a reminder that I needed to stop clenching my teeth, something I tended to do when I'm frustrated or angry. The only one in the room who may have had more clues was Nicole and she wasn't in any condition to answer questions. I looked over at the bruise on Bethany's head. It was dispersing at a rate that usually takes days as the blood seeped under her skin and turned her sweet sun-kissed face into one giant bruise. "Roberts, Coumadin comes in several colors depending on the strength. If she took a handful of a blood thinner, it could explain this. PTT?" I asked. The partial thromboplastin time, or PTT was a test that let us know if her clotting has been affected. Usually we use this blood test to monitor blood thinner doses in patients or to explain unusual bruising, but I thought it was worth a shot. After all, any clue was better than no clue.

Roberts looked up and said to his nurse, "Yep, let's do it. We also need a head CT."

"Got it," said his nurse. She was a pleasant and quiet lady in her mid-40's with brown curly hair. I watched her and she was quite impressive, never missing a beat. She was to Roberts what Mary was to me. These were the nurses that make us look good, who, if we're being honest, saved our asses in the trenches every day. Every doctor had to have one in order to do his best work through interminable shifts, and it was cases like these that defined the "one."

Nicole's parents didn't speak much. They just held each other in a tight side hug, each one with their arm wrapped around the other.

Everyone handles stress differently. Most parents fit into three categories: loud and angry, grief-stricken and wailing, or somber and prayerful. But Nicole's parents were eerily somber. It made me a bit nervous, until I saw them embracing in prayer and a few tears fall. It was sweet to see them holding each other tight, eye's closed, bowed heads and a faint, reverent whisper coming from the dad's lips. It may sound strange, but the ones that don't cry worry me the most. Once, a few years back, I had a dad who sat there expressionless as his child died. A few days later he came back with a gun and threatened to shoot the place up. Luckily, he didn't, but that incident left us all weary of the rare fourth type – the silent and deadly ones.

Those two girls took up more than a few hours before we stabilized them and sent them up to ICU where they could be watched more carefully. From the best we could gather, Bethany had ingested blood thinners and most likely a beta blocker, a blood pressure pill that slows the heart rate. She probably passed out at the party and hit her head. Lucky for her the CT was negative for a brain bleed. I said it was a miracle, but Roberts gently reminded me that faith was still the best medicine in times like these. Well, Nicole's parents certainly had enough of that to go around.

Nicole was the real mystery. Roberts and I treated her with IV Benadryl, which reversed the extrapyramidal reaction. Right before our eyes her clenched hand released and she regained control of all her motor skills. She was still drunk, but at least her body wasn't contorted anymore. It was a real crap shoot, but we did the best we could.

It was amazing how fast time passed when your internal clock was charged with adrenaline. When I looked up again it was 8:00 a.m. and now Roberts was back on my shift. He didn't seem to mind though. After a night like that, I doubted he would've been able to sleep anyway. I honestly didn't know how night shifters did it. I couldn't, that was for sure. From what I knew about Roberts, he got about six hours of sleep in the morning after a shift and then spent the rest of the time with his wife. He was the old school type, mowed his own lawn, and even found a few hours here and there to spend out on the green improving his swing. He brought his food to work in a metal lunch box every day. I once peeked inside and saw a handwritten note on a napkin: "I'll miss you tonight, sweetheart. Don't work too hard. Love you!" I never told him but that note made me green with envy, and reading it, I couldn't help but secretly wish I had his life. I'd even take his nearly bald head if it meant I could have a home life like that, and a wife to come home to who really loved me.

"I tell you what," said Roberts. "I'll stick around one more hour if you want to make a move." He was talking about the chessboard. I could see by the smirk on his face that he had some plan to annihilate me in as few moves as possible.

I entered the lounge and saw that he moved one of his two bishops from f1 to c4. The bishops can only move diagonally but can only do so until another piece was blocking it. I was actually too tired for strategy, so without giving it too much thought I moved the black knight from g8 to f6, grabbed a cup of java and left the lounge.

Elizabeth seemed especially cheerful as she stood at the nurse's station with her hair pulled back in a scrunchy and a few red curly strands bouncing to one side of her face. Her green eyes matched the small emerald pendant that hung around her neck. I pointed at the necklace and said, "That's beautiful. I haven't seen you wear that before. Is it new?"

"No. Thanks though," she said somberly as she slid it in behind her scrubs, an action which puzzled me. Why wear it just to hide it?

Just then, Mary came out of a room and said, "We've got a four-year-old with a fever in room three. Can you two take this? I really need to get back to room one."

I looked at Elizabeth as she cocked her head in surprised. Mary never asked her to take over. Then I swooped my arm in front of me as if to say, "After you."

Elizabeth assumed the position at the computer, Mary's usual spot and began typing as I asked the questions. The little girl looked tired. Her long brown hair was drenched in sweat and her skin was a slight pinkish color from the fever. "How long has she had a fever?" I asked the woman standing beside the bedside.

She was slender and in her late 50's. "She's had a fever on and off for a few weeks. Her mother . . . I'm her grandmother . . . but, her mother took her to the pediatrician a few days ago before they left on a trip. He said she's probably fighting a bug. Apparently, there's something going around," she said with a shrug.

"Any other symptoms?" I asked, assuming the pediatrician was probably right.

"Well, she hasn't been very hungry and she's been whining a little more than usual." Then she turned to the little girl and stroked her head. "Don't worry sweetie, it's normal to whine when you're sick. We would whine too."

I leaned over the bed and with my ophthalmoscope shining said, "Stick out your tongue and say "Ahhh. And between you and me," I told her with a wink. "Boys whine way more than girls, so you go right ahead and whine all you want. I still think you're tough." I said as I reached down and pinched her big toe. Looking over at Elizabeth I said, "She's dry. Probably fatigued from dehydration. Let's start an IV. We'll get her hydrated and she'll perk up in no time."

Elizabeth's cheerful demeanor melted right before my eyes and with an urgent tone of voice she said, "Can I see you outside for a minute?"

"Sure," I replied a bit confused as to what the big deal was. "We'll be right back," I said to the mom with a smile as I exited the room.

"Aren't you going to run blood work? At least the usual?"

"Why? She's healthy. Just saw her pediatrician last week. This is just a concerned grandmother." I said, brushing it off. "It's enough trauma to start an IV, but I'm only doing that to get a little life back in her. Besides, they don't have insurance and who wants to strap some young parents with a huge ER bill." *How dare she challenge my judgement,* I thought to myself as I turned away. In the space of a moment I went from admiring her red, curly hair and green eyes, to finding it all completely annoying in every way possible. Mary, I knew all too well, would never have questioned me.

As I turned to enter the room again, she lunged toward me and said, "Wait."

"Why?" I said, unable to keep the irritation from my voice. I wondered if my rolled eyes were as obvious to her as they felt within my eye sockets.

"Didn't you notice the bruises? When you grabbed her big toe, she jerked back and the sheet fell off one leg. I noticed bruises on her shins and then I saw one on her arm?" Elizabeth reached for the emerald necklace she wore around her neck and holding the small stone between her thumb and for finger, sliding it back and forth across the chain. I could tell it was a habitual act, something she did when nervous or worried.

"So, now you think she's abused?" I asked.

"No, of course not. Think about it. Fever, fatigue, bruising. Don't you at least want to get a CBC to check her count?" She looked me straight in the eyes, without blinking. Between her serious gaze and her wide stance it was apparent that her stern tone was more out of concern for the child's well-being than some kind of need to prove me wrong. She simply planted herself there stoically and we stood in awkward silence. I'm sure it was seconds, but it felt like hours.

She was right. How could I have skipped something as simple as a blood count? It was standard protocol on a young child with a fever. I placed one hand on my hip and rubbed the other across the stubble on my face. A few seconds passed and then I threw both my arms up, dropping my head and moving it slowly from side to side, and in a small quiet voice, I said humbly, "You're right. Thank you."

And the fact of the matter was that she *was* right. The blood count came back abnormal. Nobody wanted to deliver news like leukemia over the phone, but with her parents out of the country, I simply didn't have any choice but to have the tearful grandmother call them and pass me the phone. It was a humbling experience, one that put me back in the chapel at the end of my shift. I sat there, reflecting on how important it was for me to keep my head in the game at all times, to never ever let my guard down. I knew at that moment that my home life was inadvertently affecting my work life, something that was completely unacceptable in my profession.

Before leaving I stopped to grab an apple from the doctor's lounge and noticed Roberts had made one last move before he left—a white pawn from d2 to d4. Instead of just grabbing a piece and moving it, I decided to sit on the couch with my back up against once side so I could face the board. I stared at the board, contemplating my next move, feasting on both the apple and the chance to beat Roberts. Then I had it, I picked up a black pawn on e5 and moved it to d4, taking his pawn. I was quite proud of that move and my decision to take charge of the game and my life. The game, that was easy, but my life? That would take a bit more contemplation . . .

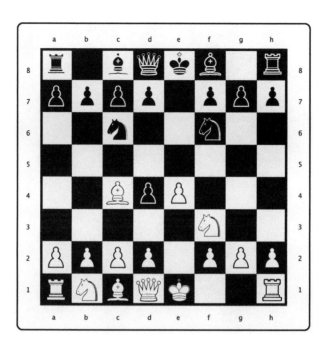

SEVEN

That night I drove home on autopilot, with hardly any memory of leaving the hospital. The next morning, I opened my eyes and caught a quick glance of BJ who was in the process of wiggling my big toe. She was already dressed for the day, but to my surprise, she wasn't wearing her usual uniform of basketball shorts and a T-shirt. She had on tan pants and a shirt with blue stripes that buttoned up the front. It was as if she grew up overnight. She tickled the bottom of my foot as she whispered, "Dad, don't you need to get up? Hey, it's 6 a.m. already."

I rubbed my hand across my face, realizing that my stubble had almost become an actual beard. The stiffness in my back and neck made me feel as if I had been hit by an eighteen- wheeler. At this point, I had lost track of how many nights I had slept on a couch instead of a bed. I lifted my head up and looked again at BJ with one eye open, then when I couldn't stand it any longer, I closed both eyes and dropped my head back down. There was an odd loss of strength throughout my whole body. It was pure exhaustion, both mentally and physically, something I hadn't felt since residency. I was always grateful that I wasn't fully warned of how taxing the residency schedule would be with all those sleepless nights, mental and emotional fatigue, as well as the feelings of inadequacy. Had I fully understood what I'd signed up for, I might have chosen a different profession.

The reality hit me that I was working myself to destruction to live in a big, fancy house where I slept on the couch. A house that I shared with a woman who didn't love me. Not only didn't she love me, she downright hated the sight of me, a feeling that by this point was mutual. *Why? Why am I doing this? What's the end game?* I thought to myself as I struggled to clear the fog from my head. Somewhere deep inside I knew that this situation was completely unsustainable. I knew that something had to give—and soon. But what?

BJ shook my right foot again, this time a bit harder and with a voice of concern asked, "Dad, are you ok? You look like crap. I mean, no offense or anything, but you can't go to work looking like, well, you know, like mom. . . after she's had one too many." I peeked at her long enough to notice her furrowing her brow.

That was enough to get my attention. Suddenly, I was wide awake. I didn't want BJ comparing me to her mother. No matter how tired I was, I needed to show her what responsibility looked like. At least one parent had to do it, and it certainly wasn't going to be Jaqueline. "I'm . . . I'm up." I said, trying to sound convincing. There was a pause and then I added, "For real." I used my right arm to push my torso up and my bicep quivered in fatigue. As my feet hit the floor and I sat up on the edge of the couch, I thought about how much I loved BJ and how grateful I was that she was such a responsible young woman with goals and dreams. "Come here, you," I said with a smile as I reached over to give her a big grizzly dad hug and a kiss on the cheek."

"Yuk," she squealed as she pushed me away. "Sandpaper face and morning breath." Then she pointed imperiously toward my bedroom door. "Go get ready, you're gonna to be late. You're never late. They're gonna think something's wrong." She paused for a moment and then added, "Unless they know about—" Her eyes rolled to the ceiling, and a small smile graced her lips. We both knew she was referencing. "She who shall not be named," was resting peacefully under the ceiling fan behind the master bedroom door.

"No. Nobody at work knows," I mumbled as I hung my head a down a bit. "Actually, I have a problem you may be able to help me with." I wasn't one to brag, so bringing up the award felt awkward. "You see, I'm getting one of those," I stopped for a minute to find the right words. "*Doctor* awards. Um, everyone is expecting me to bring your mom. And, well—"

She interrupted me with a hushed panic in her voice as she snuggled up close to me again. "No way, Dad, she'll ruin it!"

I gave her a comforting pat on the leg and quietly finished my request. "I am well aware that taking her, or even telling her about it, would be a complete disaster. That's why I was going to ask if you wouldn't mind accompanying me that night instead?"

BJ's face lit up like a Christmas tree, her lips curled to corners of her mouth and her eyes started to water as they sparkled with excitement. Her shoulders were pushed back slightly as if she was going to let out a resounding "yes."

"Wait," I stopped her, raising my hand off her leg and looking her square in the eyes. "Before you answer, you need to know something. This is a formal event and you'll have to wear a dress. A nice dress."

"Duh. I know that," she said in an exasperated tone, sitting up excitedly. "And yes, I will go. I will wear anything you want. Even if I have to wear stupid heels, I'll do it." Then she reached over, gave me a kiss on my unshaven cheek, and bounded off the couch, headed toward the kitchen. "Go get ready. Hurry, if you're late they may take that award back. And you're, I mean *we're*, going to that." Her voice was so happy, so filled with joy. It was the happiest I had heard her sound in a very long time.

I made it to the hospital in what felt like record time, the heavens smiling down on me with every green light.

As I walked across the parking lot toward the emergency room doors, I noticed the ground was wet, the potholes that littered the parking lot filled with muddy water at least four to six inches deep. The last twenty-four hours I had been so wrapped up in my own thoughts that I'd somehow missed a major downpour.

As I approached the nurses' station I thought it looked a bit too familiar, like I hadn't even left. The same white Styrofoam cup full of cold coffee was sitting on the corner of the counter. "Back for more, huh, Jackson?" Said Roberts with a sly grin. "Lucky for you, the stars must be aligned. Things were a bit quieter last night. Yep, everything's still except for those chess pieces in there," he said as he pointed the top of his pen toward the lounge.

"Now who's the one askin' for more," I replied cockily. Somewhere amongst all that exhaustion, I had found my second wind. I inhaled deeply as if to fill my lungs with new, fresh energy for the shift that lie ahead. As I opened the door to the lounge, I gazed at the chessboard on the wall. With each step closer I was zoning in on the game. Roberts made his move. He had taken his white king from e1 and moved it to g1. Then he moved his rook, which was sometimes called a castle, from h1 to f1. Castling, which was what he did, was considered one move. In fact, it was the only move in chess where a player can move two pieces at once. The point of castling was to move the king into a safer position away from the center of the board. It also brought the rook to a stronger position in the center of the board. I stood there for a moment, taking it all in.

It was a move that proved Roberts was no beginner, he was seasoned.

I stood there thinking for a moment about the game and his last move in particular. I thought about my life, particularly my castle. As the supposed king of my home, I was somehow always in a weak position, just sitting out there on the board of life, completely vulnerable and open to attack. I picked up my black knight from f6, twirled it around between my first and middle finger, and then took his pawn from e4, and placed my knight there. A smile came across my face. *I may be tired*, I thought, *but I am still in the game*, I thought with no small degree of satisfaction.

I grabbed a cup of coffee and a kolache and headed toward the door, stopping at my locker for just a moment thinking about what Sergei had said. I reached forward and started to remove that photo of me and Jaqueline, then something stopped me. *Not yet,* I thought, my hand hovering in midair. I didn't particularly want to deal with the off chance that someone would notice and start asking questions. All at once I realized that Sergei was right. I couldn't take it down because it represented the guy I wanted people to think I was. That picture, in all its falseness, represented the life I wanted people to think I had. I walked away slowly, dragging my feet a bit and feeling like a fraud, wondering who the hell I was or would even end up being. It was a nauseating thought.

Mary greeted me with a smile as I came out of the lounge. She was chipper, every hair of her bob of in perfect position. "Cutest old couple ever in room one.

Roberts asked if you would see them. His frequent flier needs his attention."

Frequent flier, I thought. It was customary for doctors to brief each other on those types. Generally, these were the patients who frequented the ER looking for prescription medication. I supposed that if Roberts thought it was serious he would've mentioned it, so I let it go.

"Something's not quite right," said a lady who was sitting on a chair next to the bed her husband was laying on. Her voice was firm but quivering. Her silver, tightly curled hair appeared as if she had just left the beauty shop. She reminded me of my own grandmother, tender and kind. Her eyes were sort of a grey color, as the haze of cataracts had turned her once blue eyes a bit milky. Her hand was wrinkled and her crooked fingers intertwined with that of an older gentleman who was laying on the bed. Both their hands covered with age spots, but their grip was strong. "When you're married for over seventy years, you get to know someone," she said with a wink. "You know when something's a little off."

I looked at the couple and thought about what it must be like to love someone enough to be with them for seventy years. I thought long and hard, but I couldn't picture it, at least not for me. As a matter of fact, the more I thought about it the more my heart sank. As sense of deep sadness came over me. My marriage had no future and I knew it. My parents and my grandparents had this kind of love. I wanted it too, but it seemed as if that ship had sailed and I missed it.

"Doctor . . . Doctor?" The older lady said as she tried to regain my attention.

"I'm wondering what you mean by the word "off," I said, snapping back to attention. "Is his speech slurred? Is he sleeping more or less than usual?"

"No. Nothing like that," she said.

I took a look at the gentleman, not noticing anything in particular that would warrant his visit. His head was nearly bald except for the few white hairs that combed over his crusty, spotted head. He was wearing a colored shirt, buttoned to the top. "Carl, how are you feeling today?"

"Oh, I'm fine," he said waiving his other hand as if to dismiss the whole thing. "Ruthie here, she worries too much."

"It's nice to be worried about. I wouldn't complain if I were you. Having someone still looking out for you at ninety is a good thing. And she's a good-looking lady at that." I winked at him and then nodded at the wife, letting her know I was taking her worry seriously.

She kept holding his hand with her right hand, while her left one clutched her little leather purse up tight toward her waist. Below the chair her legs were crossed at the ankle and she sat up as straight as she could for someone of her age. "Well, for years he's had a glass of milk and two cookies each night before bed. But the last two nights he didn't want them. He said he wasn't hungry. I don't know how that could be possible because he barely had dinner those night's either. So, I told him he needed to get in and get checked out."

I looked over at Carl who was scrunching his lips and lowering his eyebrows in disapproval. "This is nothing. I can't believe I am in the emergency room because I didn't eat my cookies," he grumbled.

Just then Ruth stood up and said, "I'm going to excuse myself to the ladies' room if you don't mind. I'll be right back." As she left, she cleared her throat. Twice. The way someone does when they're trying to get your attention. I wasn't sure if that was the case, but after a few minutes I found an excuse to leave Carl and go look for her.

Just down the hall a bit she stood with her back against the wall looking my way as if she knew intuitively that I would follow her. "Look, I don't want to embarrass him. Carl is a private man and would be mortified if he heard me talking about his underwear, but I noticed some blood and I am very concerned."

"Front or back?" I asked. "I mean was it bloody stool or bloody urine stains?"

"Back. Usually there's a brown streak, has been for years, but never red," she said quietly, peeking around my body as if to be sure Carl wasn't going to find her talking to me.

"Red, not black, right?" I asked in a serious tone that matched hers.

"That's right, red, like blood." She cocked her head back so that she could see me. I must have been at least two feet taller than her. I could see the concern in her milky eyes that darted from side to side. I found her desire to preserve Carl's dignity sweet. At the same time, one would think that after seventy years, nothing would be off limits.

"Red is much better than black," I said as I put one hand on her shoulder and bent over a bit to meet her eye to eye. "Your secret is safe with me. I can get to the bottom of this and he will never know we spoke. Give me a few minutes before you come back in."

She nodded in agreement and then turned and walked to the restroom. I supposed she needed to go to the bathroom in order to keep herself honest. As she walked away, her pantyhose made a swooshing sound against her skirt and her old-lady dress shoes clip-clopped against the hard hospital floor. I thought about how beautiful she was. It didn't matter that she was hunched over, her skin was wrinkled and thin, and the clips at the nape of her neck revealed that she was wearing a wig. She was a good woman, a beautiful woman, the kind of woman I hoped to be with when I was ninety.

I popped back in the room with Carl. "So, no appetite lately? When did that start? Any tummy trouble to go along with it?"

Carl sat up in bed, looking over to make sure the door had closed behind me. "In marriage you should have no secrets, so what I am about to tell you needs to stay between us. Ok?" I nodded in agreement and smiled at the hypocrisy of his words. He continued, "Ruth may think

I'm hiding something from her. Well, I am, but it's only because she would worry. I don't want her to worry."

They were each so genuinely concerned about the other that it warmed my heart. I reached over and placed my hand on his shoulder and said, "It's a deal."

I was expecting him to tell me to tell me about his rectal bleeding, but he let out a big sigh and said, "Mexican food."

"Mexican food?" I asked a bit perplexed. Why would that be his big secret?

"Yep, years ago Mexican food landed me right here in this emergency room. I thought I was having a heart attack. Turns out it was just indigestion." His face looked deflated and embarrassed as he continued, "Poor Ruthie. It frightened her so much that I swore on my grave that I would never touch Mexican food again."

"Let me guess," I said trying to control my desire to chuckle. I swallowed my smile and put on a straight, serious face and added, "you didn't keep that promise, did you?"

He let out an audible gulp and confessed, "I didn't mean to cheat, it just happened. One of our great grandchildren, Billy, took me out to eat on his dime. How could I say no? It was his first paycheck and he wanted to get fajitas with his great granddad."

I tilted my head and bobbed it up and down in agreement. After all, he had a point. How could he pass that up? "And then . . ."

"Billy didn't know any better when he challenged me to a hot pepper challenge. But I did. Anyways, my rear-end has been on fire ever since. I can't eat because I don't want to go. It hurts too much." He started to shift around in the bed as if the thought of it made him uneasy.

"I tell you what, let me take a look down there and see what's going on. It sounds like you may have some hemorrhoids. Any blood?" I asked, never letting him know I already had the answer to that question, compliments of dear old Ruth.

Sure enough, it was exactly as I suspected. It wasn't ten minutes later that Carl and Ruth were leaving the emergency room with a prescription for hemorrhoid cream. They were walking hand in hand, like newlyweds. Ruth turned around to wave goodbye and winked at me. I winked back with a warm and grateful smile. I was filled with envy and admiration for both of them as I looked at her and said, "He'll be back on the cookies in no time. I'd say there's at least another ten years left in both of you."

I looked around for Roberts, but no sign of him at the nurse's station and all the rooms were empty. He was right, things were quiet around there. The usual beeping of machines, cries of pain and sounds of coughing and vomiting were all missing, creating a vortex of silence. "Roberts?" I asked Mary.

She was busy typing notes about Carl and stopped just long enough to answer me. As she looked up, her brown bob shifted back, putting every hair back in its rightful place. "Nope, he left already. Said he didn't really have anyone to pass off to you. If I know him, he wanted to get home for breakfast with that sweet Mrs. Roberts." She was right, Roberts will probably be one of the lucky ones—ninety and still holding hands.

Mary was organizing and cleaning the desk, something we rarely have time to do. "Coffee?" She asked, without looking up.

"I'll go grab some out of the lounge. I've got to get a second cup in before rush hour," I said half laughing, half serious, but not knowing how prophetic that statement would be. I really just wanted an excuse to go in and look at the board. Surely Roberts would have made another move on his way out the door. And, just as expected, he had. The white rook on fı had been moved to eı. I stood there basking in the silence, planning out my next move, when my cell phone rang. It was Jaqueline. I sent it to voicemail and then looked back at the board. It rang again. Again, I sent it to voicemail. My eyes squinted in on the board as I went into deep contemplation. *If this, then that. If that, then that,* I thought. Chess, much like medicine, was a game of consequence, with each move dictating the next. You were either closer to a win or closer to a loss.

Just as I was about to make my move, Jennifer burst through the door. "It's bad, let's go." Her face alone told me all I needed to know. It was ashen and her pupils were dilated and her hands were shaking, a panic I had never witnessed on her before. It wasn't like the look of a normal emergency, it was the panic healthcare workers got when it was someone they knew. Normally Jennifer's curly blonde hair would be pulled back in a scrunchy, but for some reason it was loose and hanging down over her shoulders. As we were running, I noticed how she grabbed a scrunchy from her pocket and quickly put it in a ponytail as if she was preparing for something serious.

"Elderly couple, look to be in their eighties or so, hit head-on. Multiple fractures. She's unconscious and from the looks of the windshield, her head took quite a blow. He's also lost a lot of blood and his blood pressure is dropping." No longer had the paramedic said those words that my phone rang again. I took it out of my pocket and threw it across the room. It landed in the sink clanging as it hit the stainless steel.

"Ruth," I said looking down over her lifeless body. It felt so surreal to be looking at her like this. I was feeling a flood of emotions, from shock to sadness, and back again. Her little pink heeled shoes were pointing outward. And her lace-trimmed white slip was peeking out from below her blood- soaked skirt. I started barking orders, "Let's manage the airway. Call x-ray. We'll also need a CT of her head, alert imaging." Noticing the paramedics taking Carl to the next room, I quickly got everyone's attention. "Nope, they stay together. Let's take them into the trauma bay." It was an area large enough for us to work on both of them together. "Carl, I said sternly. Stay with me Carl, Ruth needs you. I'm gonna keep you right here, right here in the same room. Together." Carl reached for my hand, but he was weak. He tried to grasp it, but he lacked the strength.

I overheard the paramedic tell Jennifer, "It wasn't even their fault. The SUV ran right into them. That driver went to Methodist but looks like they escaped with just a few bumps and bruises."

The once quiet walls of the emergency room were now echoing with its customary symphony of sounds. Neither Carl, nor Ruth, had a good prognosis. "Tell her," Carl said using every bit of strength he could muster. "Tell her I love her." He glanced over at her and tears filled his eyes. He was growing weaker by the moment. Even if I stabilized him, it was unlikely that he would make it through the surgeries he would need for the compound fracture of his femur. A large, broken bone, like a femur, usually spelled disaster.

I looked up and noticed how everyone was just going through the motions, on autopilot, as if they were hiding their emotions by being hyper-focused. Then, I did something extremely unconventional for most doctors. "Hold up," I told them. "Help me push these two together." Mary and Jennifer looked at me for a brief moment as if I had lost my mind. How could we work on each of them from only one side of the bed? I didn't know, but at the moment, I didn't care about logistics. Elizabeth never looked at me nor questioned my request, she just started moving the beds together, as if she'd read my mind. Her face was as red as her curly hair, and I could feel that she and I were on the same page without us having to say a word.

Carl reached over and rested his hand on Ruth's arm. "Ruthie," I heard him say faintly. "Ruthie, I'm here. I know you can't see me, but I'm fine and I'll stay here and take care of you." Those were the last words that Carl ever said and the last words that Ruth ever heard. As if on cue from the great conductor in the sky, both of them flat-lined. And just like that, they were gone. Nobody moved. We all just stood there, sad and relieved at the same time. Somehow, I couldn't help but imagine that this was how they would have wanted it. I scanned the room, but one person caught my eye. Elizabeth. Our eyes met and the glance was just a few beats too long. Long enough for me to read her thoughts. I could tell that she got it, she knew exactly why I did this and by the look in her eye, she agreed with my choice.

It wasn't long before I was sitting in the hospital chapel contemplating God's big plan. The quaintness of the room, with its wooden pews, and low ceiling was comforting. One couldn't really witness something like what had taken place and not think there was some sort of great orchestration. I cried and chuckled all at the same time as I thought about how ironic it was that Carl and Ruth, just moments earlier were so concerned about such trivial matters as underwear and Mexican food.

Elizabeth suddenly appeared right next to me in the pew, her eyes ringed with mascara as if she had shed a tear or two. I never even heard her come in. She put one arm around my shoulders as if to give me a side hug. I was taken a bit off-guard, since before that moment, I'd only imagined her touch. She whispered, "So, this is where you disappear to." Then she sat next to me quietly for some time, neither of us saying anything, just sitting there and comforting one another with our presence. I was thinking about Ruth and Carl, but I was also thinking about Elizabeth and how deep her green eyes seemed in that moment we'd shared. It was as if we were looking at the other's soul.

Elizabeth had been holding that emerald stone around her neck, sliding it back and forth across the chain. "It's weird, isn't it? We never really know when our lives will change. It can happen so fast or it can happen gradually. I'm convinced that no matter how it happens, we're always surprised." Another three of four minutes went by. Then she turned toward me, and looking down at the stone she said, "You asked me about this necklace once. I think I'm ready to tell you."

I turned toward her, ready to give her my undivided attention. I don't remember being that close to a woman who smelled that good and looked so genuine in a long time. Her perfume was floral with a hint of Jasmine, but not overpowering. The Jasmine scent reminded me of my mother's garden growing up. Being this close to her I could notice the freckles she had worked so hard to disguise behind her makeup. I never understood why women choose to cover up the very things that make them beautiful and unique. "Emerald is the birthstone of May. My daughter was born in May."

"Oh," I said with a tone of surprise. "I didn't know you have a—"

"I did." She stopped me. There was a pause. I could see her eyes watering a bit as she swallowed a few times. "She had leukemia." She paused again and her chest was starting to flush, like people do when they're choking back emotion. She swallowed hard. "When she got sick, my husband said he couldn't handle burying his own child. He left and I took care of her. I always knew it was coming, that last day, but no matter how you plan for the end, it always feels like a surprise." She turned her head and I heard a faint whimper escape her throat. I wanted to grab her and hold her, wipe away her tears. Instead, I just sat there, keeping my hands to myself and trying to think of a way to comfort her.

I thought back to that case several days back. That must have been why Elizabeth was so adamant about the blood test on that little girl, the one with the bruised leg. "I'm so sorry. I wish I could say that I can't imagine what that feels like, but unfortunately I can." Our eyes became locked as I described the pain we both knew all too well. "It hurts. It's a searing pain that pierces your heart again and again, each time you think about it. It sucks the life out of you, ripping at your very soul." She nodded as if she agreed. Her voice cracked a bit as she choked back emotion, "It's unnatural, you know." I went on, "Burying your own child."

Elizabeth and I, as if on cue, both turned and faced forward again. But this time she reached over and grabbed my hand, wrapping her long fingers around my own. We sat in the silence, soaking in a bath of our own tears for what must have been fifteen minutes, but felt like an eternity. The first time, since Jeremy died, I felt like someone understood me, that I didn't need to run from my pain any longer. Elizabeth was giving me something that I needed: a friend, a confidant, a shoulder to lean on. Not just any shoulder, but one that had carried a similar burden. In that moment of weakness, I felt strong.

It was as if this enormous festering despair had finally come to a head. For the first time, I felt as though I might someday be able to heal. In medical terms, it was like having an abscess. The pain was unbearable, and no matter how many antibiotics you threw at it, the only way to cure it, was to drain it. While nobody looked forward to having their abscess lanced open, I've never once heard someone complain about it after the fact.

The rest of the shift was somber, as if the whole team was mourning over Carl and Ruth and their fatefully tragic day. It was as if they became all of our surrogate grandparents for a day and then, just like that, they vanished. Then about an hour before my shift ended, Mary handed my cell phone back to me rolling her eyes. "Someone really wants to talk to you. That thing's been buzzing all day."

Just as she handed it to me, it rang again. I slid into an exam room to answer it. "Hello."

It was Jaqueline, and by the volume and tone of her voice, I could tell she was furious. "Hello? That's all you have to say? I've been calling you all day and now you just say hello?"

I let out a sigh and forced myself to converse with her. "It's been a heck of a day around here. What do you need, Jaqueline?"

"What do I need? I need you to answer your damn phone when I call. I needed to schedule the plumber to come out and how can I schedule him if I don't know your schedule?" She ranted, barely stopping to take a breath.

"Why do I need to be there?"

"Seriously?" she huffed, "You expect me to sit around here all day waiting for a plumber? Sorry, that's your department."

My skin crawled and my blood pressure shot up with the very sound of her voice. Especially after the day's events I felt trapped like never before. I stopped thinking about getting through one more day and started thinking about the next sixty years. The very thought of a future with Jaqueline was chilling. The kind of chill that goes down your spine during a horror movie. Except that horror movie was my life.

I ended up hanging up on her, even though I knew I would pay for it later. I slid my phone back in my chest pocket and tried to forget she even called. But, the more I tried to get her off my mind, the more she haunted my every thought. *I need to get away from her, forever,* I thought. I imagined how much better my life would be, and BJ's, if she was just gone. I saw myself smiling, enjoying life. I even imagined myself going out on dates or fueling my romantic side with whimsical trips to far off places. My fantasy of a life without Jaqueline was turning into an obsession.

As I walked past the medication cart, I remembered something an old professor once told the class. He said if someone ever wanted to get away with murder, all they would really need was a vial of insulin. I stood there staring at the medication cart, contemplating how easy it would be. All I needed was a diabetic to come in and I could conveniently sign out enough that nobody would ever miss it. I even imagined injecting it between her toes when she was passed out drunk. Nobody would look for a needle mark there. Perhaps, after the next drunco party . . . I stopped in my tracks, my mouth falling open in disbelief at the depth of my own twisted thoughts. *What the hell am I doing?* I thought, shaking my head as if I'd been asleep, trying to snap myself back to reality. *How can I seriously be thinking about murdering Jaqueline? Have I gone mad?* I shook my whole body, like a shiver, as if to shake the very thought of it off.

As I walked down the hall toward the nurses' station, I decided that I wasn't crazy, but that I just needed to get a good night's rest. Surely, a few hours of real sleep in real bed would turn me away from these insane, dark thoughts. Then I remembered that I never made my move. I stopped in the lounge just before leaving and picked up my black pawn from d7 and moved it to d5. Not exactly the most exciting move, but chess, like life, was a game of strategy, not speed.

And I needed a strategy if I was ever going to get out of this mess.

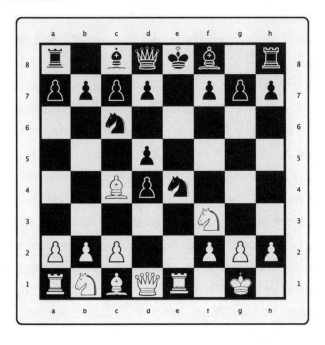

EIGHT

"Good morning, sunshine," I said to BJ as I entered the kitchen. She was already up and making breakfast, something that I don't usually see her doing at six a.m. on a Sunday. She was wearing plaid pajama bottoms and a T-shirt with a basketball sailing across the fabric and into a hoop, the words "Yeah, I play like a girl. Want a lesson?" written across the top. I'd bought that shirt for her last Christmas and she wore it quite religiously, especially on the weekends. She loved basketball, but I just wished she'd loved calculus class as much. "Hey, finals are coming soon, so be sure to get a few hours of studying in while I'm at work," I suggested in a very parental way.

She rolled her eyes a bit and then smiled, "Yeah, yeah, Dad. I know," she said distractedly as Honeysuckle wound herself back and forth between our legs, meowing as if she was trying to get our attention. BJ reached for her soft, furry head and scratched between her ears before picking her up. "See this face?" she said as she brought Honeysuckle a bit closer to me. "How could anyone not love this face?" As if the cat could hear everything BJ was saying, she purred louder and louder, swishing her big, plumed tail back and forth.

I reached over and stroked her from the head to her tail, looking deep into her gold eyes and thinking about my mother. "I think everyone *does* love her." Just like my mom, Honeysuckle was always loved by our family and friends. She wasn't a shy cat, she was more like a dog in the sense that she loved being the center of attention.

As BJ placed her back down on the floor, she said in a disapproving tone, "Everyone *but* Mom." She reached for the mixing bowl. As she cracked the first egg she asked, "Two or three?"

I signaled back to her with two fingers as I grabbed a coffee pod for the Keurig.

"Oh, and the athletics banquet is coming up. I need a dress, a nice one," she said as she cracked the second egg against the side of the bowl.

Wow, a fancy dress, I thought. *Impressive.*

"I wish Jeanie wasn't so sick, we could go shopping together. I love her so much, Dad, and I'm going to miss her when she dies." Her eyes welled up with tears, but none fell out. Just like any normal teenager, her emotions flipped almost in an instant and she became a bit hardened as she announced, "There's no way I'm asking Mom, otherwise known as the cat- loathing, daughter-hating monster."

I took in a deep breath and let out a sigh before speaking. "That's a little harsh, sweetheart. Don't you think? She doesn't *hate* you. Maybe the cat, but not you." I chuckled a bit, trying to make light of her comment, but inside I wondered whether or not she didn't have a point. But I knew I had to say it, even if I didn't believe it myself. No girl needs to think her parent hates her. "Besides, hate is a strong word. She loves you, she just doesn't know how to show love. I mean, I'm not making excuses for her. Trust me—I understand how you feel."

There was an awkward pause that filled the air. BJ cracked the eggs with such purpose, as if she was taking her frustration out on each one. "I'm just sick of trying, that's all," she said in a defeated tone.

"I know. And you could probably care less, but today *is* Mother's Day."

The very thought of asking BJ to do something nice for Jaqueline seemed wrong, but not recognizing Jacqueline at least in some small way would have devastating consequences for both of us.

BJ slammed her hand down on one of the empty eggshells. The sound of the shell crumbling seemed to mirror the state of her own crushed heart. "Seriously?" She mumbled. Then she grabbed a paper towel to clean up the mess.

"Look, just make her breakfast. You'll be doing both of us a huge favor," I begged with a bit of desperation in my voice. "Nothing fancy, just a little something." I held my hands out in front of me, practically pleading with her.

"Fine," she said curtly as she wiped the counter with the paper towels, rubbing so vigorously that they immediately began to tear apart. "Why don't you just divorce her? I hope you're not doing that 'stay together for the kid thing' that I hear about. Trust me," she said, unable to keep the bitterness from her voice. "I'd be better off without daily interactions with Cruella De Ville."

That was the first time the D-word had ever come up. It was as if BJ had been reading my mind and could see into the deepest recesses of my brain to the dark thoughts hiding in corners up there. But I didn't have time to have that conversation, not right before work. "Later, BJ." I said, brushing off her comment as I reached down to put food in Honeysuckle's dish. BJ usually fed her during the week since she was the first one to the kitchen, and I took weekend duty.

As I drove into the hospital, I thought about what BJ had said. She had no idea that I'd once visited a lawyer about divorce. I remembered it like it was yesterday. The lawyer's office was wood paneled and he had a large, mahogany desk with carved legs, a desk he sat behind and told me that divorce would be expensive and that I would probably have to give her everything. At the time, I had just started making the first real money of my career and I couldn't imagine starting all over again. Jaqueline texted me while I was sitting in his office. It was her usual demanding, rude text. It was enough to convince me starting over would be worth it.

About a week after that, Jaqueline found the card while doing laundry. She went nuts, yelling and screaming in my face, her eyes wide and crazed looking, spittle flying at my face. It was a few years back and BJ was much younger, but Jaqueline's threats of ruining me, my career, and moving away with BJ paralyzed me with fear and I never followed through. I guess I was doing that "stay together for the kids" thing BJ was talking about.

As I entered the emergency department, I noticed that things were quiet, which was typical of a Sunday morning, but I knew that with it being a holiday, it wouldn't last long. "Working on Mother's Day, huh?" said Jennifer. Her curly blonde hair was pulled back in a scrunchy and her hazel eyes matched her eyeshadow. "I hope you remembered to send your mother something."

I looked at Jennifer, my mouth falling open, then closing shut again. I guess I had never told her my mother had died of cancer a few years back. "Well," I started, not knowing what to say next and hoping she'd just drop it.

"Well what? Did you? If not, you should get on that computer right now while there's still time and send her something. I was lucky enough to have a husband who got the kids up super early for a pancake breakfast." She smiled and added, "And they even remembered that momma needed a new yoga mat. Good thing I sent something to my own mom a few days ago, or I would have forgotten too."

Well, that was an assumption, I thought. I hadn't forgotten my mother at all. Actually, I'd been thinking about her all the way to work, wishing I could call her and talk about my dilemma with BJ and Jaqueline. Thinking back, Mother's Day was the only day we'd been allowed to mess up her kitchen without getting into trouble. Standing there, smiling weakly at Jennifer, I would've given anything to make my mother breakfast in bed again. Finally, I cleared my throat and said, "I did send flowers, but they were sent to my mother's grave a few days ago. I'm sure somewhere, somehow she appreciated them."

"I—" she stopped, her eyes growing wide, and then she looked down at her feet and back up at me again, her cheeks flushing bright red. "I am so sorry. I never should have—"

"Don't worry about it." I said with a wave of my hand, trying to brush the whole thing off. "I know you meant well." I noticed a white box on the nurse's station ledge. "What's this?" I asked, my mood brightening. "Pastries?"

Just as I reached to pop the corner of the box up, Jennifer slapped my hand and said with "None for you, Mister. I made those for the mothers." It was well-known around the hospital that Jennifer was a great baker, one who's pastries would rival even the fanciest bakeries in town. She once told us that if she hadn't become a nurse, she would have opened a bakery of her own. I could envision her doing that. Someday, instead standing behind a nurses' station, she could be standing behind her own display counter, the glass case filled with raspberry tarts that sparkled like jewels.

As I entered the doctor's lounge to grab a bite of non-forbidden breakfast, there was Roberts doing the exact same thing. His glasses were tucked into the pocket of his shirt, and his blue scrubs looked like they were still freshly pressed, not like he'd just worked a twelve-hour shift. I must admit, he was the only doctor I'd ever met that actually *ironed* his scrubs. He looked at me, cocking his head to one side and with a smirk he said, "We need a new policy. The physicians need to have full access to all food at all times."

I chuckled a bit at his suggestion. "Yeah, I like that." Over the last few days the chessboard had seen some serious action between us. He moved his white bishop from c4 to take my pawn on d5 and I moved my black queen from d8 to take his bishop on d5. Then he moved his white knight to from b1 to c3 in an effort to attack my queen. Having no choice, I moved my black queen from d5 to h5. I couldn't help but think *strategy, strategy* with each move, but much like in my life, I felt I was playing more defense than offence. Over the past few days, I had meant to see an attorney, but just couldn't seem find the time. At least that was what I'd been telling myself.

Roberts walked over to the board, turned to me and said with a smirk, "I almost forgot." He proceeded to take his white knight on c3 and capture my black knight on e4. He turned away from the board and looked at me with a sly smile, the kind you make when you want to brag with your words, but it would inappropriate so you hide behind your look instead. The smile only fell so that he could take another bite of his cream cheese smeared bagel. Without uttering a word, he just chewed all the way to the door. I stood there, looking at the board, feeling deflated, knowing I needed to make a move, a good move. It was time to activate my bishop, so I took him off c8 and moved him to e6. It wasn't one of those moves that takes a piece of his off the board, or puts the king in check, but it was definitely strategic. Good strategy often was about small steps in the right direction. Which was a reminder that I needed to take the time to make small steps in the right direction—not just for me, but for BJ as well.

After I walked back into the ER, things stayed quiet for another fifteen or twenty minutes, then a skinny, agitated woman entered through the automatic doors. She was around thirty-five and had wide, paranoid eyes. Her hair was stringy and looked as though it could use a good brushing. The short, cotton skirt she wore was hopelessly wrinkled, and the loose white button-down shirt she wore had what appeared to be an old coffee stain across the front. "Where is he?" She said. "Dr. Roberts. Did he leave?"

Just then Mary came around the corner. I was surprised to see her working on Sunday, as normally, she tried to take the day off. Since she'd been there the longest, she had the most flexibility in her schedule. "Well, she's an hour late. Let me handle this." Mary said in an authoritative tone as she walked toward the woman and very calmly said, "Yes, he left a few minutes ago. Dr. Jackson is here and he can see you."

The woman pursed her lips, squinted her eyes, and said in a loud, aggravated tone, "Oh hell no." I had to admit, it was the first time I had seen a patient so put off at the thought of seeing me. "When's he back? Tomorrow?" she asked, her tone desperate.

Jennifer walked up at that point and without any compassion blurted out, "No. He won't be back for a few days." With that, the woman turned in a huff and stomped back toward the sliding doors. Right before she exited, she turned to give everyone one last dirty look.

"What was that all about?" I asked. At that moment I felt like there was a story here, and I was the only one who was out of the loop.

Jennifer rolled her eyes and said, "Oh that's Lynn. She's a frequent flier. Usually showing up an hour or two before Dr. Roberts's shift is over. I don't think he likes her either. At least he spares us the pain of dealing with her."

Mary added, "Yeah, he usually deals with her alone so we can focus on the real patients. She's obviously a drug seeker or a hypochondriac or both. She's been coming here for years, but lately she's gotten worse."

"Well, in that case, I'm glad she doesn't want to have anything to do with me," I said. I had a fleeting thought about the oddity of Roberts never mentioning her to me, but then I let it go. After all, I didn't know everything about his days, or his life for that matter.

I heard the doors swoosh open and I assumed it was her again, but instead it was a woman holding her husband's arm, flanked by two young girls on either side of them. The mother, who looked around fifty, seemed to be having trouble breathing. As she moved, she bent over slightly, her hand hovering across the upper part of her chest. She looked a bit panicked, but not quite as panicked as her husband and two daughters, one blonde and one brunette. They were all dressed up as if they were on their way to church. The mother was in a flowing floral dress that buttoned down the front. Mary immediately triaged her into the first room on the right.

She was raspy, but her airway wasn't completely blocked off. As I unbuttoned the front of her dress to listen to her chest I asked, "Any history of asthma?"

"No," she replied. It was a faint answer that sounded more like a whisper.

Mary was standing as if at attention at the computer. "Any allergies to medications?"

"Penicillin," her husband answered as he pointed his index finger in the air.

"Anything else?" I asked, thinking it was seeming more like an allergic reaction at this point, than asthma. It appeared as if it was getting harder for her to move air and her heart rate was going up.

"No," the brunette daughter answered. Both girls looked like they were in their early twenties. Old enough to be out of school, but perhaps not old enough to have any children of their own. The brunette was dressed conservatively with a pencil skirt and button-up blouse, while the blonde was in a loud colorful maxi dress that went down to her platform sandals. I couldn't help but notice how one seemed to favor the mother and the other their father. Since both girls were with their mother on Mother's Day, it was a dead giveaway that neither had children of their own yet.

"List of medications?" Mary asked as she tucked her bobbed hair behind one ear. She was mostly directing her questions toward the husband. "Did you happen to bring them with you?"

"No, we don't have them here, but I know what they are. She only takes a baby aspirin and something for cholesterol. Oh, um, I think it's called Simva-something"

"Simvastatin." I said looking at Mary. I don't know why I bothered to tell her, she had already figured it out and typed it in. Looking back at the woman and her husband I asked, "Ok then, any supplements?" Most people forget to report that they take vitamins and other things because they consider them innocuous. I always told my patients, "If you put in your mouth and it's not food, I want to know about it." It was a good rule of thumb, one that I learned during residency.

The husband shrugged and responded, "Nope."

Then, the wife shook her head frantically in the affirmative as she pointed to the daughter who had been silent. The daughter's brown eyes seemed to grow larger as she started digging through her purse. It was a large, leather hobo-type bag. I couldn't imagine why she would have needed such a big purse. I guess purses were something I never quite understood about women. Some could fit everything they needed into a small clutch, while others carried around a purse that looked more like luggage. Finally, she pulled out a large white bottle and read off the front label. "Glucosamine. I bought this for her knees," she said holding out the bottle so I could see. "It says it helps with joint pain. Mom's been complaining about her right knee, so I thought we'd try this."

By this time, we had oxygen flowing through a mask to help the mother breathe. I looked over at the husband who was at the head of the bed with one arm stretched out so he could stroke her wavy brown hair. His tailored suit still perfectly pressed for church. "By any chance does she have an allergy to shellfish?"

The woman pulled off the mask and let out the loudest whisper she could muster. "Yes!" Then she put the mask back on, her expression weary, as if that one small gesture had taken all her remaining strength.

"Oh yeah," he said concerned. "I mean, she almost died once when we were at a seafood restaurant. The kids were little back then. I have made double sure she hasn't had any shrimp, crab, or anything like that since. Whew, that was scary stuff. But, why is that relevant, Doc?"

"Holy crap!" said the girl holding the bottle. She ran her hand through the top of her straight blonde hair. "I forgot about that. I am so sorry, Mom."

"Ok, I'm confused," said the husband as he looked around at everyone. He reminded me of myself earlier with that crazy patient looking for Roberts. Everyone in the room but him seemed to have caught on to what was going on.

The other daughter grabbed and turned the bottle around in her hand and read the warning, "contains shellfish." Then she rolled her eyes. The eye rolling seemed to be contagious as the rest of the family followed suit.

I got up close to the woman, who was visibly shaken by the shellfish announcement, her face ashen. "It'll be ok. Epinephrine, which Mary's about to give you, will help reverse the allergic reaction. Keep in mind, this medication will most likely make you feel anxious and may make your heart race, but that will pass. In a matter of minutes your airway should open back up and you'll feel much better." I smiled at her and then nodded at the husband.

No sooner had Mary given the medication that the mother's skin began to turn a nice shade of pink. "This is all too common," I said to the family. "People assume that all supplements are safe and harmless. That's not necessarily true, and when you have allergies like this one, you have to be extra careful and read labels."

The room seemed to nod in unison, then the brunette looked at the blonde with the big purse and said, "Way to go. You nearly killed our mother . . . *on* Mother's Day at that." It was sort of a tongue-in-cheek comment, she seemed to be half kidding and half serious. While it wasn't funny, it was a bit ironic. Their banter reminded me how nice it was to have siblings. I wish I could see more of my own sister, but after mom died she and her husband moved to Colorado, so an occasional call was about all we did these days. Watching these sisters made me think about BJ. She had lost her only brother and was going to miss out on so much because of it. Just thinking about BJ growing up without a sibling made my heart sink in my chest.

Later while Mary, Jennifer, and I were at the nurse's station, Elizabeth came in. "HR told me this is the slowest day of the year so they asked me to work a half shift." She seemed disheveled and sad. Her red, curly hair was a bit unruly, and her face was impassive, void of emotion. I knew that Mother's Day must've been hard for her, but I didn't let on. I was pretty sure I was the only one who knew about the loss of her daughter.

"You haven't missed much," I said. Everyone kind of nodded in agreement. It was indeed a slow day, one of the slowest I had seen since I'd been there. Then the doors opened and a man carrying a vase of yellow roses walked toward the nurse's station. "Somebody loves their mother," he said as he placed the vase next to the white box on the counter.

"Who's the lucky girl," I said as I reached for the card. Jennifer and Mary were both thinking it was them, so they stood there with big smiles of anticipation. Luckily, I read the card to myself and not out loud. It said: Lizzy, Thinking of you this Mother's Day. Love, Mom." I swallowed hard and knew I had to think fast. Something told me this wasn't something Elizabeth wanted to explain, at least not today.

"And??" Jennifer insisted. I could tell she thought they were hers by the way she asked, and the devilish grin on her face.

"Sorry ladies." I said sweeping the flowers up with one hand. "These are for someone upstairs. I know her, so I'll take them up." Everyone was deflated, I watched as one by one their faces fell, all except Elizabeth's. She had tried to appear preoccupied, shuffling paperwork, but as soon as I'd finished she looked at me and gave a small, almost imperceptible sigh of relief. I gave her a quick smile, then walked down the hall a bit. When the coast was clear, I slipped into the doctor's lounge with the bouquet.

The morning remained relatively slow. There were a few lacerations that needed to be stitched, a case of food poisoning, and one chest pain that turned out to be indigestion from too much barbeque. At one point, Elizabeth caught me in the hall, grabbing my arm gently as I passed, and with a humbled and quiet voice she said, "Thank you."

"No problem," I replied with a faint smile. "I didn't quite know what—"

"What you did saved me some heartache today," she said quietly. I looked at her sad green eyes. I noticed the whites of her eyes were a little red, as if she had been crying before she got to work. I wanted to say something, but I just stood quietly, lost in her watery, glistening eyes.

She looked down at her feet and said, "I knew they were mine, but I froze. She does that every year. Roses. Yellow Roses." Her voice grew stronger and a little louder.

"She thinks it helps, but it doesn't." She looked back up and our eyes met again. I could feel her frustration, her pain. I knew exactly how she felt. When Jeremy died, everyone tried to do things to make me feel better, but most of it was just a reminder of the pain.

I wanted to reach out and grab her, pull her to me tightly, and let her cry on my shoulder. I knew I was the only one in that emergency department who could under-stand how holidays, like Mother's Day could hurt. It was the same pain I felt every Father's Day since my own son died. As much as I wanted to gaze into her beautiful green eyes forever, I knew I had to stop. I looked away and said with a bit of a chuckle to lighten the mood, "I can take care of the flowers for you, but if you want to partake of those Mother's Day pastries, you're on your own."

She smiled back, leaning toward me almost expec-tantly, those green eyes hypnotizing me until I almost had to reach out and . . . But just then, the dinging sound of my phone broke the moment, and I reached into my pocket. It was BJ, sending me a text of the breakfast she made for Jaqueline. She had gone all out with pancakes, bacon, coffee, and a little orange juice. "Proud of you," I texted back.

"Sorry, it's my daughter," I said, hoping Elizabeth and I could simply continue our conversation and that she wouldn't just walk away. "Look, what a sweet girl," I said, holding the phone out for her to look at. "She made this for her mom this morning."

"Wow, quite a girl you've got there." Elizabeth said with a smile, "a real keeper."

"She's special all right," I said, trying not to be too over the moon about BJ for fear of hurting Elizabeth on what I knew was already a difficult day. It felt wrong somehow to be bragging about my daughter when she'd lost hers. Then my phone dinged again. When I pulled it back out, I read, "Don't get too excited. She didn't eat it. She looked at it and complained about the carbs. Oh, and she told me that I shouldn't eat it either unless I wanted to put on more weight." She added an emoji with a sad face and a single tear.

I felt the smile from my face transform into a scowl. My head felt flushed and hot and I could hear my own pulse in my ears. I knew my blood pressure had just shot up from the hormone surge. Elizabeth noticed the change in my demeanor and said, "What? What's wrong?"

I huffed and took a few deep breaths, rereading the message as if it was more than I wanted to believe. "Got a minute?" I asked. "Actually, this may take more than a minute."

"Of course," she said, still concerned and looking a bit confused as her eyebrows turned down. "Let's go to our *other* office." We both knew what she meant and headed toward the chapel.

I spent the better half of twenty minutes unloading all my emotional baggage. I told her how there were signs and I ignored those signs and married Jaqueline anyway.

I told her about missing my mom, being confused about divorce. I even told her what BJ said that morning. But, the most shocking thing, by the look on her face was when I let her read BJ's last text.

"I had no idea. I'm so sorry." Her face crumpled as if she was experiencing my pain right there with me. There was a bit of silence and then she reached over, took my hand in hers. "How can I help?" she asked with a smile. Her teeth were so white against the redness of her lips. I looked at her and thought about how perfect she was, even with the little brown freckle at the top of her nose bridge.

Marry me. Take me away from this nightmare. I said with my inner voice while my outer voice simply said, "You've already helped. Thanks for just being there."

As we left the chapel, I felt better, as if Elizabeth had helped me somehow by sharing my emotional baggage. Unbeknownst to us, Sergei had been right outside the chapel the whole time. He started whistling as he mopped, as though he was in his own world, paying no attention to us whatsoever. But, as Elizabeth and I continued down the hall, I stole a glance back at Sergei, who looked up from his duties, smiled and gave me a wink of approval. I had mixed emotions. On one hand, I was worried that Sergei might tell someone. On the other hand, I'd never known him to be a gossip, as he mostly kept to himself. And we'd shared a moment that day at my locker. He was the only one who'd figured out that my life wasn't all it appeared to be. Between this moment and his locker comment, he was most likely putting two and two together. But strangely, that idea didn't panic me. Somehow, I knew my secret was safe with him.

The rest of the shift I was thinking about Elizabeth, the way she'd looked at me, her huge, green eyes seeking my own. Was something happening here? Something that everyone else realized but me? The cases to follow were more like background noise to my internal dialogue. *Does she feel what I do, or was I imagining it? Maybe we were just really good friends . . .* All shift, I couldn't help daydreaming about what it would be like if BJ met Elizabeth and the two of them hit it off. *What if I could have a good marriage, one like Roberts has?* I thought tentatively, although even thinking of it felt like a betrayal. Even if nothing came of these feelings for Elizabeth, the thought that a new life, a better life, was indeed possible, strengthened my resolve to go and see that attorney once and for all.

It was 6:00 p.m., with just an hour to go in my shift, one we were all about to mark as the easiest shift in emergency room history, when the roar of the ambulance siren cut through the peaceful day like a loud protester during the solemnity of wedding vows.

"Suspected heroin overdose," said the paramedics. "Looks as though we got there too late. We actually found her on the side of the road as we were headed back from another call across town. She was real close, just a few blocks away from here."

I looked down at the patient, her skinny body was limp and her hair was soaked from foam and vomit. Her eyes were closed, her white shirt with the coffee stain even more soiled. Her legs protruding from her miniskirt were thin as sticks, and unnaturally still. "Lynn," I said as we all started working frantically to pull her out of it. Heroin was nasty stuff. If you caught it fast enough, a shot of naltrexone could pull a patient right out of it, but if you were too late, you were just too late. As I watched the woman's face as it went from being devoid of color to a light blue, I knew this was a case of being too late. It was over as fast as it had begun. I called the code. "Time of death, 6:20."

It was oddly calm in the department after that. Mary and Jennifer seemed totally indifferent to the patient's death, as if they'd expected it. After the morgue came up to take the body down, I asked if one of them would look through the patient's medical record to see if she had a next of kin. Mary agreed.

Sergei came to clean up the room. Afterward, he handed me a small, folded piece of paper. I thought he was passing me a note, the kind you got back in high school. I gave him a half smile as I took it. He didn't smile back. Instead there was a serious look on his face. He leaned toward me and said quietly, "Don't read it now. Later. I found that note on the floor, and I'm guessing it fell out of her pocket."

I found it odd that even Sergei knew this patient's name. She really must have been a frequent flier for even the janitor to know who she was. Nonetheless, I did just as Sergei asked. When the shift was over, I disappeared to the lounge. I plopped down on the sofa and exhaled before taking the note from my pocket. It was a bit wrinkled and stained, as if she wrote it days, if not weeks ago.

In shaky handwritten letters it spelled out:

John, or should I call you DOCTOR Roberts? I'm not going to play your games any longer. Either give me what I want, what you know I need, or she's going to find out. I will ruin your career – your marriage – your everything. It's a simple request so stop jerking me around!!

What the hell? I froze for a moment in disbelief. When I'd unfolded that paper, I had no idea I was about to unfold so much more.

NINE

On the way home, my mind was racing. I thought of every scenario in the book, but couldn't possibly figure out how Roberts, the man I thought I knew, could somehow be mixed up with an addict like Lynn. I pulled into the garage, numb from the day's events. I knew I'd never get to sleep if I couldn't get some answers. As I thumbed through the contacts in my phone, hovering over Roberts' name, I stopped to wonder what the hell I was going to say. *Hey John, some drug addict with a note addressed to you died today* probably wasn't going to cut it. Taking a deep breath, I pressed his name and then again on his number, not knowing what, if anything, I'd say when he answered.

Roberts answered the phone, seemingly wide awake. It was always a bit tricky calling someone who worked nights. You never knew their sleep schedule, so it was a gamble. "Hey Jackson, what's up? Shouldn't you be home by now?" Roberts always called me Jackson, most of the other doctors at the hospital call me Bob or Bobby, but Roberts and I were on a last name only basis. He called everyone by their last name though, probably because he spent his whole life dreaming of going into the Air Force and becoming a fighter pilot. He even did ROTC through high school and his first year of college. He didn't find out he was color blind, an exclusion for Air Force pilots, until he was twenty. He told me that story once, between shifts. I could tell by his tone and the way he kept clearing his throat that thirty some years later, it was still a painful disappointment.

"Actually, I'm sitting in my car in my garage," I said, letting out a little nervous and muted cough. I was trying to think of what to say next.

He seemed to sense my hesitation through the phone. "Everything all right? I can count on one hand the number of times you've called me after work. What's up?" He asked with a chuckle.

I stalled for a moment, but then it hit me that I didn't want anyone to overhear this conversation, especially his wife. "Are you alone right now?" I asked, somewhat cryptically.

"Hold on a minute, Jackson, let me find that for you," he said in a serious tone. His footsteps seemed to echo across the wooden planks in his house. I heard the creak of a door and then the latch catch. "I am now. What's going on?"

My heart was racing a bit and I felt slightly nauseous. I knew that in that moment, that conversation, in some way was going to change the life of John Roberts. "Do you know a patient by the name of Lynn Seldeen?"

There was a long pause. The kind of pregnant pause that can make sweat form on your brow. The kind that people give when they've been caught doing something wrong.

"Oh, be right there, honey," he hollered out in response to the knock on the door. Then he said very business-like and loud enough to be purposely overheard, "You know what Jackson, it's probably best if I show you that procedure in person. I'm actually up, so how about I come down there."

I knew exactly what he was doing. This was cover talk, the kind that's code for "someone is way too close for a real conversation."

"Meet you at Al Bernat's." I said as I hung up and reversed down the driveway. I stopped only long enough to text BJ that I had to run back to work, so not to wait up.

The restaurant was lively, with white linen covered tables for four filling the center of the room, and only a limited number of booths lining the sides. Luckily, we managed to get the last booth, one in the far corner which offered a bit of privacy. After we each slid across the leather seats and settled in, our eyes met, both of us knowing this had the potential of being an incredibly uncomfortable conversation. Roberts was fidgeting and making meaningless small talk. I was hoping to order quickly and get the waiter out of our space. I knew, even without John saying a word that this was the type of conversation that should never be overheard.

"Look, before you tell me what you're going to say, I want you to know that I'm here as a friend. Whatever you tell me about Lynn, know that it won't go past this table." I looked him dead in the eyes and paused to let him know I meant it. His brow was sweaty and his face was flushed. I felt sorry for him. He was upset and he didn't even know yet that she had died.

"Look, I love my wife," he said as tears welled up in his eyes.

"I have no doubt that you do." I said, knowing that it was true. "You're a good man, I can't quite figure out the connection here. Were you—"

"No," he said emphatically. "Well, only once." He paused and rubbed both hands across the front of his face like he was trying to scrub off the guilt. "It was like ten years ago." He looked around nervously and then down at the table.

"Ok." I said, trying not to sound as shocked on the outside as I was on the inside. "Well, what happened? And, what's the deal with her coming to the emergency department looking for you?"

He looked around again to be sure nobody was within ear shot. "Look, I met her a decade ago at a hotel in California. I was there for some continuing education credits, ironically for mental illness." He suddenly sat up straight and got stoically quiet. Then he looked at the waiter and smiled. Once the coast was clear again, he continued. "I was going through a rough patch, feeling pretty sorry for myself, feeling old and washed up. I was realizing all the things in my life I hadn't accomplished. Lynn was at the bar that night and said all the right things. She told me I was smart and handsome. She even laughed at all my stupid old jokes. I felt alive, young, and manly. Oh jeez, I can't even imagine how stupid and corny this must sound to a young, handsome guy like you."

"It doesn't sound stupid at all. Hey, I get it." I made eye contact with him after a long pause. "Really," I added, hoping he could see that it was sincere.

"It was one time and I've busted my ass trying to make up for it ever since. By the way, Ellen knows nothing about this and I'm doing everything in my power to keep it that way."

"I'm a bit confused. How did this girl from ten years and ten thousand miles ago end up back in your life?" I asked.

"He sat back, took in a deep breath, rolled his eyes, and then asked, "I don't want to tell you anymore. Well, I want to tell you as a friend, but I can't."

"Why not?" I asked, a little taken back by his demeanor.

"I don't want to put you in that position."

"No position here. I'm here as a friend and a confidant. Nothing more, nothing less."

We sat and ate for a few minutes, but I noticed he mostly picked at his food, pushing it around his plate. A grown man who can sit in front of a Texas-sized steak and refuse to eat it was one tormented soul. Finally, like a pressure cooker that couldn't hold it in any longer, he began to spew. He told me how she showed up a few years back in the emergency room demanding Vicodin. Apparently, her dentist had been giving it to her for years and then he retired. Surprised and afraid, he gave it to her. That turned into regular threats that were defused by prescription after prescription. "Since the DA tightened up the rules of opioids, I started refusing her requests. Lately, she's been coming in a lot. I've done everything to try to keep the staff and the hospital out of this. I guess she came in to see you today?" He asked in a rhetorical way.

"Yes, yes she did. Twice as a matter of fact. Once she came in looking for you. Then she came back again later, just before the end of my shift," I said. I took in a deep breath so I could blurt out the big news, but before I could he interrupted my thought process.

"Look, I'm sorry. I can't believe she's bugging you. Did she tell you all this? Oh man, I hope she didn't tell the staff." His eyes grew big with fear and his voice became a bit more panicked.

"Before I tell you how I know, I want you to know that cutting her off was the right thing to do. And what I am going to tell you is going to be just between us."

"Ok," he said in a quivering voice.

Then I handed him the note. He read it, silently and without expression. He crumpled it in his hand and then looked at me and asked, "Who's seen this?"

"Just me, none of the nurses. It fell from her pocket. Actually, it was under the gurney. The one she died on, Roberts. Lynn came in with a heroin overdose, but there was nothing we could do."

His eyes filled with tears, but I wasn't sure if they were tears of sorrow, or relief, or both. I didn't ask and he didn't say. We just sat there in silence for a good five minutes, but that five minutes felt like thirty. He took his black cloth napkin, wiped his eyes, then took his first bite of steak.

"I guess it's time to get back to your day off," I said, trying to break the silence that had fallen between us like a heavy black shroud. "Hey, I know you have a vacation coming up. Take that time to relax and love on Ellen," I said, looking him in the eye. "Your nightmare is over now." He curled his lips in, then smiled faintly as he hung his head, and nodded in agreement. In an effort to break the tension, I added, "But that chess game, my friend, that's another story."

As I drove home I reflected on how Roberts had been dealing with so much, but never chose to share his pain with me. I could have been there for him. He must have felt lonely and afraid through it all. Guilt can be such a heavy yoke around the neck. I felt sorry for Lynn too. On some level, one had to feel sorry for those caught up in the opioid crisis. Being in the emergency room, we saw all walks of life, from the elderly to executives, to blue collar workers who've had their worlds turned upside down, all from a seemingly innocent prescription.

Then, as I stopped at a red light, it hit me, Roberts didn't know much about my life either. His comment about my being young and handsome showed how he viewed me. I thought back to that time Sergei commented on the photos pasted up in my locker. He was right; we all projected what we wanted people to think our lives were like, basically, what we *wished* they were like. After seeing the relief on Roberts' face once he opened up, I realized that I wanted that kind of relief too. I had to change my life, or come ten years later, I would still be in the same situation—only worse.

TEN

I couldn't help but think about Roberts for two straight nights, tossing and turning as I tried in vain to find sleep. I had a strange sensation in my heart, one I hadn't felt before. It wasn't pain, or pressure like you get when you're having a heart attack. It was more of a warmth. While I'm sure my parents weren't perfect, I never saw their faults. Perhaps that's why I never wanted anyone to see mine.

Throughout my life, I'd had countless college buddies and many professional colleagues, but none that I considered true friends. I wasn't even sure if I really knew what a true friend looked like, but despite that fact, I couldn't help feeling some kind of empathy for Roberts. After our conversation, I couldn't shake the fact that we were becoming friends, real friends. Through our talk, I oddly understood a new truth about life—we were all flawed. Even people we thought were perfect, or close to perfect, weren't perfect at all. Maybe it was time to stop beating myself up over my decision to marry Jaqueline all those years ago.

My mind was restless, so I went to the hospital a bit early. "What are you doing here at 4:00 am?" Roberts asked, a tinge of nervous energy in his voice. It was as if he couldn't take any more surprises. He was sitting behind the desk finishing up a note. He looked up out of the top of his glasses, staring at me, waiting for me to answer.

"No reason to be here," I said with a reassuring glance. "Except for the fact that I couldn't sleep." He let out an audible sigh of relief. I looked around noticing that the emergency room was empty and quiet. "Slow night?"

"Yep, just tucked the last one in upstairs. Looks like she'll be here a few days. Pneumonia." There was this awkward silence, as if he wanted to talk, but was afraid that other's may overhear our conversation. "Umm," he said, pushing against the desk to roll his chair back away from it. "Awake enough for a few moves?"

"Oh, you're due for some punishment this morning," I said with a wink. "I'm always up for moves. Besides, we should make use of our time. I'd like to finish this game before you head out on vacation. What's that, like a few weeks from now?"

"Not soon enough," he said as we walked through the lounge doors.

Before I arrived, he had already moved his white knight on e4 to g5. "Oh, I see you've had some time to think about this already," I said as I moved my black bishop from f8 to b4. I wanted him to know I was always up for a good counter attack. I stood there trying to hide my smirk, hopeful that this would stump him, or at least slow him down a bit.

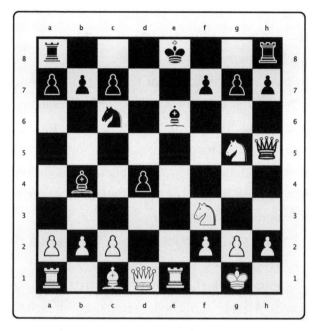

Without so much as flinching, as if he was anticipating my move, he picked up his white rook on e1 and captured my black bishop on e6. I winced, frustrated that I hadn't anticipated it. "Yep, it's time for a cup of java," I said, making my way to the pot on the lounge counter.

He chuckled a bit and then said, "It's fresh, just made it about an hour ago." Then he stopped and looked up at me in confusion. "Wait a minute, I thought you didn't drink that stuff? Word has it you're a bit of a coffee snob. Aren't you the one who put in the request for one of those by-the-cup machines?"

"Listen here, old-timer," I said sarcastically. "Those by-the-cup things are called a *Keurig*. And yes, I did. You don't know what you're missing. You see, you like this institutional tar because you have an unsophisticated palate." I started to laugh. So did Roberts.

"Listen here, Ken doll," he said, raising an eyebrow. "This old-timer still has what it takes to make you look like a patzer." He used the word "patzer" with such conviction, but I had no idea what the heck it meant.

As soon as I moved my black pawn off f7 to take his rook on e6, I stepped away with a big smile. Roberts stood in front of the board, his arms folded, studying it. He narrowed his eyes, deep in concentration.

I pulled out my phone to Google that word. *Patzer: a poor chess player.*

"Are you back there looking up patzer?" he asked with a chuckle. I couldn't believe it. It was as if he had eyes in the back of his head. Before I could answer, he moved his white knight off g5 to capture my black pawn on e6.

"Maybe I was, maybe I wasn't," I replied coolly. "All I have to say is that despite certain people's beliefs, I'm not particularly bad at chess."

Roberts started laughing, looked at me, pointed and stepped backward. "You did look it up!" Suddenly, we both were chuckling, the kind of chuckling that's contagious.

The door to the lounge opened, and nurse I had only seen a few times before looked in. She was wearing green scrubs and had jet black hair. By her frown, I could tell she was not amused by our loud laughter. She put one fist up on her very large left hip and said, "Party's over, doc's. We've got patients out here." Then she walked away and the door shut behind her.

I'm not sure why, but it just made us laugh harder. Perhaps it was the way she'd entered the room with such authority, reprimanding us like she was our mother. It was the same look my own mom would deliver when my friends and I were laughing and carrying on down in our rec room well past midnight.

Soon as we walked out, the party was over. Two stretchers were rolling through the door. "Young couple, early twenties," the paramedic said. "Looks like a domestic violence case. Gunshot wound to the groin," he said pointing to the male.

"And the female?" Roberts asked.

"She's out of sorts. We noticed several bruises on her arms, but she's talking gibberish, so we can't confirm what really happened."

The bossy nurse was standing over the male patient, her face expressionless, seemingly without sympathy for the boy, as if she was the judge and the jury, convicting the patient of domestic violence in ten seconds or less. He was grimacing in pain, beads of sweat dripping down the sides of his face. His pale complexion was a tale tell sign that he was most likely bleeding internally. His pants and chili pepper boxers had been cut away by the paramedic, exposing his thin frame, and his black hair was drenched with sweat.

"Wanna give him something for the pain?" she asked Roberts in a way that clearly indicated she was indifferent to the idea. It looked as if the two patients had been up all night since they were both fully dressed at 4:45 am.

"Start an IV and morphine drip," he said. She rolled her eyes at Roberts a bit, but I don't think she realized she had. Roberts noticed it though, and by his stern look, it appeared he didn't appreciate the insubordination. "Look, we've got to get an x-ray before we do anything else," he said. "Morphine is the least we can do right now."

Then the young boy reached out, grabbed the nurses arm. "Am I gonna—" He started to ask the question he feared, then took a deep breath and blurted out, "Am I gonna lose my balls?" His eyes were as large as porcelain saucers, bulging with panic.

The nurse jerked her arm back and said, "Maybe, maybe not. Hard lesson to learn, young man."

"Whoa," I said, stepping in and pushing the nurse out of my way. I looked at her with disgust as I turned my back to the patient and mouthed to Mrs. Man Hater, "Not appropriate."

I then looked the young boy in the eyes and said, "This nurse here needs to attend to another patient, so let me answer that for you. Nobody wants to think about losing their balls, not me, not you, not anyone. I think it's too early to think about that, so let's just focus on getting the x-rays right now, ok?"

The fear began to melt from his ashen face. "Ok. Can I still get that morphine?" I nodded in agreement, as I inserted an IV into his forearm. Then the young, terrified man continued, "Look, I don't know what happened. We had been driving all night back from a weekend in San Antonio." He groaned in pain. "We were supposed to stay one more night, but she said we had to leave. I told her I was too tired to drive, but she didn't care." Then his eyes closed and he let out a howl of pain. "She said something about the bottle in her purse being empty."

"Alcohol bottle?" I asked.

"I don't know, but I can tell you that after this trip, I got to see the real her. After we got home, I told her we were over, then she shot me." His eyes grew wide and he pointed at his crotch with both hands. "She freakin' shot me!"

"Roberts, check her purse." I said, pointing to the denim purse on the gurney next to her. I would have done it myself, but I needed to get the morphine in that poor guy's IV line.

He looked back at me and grabbed the girl's bag, shuffling through all the contents. Then he took a bottle out and read it aloud, "Clozapine." His lips pursed and his head bobbed slightly. "Ok, the picture is becoming a bit clearer."

"What?" said the young man as he lifted his head up off the gurney. "What's that for?"

I suddenly felt unbelievable empathy for this young man. I also felt mildly guilty that we all judged the situation a bit prematurely, especially the nurse. "Well," I said and took a brief pause, "has your girlfriend . . ."

"Ex-girlfriend!" he interrupted.

"Yes, ex-girlfriend. Has she ever told you that she takes a medication for schizophrenia?"

"Hell no!" he yelled. I could tell from his response that the morphine hadn't quite kicked in yet.

"She's on the type of medication that works on resistant schizophrenia. Therefore, going without it could explain all this."

The portable x-ray arrived, but I asked them to wait just two or three minutes until the pain meds kicked in. I couldn't imagine jostling him around just yet since he was in such incredible pain and shock to boot. Not only from the injury, but because I'd basically just told him his girlfriend was crazy . . . or at least crazy when she wasn't on meds.

"Doc," he said, motioning me to come over to the head of his bed. "Look in the pocket of my jeans. There's a diamond ring. Can you make sure it didn't get lost and put it away somewhere?" His eyes were filled with tears, but this time it was emotion, not physical pain making him cry. There was an old saying that emotional tears fall slower and much quieter than tears of pain. I personally found that tears of pain fall out of the inner most portion of the eye, by the nose, and emotional tears originate from the outer aspect. "I almost made the biggest mistake of my life. How could I not see it?" And there it was, another single tear leaking from the outer corner of his eye and slowly traveling over the cheek bone, "I mean—"

I reached in his jean pocket and found a little grey velvet covered box. I held it up to show him and he let out a small sigh of relief. "Don't beat yourself up over this," I said. "You didn't make that mistake. This bullet wound may hurt for a little bit, but it's better that you found out now." I was actually a little envious of his bad luck. Not that I wanted to be shot, but I would have liked some sort of big sign that I should've had second thoughts about my own wedding. "On a more positive note, your scrotum is intact, and I think the surgeon will probably just remove the bullet and sew you back up. I don't anticipate any long-term damage. Maybe you took this bullet to dodge another, bigger and more painful one."

I wasn't sure if it was the pain killer finally kicking in or if he really understood his good fortune, but he smiled through the haze of his tears and nodded his head.

In the meantime, as the ex-girlfriend was sent up to the psych ward with a police accompaniment. The nurse, whose bullish demeanor seemed to have softened, walked over and with much more respect in her voice said, "I owe you and that boy and apology. I was out of line."

"Yes, you were," I agreed, holding her gaze. "Just learn from this. If life has taught me anything lately, it's to not judge a book by its cover." Of course I was also thinking about Jacqueline and how deceiving her beautiful, polished exterior had turned out to be. How to look at her lithe body, golden hair, and brilliant smile, one would never guess the monster lurking inside. Even Roberts, who I had pegged as strait-laced man with a perfect marriage, had a secret side.

After a few moments, things were quiet again and Roberts and I finished signing off on our case notes. "Meet you in the lounge," I said. "It's time to show you I'm not a patzer."

Before we'd so much as exchanged two words, I'd moved my black queen off h5 to f7, and Roberts quickly picked up his white knight, moving it from f3 to g5. I began to think we were on a roll and that we might even finish the game before he left for vacation. I moved my black queen from f7 to e7.

But just when I expected him to make another quick move, he went over to the breakfast bagels that had been delivered while we were attending patients. Roberts smeared cream cheese across a half bagel slowly and methodically. Then he turned and leaned his backside against the counter. He had one arm across his abdomen and the other was bent at the elbow, holding his bagel off to one side. "Not sure if you noticed, but I wiped one of those bruises off that girl with an alcohol swab after I happened to notice her arms matched her eye shadow." He shook his head in disbelief as he raised his bagel up. Before he took a bite, he asked, "Do you really think that young man didn't see any signs of mental instability before this weekend?"

"Maybe. Or there were signs and he ignored them." I felt myself tensing up, sweat breaking out under my arms the way it always did when I was nervous. This was it, this was my moment to get real with Roberts, to tell him about my life.

"Well, you and I lucked out. We both married normal, stable women," he said as he took a bite, the cream cheese squishing over his upper lip.

There was a long pause, one where I could hear him chewing thoughtfully, and I knew it was now or never. I took a deep breath and let it out slowly, trying to slow my suddenly racing pulse. "I think you should know that only one of us married well and it wasn't me," I said, trying my best to maintain eye contact when all I wanted to do was run from the room.

He put down his bagel, wiped his lips with a napkin and stared at me for a moment in surprise, his eyes widening. "Ok," he said slowly, carefully, as though he was afraid to probe too deeply at first. "Can you expand on that? You know my story," he said with a bashful shrug. "So what's yours?"

The nurse came in and interrupted just as I got my nerve up. "I have a suture removal here, can one of you come out and take a look?" Her voice was much softer and her stance much more relaxed. She had definitely been humbled. "If you clear the wound, I'll take the stitches out for you."

A few more cases trickled in before Roberts' shift was over. At around 7:15 a.m. he came from the lounge and stopped by the treatment room I was working in. I turned away from the young girl I had just diagnosed with a bad case of strep throat and acknowledged Roberts with a nod of my head as I tossed the tongue depressor into the trash. "Heading out, Jackson," he said. Then with a wink he added, "I took care of that important fair lady in the lounge. And about that other conversation— we'll continue that later." I had no idea what lady he was talking about until the end of my shift when I saw he had moved his white queen, from d1 to e2.

I stood there, my feet hurting from the fifteen-hour shift and picked up my black bishop from b4 and held it in my hand, rolling it between my fingers for a bit. I thought about the chessboard and how the bishop symbolized the church and religion. The bishop I currently held was the only one I had left. The other was taken earlier in the game. I couldn't help but wonder what the church would say about my decision to leave Jaqueline. It wasn't like I actually went to church anymore, the Catholicism was more of my mom's thing, not mine. But, what if I wanted to go back to the church someday? I would be a divorcee, which was frowned upon, to say the least. Just as I'd chosen to stay in my marriage for BJ, I knew plenty of people who remained in their bad marriage due to their religious beliefs. I looked down at the bishop in my hand and said, "Too bad, buddy. I guess I'm going to take my own bullet for this one." Then I placed him on the board at d6.

On my way out, I stopped by the hospital room of the gunshot victim. His surgery had gone well and just as expected, he would be discharged soon. "Here you go," I said handing him the small, velvet box. "Let this be your warning shot. The right girl is out there and she's going to make you a happy man someday. Choose carefully and pay special attention to how she treats other people, animals, and your mother. And be sure to have at least one big fight before you propose. A patient once told me that women are like a tea, you never know what flavor you have until they're in hot water."

The young man looked at me with a weak smile, clearly still dazed from the anesthesia, and nodded slowly. "I guess I should thank you, Doc," he said reaching out to shake my hand. "You saved my ass *and* my balls."

ELEVEN

Everything's bigger in Texas, even the storms. The night had been filled with large crashes of thunder, preceded by flashes of light that pierced the darkness repeatedly. The flashes were so frequent that it gave the inside of the house a strobe-like effect, the brilliant flashes of light illuminating objects and walls momentarily, highlighting them eerily. The next morning I woke on the sofa with Honey nestled in my armpit, her whiskered face buried as if to hide from the howls of the wind and rumbling of thunder. I stroked her soft back and nudged her awake.

Walking toward the kitchen I was reminded of an old saying in college: *It's not the night before, it's the night before the night before.* A saying that had never felt truer than it did right then. With each step I felt as though I was walking in water, just slogging along as if in a dream. I was so tired that I barely remembered taking a shower, grabbing my coffee, or getting in the car. The raindrops that pelted the car were large, hammering against the windshield. I sat up tall in my seat, my hands clenching the wheel. The wipers tried their hardest but couldn't possibly keep up. It was a torrential downpour, making it hard to see anything on the road ahead. Had it not been for the familiarity of the path between my front door and the emergency room, I probably would have pulled over and waited it out.

As I neared the hospital, a flash of lightening illuminated the street. I could see a driver pulled to the side, his flashers blinking. My first instinct was to stop and help, then I started playing the mind game, the one we play when we try to justify not doing the right thing. "Well, they probably have roadside assistance," I told myself. "Besides, you're a doctor and you have patients waiting." Then my own mind started arguing back, "But what if they *don't* have AAA? What if it's a woman or worse yet, a woman with children?" I realized it was an argument that I wasn't going to win.

It was as if I could hear the whisperings of my mother in my ear, "Always treat everyone as if they were your mother, your brother or your child. That way, you'll never go wrong."

"Need some help?" I hollered. My words were swallowed by the pelting of the drops.

"Dr. Jackson?" The silhouette of a familiar frame became clearer as I approached.

"Sergei?" I asked, "Is that you?" I would recognize his accent anywhere, so the question was rather rhetorical. As I approached I could see that the tan scrubs he wore were completely soaked and he was holding a jack in one hand. I was thankful for my mother's whisper. *What if I hadn't stopped*, I thought. "Here, hand me that." I said with my hand extended.

He stood there smiling ear to ear with wide eyes filled with gratitude. "Thanks, I'll get the spare."

Once the tire was changed I looked down at his feet. "What's your size?" I hollered through the intense sound of the rain.

"My shoe size?" He questioned with a turn of his head. He squinted his eyes, partially in confusion and partially as a way to keep the water out.

"Well, you can't walk around in those all day. We have extra Crocs in the doctor's lounge." As I started to walk away I looked over my shoulder and said, "I'll meet you in there."

When I arrived at the emergency department, Mary, Jennifer, and Elizabeth were all gathered around the nurses' station talking to Roberts. They turned and looked at me standing there in a puddle of water, my green scrubs sticking to me like a second layer of skin. Jennifer started chuckling, which eventually turned into full-blown laughter. Roberts came around the front of the desk, trying in vain to cover his smile with his hand. "Ok, Jackson, it's not that long of a walk from your parking spot to the door. What'd you do, go for a run?"

"No, not quite," I said as I used my finger to dislodge the water from my right ear. "Can I get a towel?" With a look of surprise that they hadn't moved yet to help me, I added, "Please?"

"Certainly," Mary said as she scurried toward the cabinet. I could always count on Mary. She was the only one not laughing or smirking at me.

"Well?" Elizabeth said with her hands on her hips and a smile as wide as the Grand Canyon.

"Well, what?"

"What's the story? Why are you so soaked? You can't walk in here looking like that and not give an explanation." Her tone was bossy and her curly red hair danced around her face. I couldn't help but admire her as she stood there demanding an answer. When Mary brought two towels, Elizabeth grabbed one and started to help dry me off. "Oh, I see, now you want to help me." I said, acting annoyed but deep down I was secretly enjoying being doted on. It was so different than what I experienced at home from the woman who was supposed to love and care for me.

Just then Sergei walked through the doors, equally drenched, his shoes squeaking, the water squishing through onto the floor and making small puddles with each step he took. Jennifer looked up, and as she twirled her blonde ponytail in her finger she snickered and said with the most sarcasm she could muster, "Looks like we need to call housekeeping to clean this mess up. Oh wait, housekeeping *made* that mess!"

"That man is a saint," he declared as he pointed at me. "Car after car passed me by out there. Not him, he stopped. He even changed my tire. Imagine that. Saint, saint I tell you."

Elizabeth looked up at me with a sheepish grin, her green eyes sparkling with admiration. "Very nice," she said under her breath. She smiled at me, and our gaze lasted a beat or two too long. As much as I enjoyed it in the moment, I hoped nobody noticed.

As Sergei and I entered the lounge, he placed a beat-up leather briefcase on the sofa. It was stuffed to the point it was bulging on both sides. As I went to grab a pair of scrubs and Crocs for him I was thinking, *why would a janitor bring a brief case to work?* I resisted the urge to ask and simply handed him the stack. "One pair of medium scrubs and one size nine-and-a-half dry shoes. Sorry bud, we don't have extra underwear so I would go commando and stay untucked if you know what I mean." I winked and walked back to get myself a pair.

When I returned, fully dressed in a pair of dry scrubs, I saw Sergei sitting on the sofa sifting through papers from his case. "Ah, here it is," he said, pulling out a small notebook and a pen. "Mind if I ask you a question?"

I stopped dead in my tracks. *Had Sergei been keeping notes on me? Oh, this is not good. Was he going to ask me about Elizabeth?* I swallowed hard. "Sure, what's up?" I said as I plopped down next to him trying not to act suspicious.

"This case, one from a few weeks, the lady with hematuria and extreme fatigue. The tall blonde."

Did he just say hematuria? That's not a word you hear janitors spouting off often. I looked down at the paper and noticed that he'd even spelled it correctly.

Hoping he didn't notice how pleasantly surprised I was that he knew the medical term for blood in the urine, I replied, "Yeah, I remember that one. What about her?"

"You ordered a urine test for acid fast bacilli and a TB skin test," he said, pointing toward his notes.

All right, this is a bit weird, I thought. *But, I'm willing to play along.* "I did, yes," I said, still not quite sure where this was going.

"How in the world did you come to that decision? That diagnosis? Most doctors would assume a urinary tract infection and send her on the way with course of Cipro or Bactrim," he said with his head tilted to one side and a puzzled look on his face.

"I probably would have too, if she hadn't been a nurse. A nurse who worked in the ICU. I knew it was a long shot, but renal tuberculosis just fit." I said with a shrug, although I was rather impressed with my diagnosis in retrospect.

He shoved the notebook back into his briefcase, stood up, and headed toward the door. "Thanks again," he said with his right hand over his heart and this left hand on the door.

"Hey, no problem." I replied. I stood there a few minutes literally scratching my head. My scalp was still damp from the rain, and I wondered exactly who Sergei was.

About that time, Roberts came in, looked at me with a smile and said, "Saint, huh? Yep, I believe that. It looks like you have everyone's back these days." He moved toward the chessboard on the wall, hesitated for just a moment and then picked up his white knight that was on e6. He turned and looked at me, looked back at the board and said, "Sorry, but I have to." Then he removed my black pawn and placed his knight on g7. "Check," he said as he faced the board.

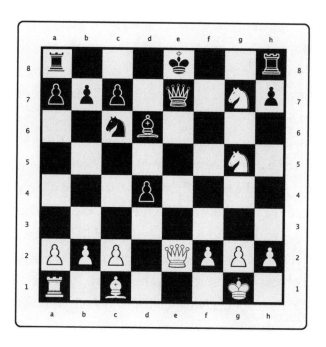

When he finally turned around, I locked eyes with him and pursed my lips. There was an awkward silence and then I stepped toward the board and moved my black king from e8 to d7, taking it out of check. "Nice try," I said, cocking my head to the side as I raised one eyebrow. "Oh, and no more Mr. Nice guy."

He moved his white queen from e2 to g4. "Check," he said with a bit of a sideways grin.

I took in a deep breath and then exhaled loudly. I reached for my king again and moved it to d8. "Enough," I said a bit deflated. "I've got patients to see."

"Really?" he replied, raising his voice to be sure I heard him as I exited the lounge. "Emergency room's empty."

I popped my head back through the door to get the last word in. "Famous last words. Are you trying to curse me? Never speak those words," I ordered, pointing right at him as I chuckled under my breath. "That's the call of the *wild*."

After about an hour I was beginning to think it was going to be a quiet empty day after all. Nothing could be further from the truth as the doors swooshed open and a bearded man walked through the door, each step hitting the floor with purpose. He was dressed like a biker with his leather jacket and jeans. He even had one of those silver chains that attached to his wallet. "Get me a barf bag!" He growled, "Now, damn it, unless you want to spend the ten minutes mopping up my puke!"

Sergei was the closest and went to hand him one of the blue plastic bags. "Here you are sir, and if you miss, don't worry about it, I'll get it cleaned right up." It was rather amusing how joyfully he said those words, as if he really didn't mind cleaning up after vomit.

"Oh, *hell* no," he said raising his voice. "No way I'm taking anything from a rag head terrorist."

I felt my blood boil, and I stepped right in front of Sergei, placing myself between the two of them like a human shield. "We'll help you sir, but you will *not* insult my staff like that." I grabbed the bag from Sergei and handed it to the patient. "Don't miss," I said sternly. "No way I'm going to have my friend here cleaning up after you." I knew I shouldn't have said that, but I was so angry. "Jennifer, triage him," I barked.

She did just what I asked, but I could still hear him all the way at the nurses' station. Every other word was an F-bomb. I just wanted to get him out of my emergency room and on his way. Finally, Elizabeth looked at me and said, "You know, the only way to get him out is to go in there and treat him." I rolled my eyes in response and reluctantly got up.

"Have you been drinking, sir?" I asked.

He looked at me with bloodshot eyes and a stare that could penetrate a brick wall. "For God's sake it's 10:00 a.m. What do you think?"

"Headache with vomiting. Recent history of migraines," Jennifer said.

"Ok. What usually works for you? Imitrex? Toradol?" I said, not making eye contact. I couldn't bring myself to look him for fear that I may tell him off with a few choice words of my own.

"Nothing. Nothing works," he said angrily through a half-closed mouth. "I don't even know why I'm here." His voice grew louder and more disgusted. "None of you clowns can help me. I've lost just about everything. My wife, my job, and if you can't get this damn thing under control, I'm going to lose my sanity too."

I stepped away with Jennifer for a minute to discuss a plan of treatment. Normally, I would just talk in the room with the patient, but this was one room I didn't want be in, so we went to the nurse's station to huddle our next move. As I rounded the corner back toward his room, I saw Sergei hanging out close to the door frame. I couldn't believe he would come within a hundred feed of this racist bully. "Just stay away," I said to him. "It's not worth it. I'll get him out of here."

Sergei shooed us back with one hand and placed his finger over his lips with the other to quiet us down. He stood completely still, except for his eyes which were darting back and forth as he listened. Then he walked towards us, stretching his arm out and pointing for us to meet him at the corner. Honestly, I felt like I was in the Twilight Zone, but I obliged anyway.

"What?" I said rather impatiently. All I wanted to do was give this guy a shot and get him out.

"He's not racist," he said.

Jennifer and I both looked at Sergei like he was the crazy one. I even let out an audible sigh as if to say he was wasting his breath defending this idiot.

"Just hear me out," he said with great enthusiasm.

"He lost his wife, his job. He came in a place where he needs help and risked being thrown out. He has a headache, vomiting, and he's in there completely hallucinating. He's swatting at flies that aren't there and saying we need to get an exterminator for all those spiders on his bed." Sergei was filled with enthusiasm, with a fire that I recognized. I often saw it on the face of first year residents when they cracked their first case. It was an undeniable look. Even seasoned doctors got it once in a blue moon when they solved a particularly mysterious case.

"Ok Sherlock, I'll humor you." I said with a downturned smile and a slight bob of my head. "Jennifer, send him up for an MRI with contrast. If they're busy, get a CT instead. I don't want him sitting around offending people."

"Thank you," Sergei said. "I think I'm right on this one." He had a smug grin as he walked toward his janitorial cart and started pushing it down the hall with his shoulders back. As I stood there, I couldn't help but notice that our scrubs and shoes matched. Maybe there was something to his theory.

The rest of the morning was filled with hum drum cases; the usual broken arm, a stomach ache, some lacerations. When things quieted down a bit around the lunch hour, I made a run to the cafeteria. The food in the cafeteria wasn't that great, but there were a few staple items I could always count on, like the turkey chili or the club sandwich. As I got closer the smell of the grilled onions hung in the air.

As usual, I scanned the room. Some people loved to people watch at the airport, but the airport had nothing on a hospital cafeteria. There was a story to be told in each booth. While I waited for my food I looked around trying to decode the looks on their faces. *That one must have been here for days, probably a sick husband.* I thought. *Yep, know that guy's story. He's a new dad. Super happy and loading up on carbs as he smiles at each passerby. Oh no, that one's crying in her salad. Probably the first meal since the bad news.*

"Oh, sorry," I said as I turned to look at the cafeteria worker who was so patiently waiting for my order. "I'll have the club," I said.

Just as I was going sit down in the corner booth and eat my sandwich in peace, I noticed Sergei from across the room. He didn't see me because he was buried in those papers of his. I ate my whole sandwich without taking my eyes off him. I couldn't imagine what all those papers were or why he had them sprawled out across the table. After a few minutes, I just couldn't take it any longer. As much as I wanted to give him his privacy, curiosity got the best of me.

I walked toward him, not sure of what to say, but knowing I had to get to the bottom of this. "Hey man, you're so engrossed, I hate to bother you."

He looked up a bit startled. "Oh, no bother at all." He started to move the papers and stack them on one side of the table. "Here, have a seat. I was just—"

Just what? I thought. Why didn't he finish that sentence? An awkward silence filled the air as I sat there looking at him and his stack wondering how Sergei went from just being a janitor to being the most mysterious person I'd ever met. Just then, as if on cue, my phone rang. "Yep, Jackson here." I said. "Oh wow . . . Seriously? That's fascinating. Yep, we'll get him admitted and call in the neurosurgeon."

Sergei hung on every word. By the impatient, wide-eyed look on his face, he knew it was about that case. He leaned in, knowing I was going to give him some interesting news. "Well?" He said as he paddled his hand in the air as if to speed up my response. "I take it that was radiology? And?"

"And, you probably saved that guy's life. Turns out he's got a brain tumor."

"Let me guess, occipital lobe?" He asked, almost as if he already knew he was right.

I sat there stunned. Then I realized he must have overheard the conversation. "Oh, you heard," I said.

He frowned a bit and replied, "No, I couldn't hear what they said. It just fit, with the hallucinations."

I sat back in my chair and put one hand on my chin. I looked at Sergei for a minute with my head tilted slightly to one side. "Ok, what gives?"

"Gives? What do you mean?" he asked in that undeniable accent. A look of confusion washed over him.

"This." I said a bit animated as I stretched my arms out. "These papers, your medical terminology. All of it."

He sat quietly. Then he said in a quiet voice, "I just miss it, that's all. I miss being part of the action, using my brain. Doing what I was trained to do."

At this point I was thoroughly confused. "You mean you went to medical school?"

"In Russia," he said. "I was a doctor there, had my own practice. Before . . ." He stopped and looked away, swallowing hard. "Before things go so bad that we had to leave. Chechnya is no place for a family."

"I'm so sorry," I said, in a state of disbelief at what I was hearing. "I didn't know. I mean, I really had no idea." A few minutes of silence filled the air and then I asked, "Do you hate it?"

"Hate what?" He asked.

"Hate being a doctor who's posing as a janitor." I didn't mean to offend him, it was just that I couldn't imagine myself going to medical school and then pushing a mop around and living off such meager pay.

"I'd do it all over again," he said. "Money, prestige, it means nothing if your family isn't safe. Growing up, my parents taught me that it doesn't matter what you do, it's how you do what you're doing. That's why I take my job so seriously." He paused for a moment before continuing, "I may be just a janitor to some people, but I'm a working man who loves and supports his family. If I have to be a janitor then I'll be the best janitor I can be."

"Would you go back?" I asked.

"To Chechnya?"

"No, of course not. I mean to medical school. It's obvious you miss it. You could go to an American school and then write the America boards." I was imagining Sergei living out his dream for real, not just on the papers spread out in front of him.

"I'm afraid American medical school is not exactly affordable on my salary, "he said, a note of wistfulness in his voice. Then he smiled and said, "One day. Maybe. But for now, I'll just keep doing what I do."

I stood and motioned for us to head back to work. "Hey, anytime you want to discuss cases or play mystery diagnosis, I'm happy to."

An enthusiastic smile came across his face as he reached out to shake my hand. "You got yourself a deal," he said.

That evening as I drove home I thought about all the events of the day. I couldn't believe I had almost missed that brain tumor. It was so ironic how Sergei was the one to point out something that should have been so obvious. To him it was right there in plain sight, but I couldn't see it. I had already formed an opinion about that patient. I guess in some ways, Sergei and his brilliance was right there in plain sight too and I had missed it entirely. Luckily, I didn't miss what Roberts was up to. He had my king in check by moving his knight from g5 to f7 before he left. That knight was taken by my queen. One thing was certain, that chess game, much like my life, was taking some interesting turns.

PULSE

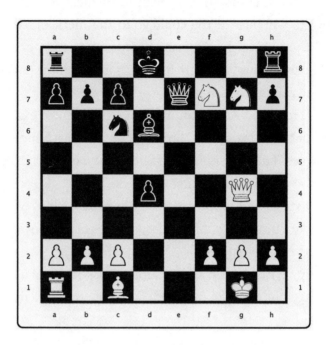

TWELVE

When I walked into the kitchen that evening, Jaqueline was bent over an aromatic pan of chicken and veggie stir-fry. She was dressed in a green silk blouse with a black skirt and heels. The apron that wrapped around her slim body was one I had gotten her a few Christmas' back. It was the first time I'd seen her in it. The house smelled like freshly grated ginger and sesame oil—like someone cared. Like a real home, the air heavy with the kind of rich scent I'd often imagined lingered behind the doors of the neighbors on our block.

"Smells good," I said with a tentative smile, hoping she'd respond in kind. If so, it would be the first cordial exchange the two of us had experienced in well over a year.

"Thanks," Jacqueline replied as she looked up and smiled back. In that smile I held out hope that the evening would be uneventful, maybe even downright pleasant.

Still, the irony didn't escape me. I'd finally decided to divorce her, and now here she was behind the stove, practically Martha Stewart. I'd always thought that Jacqueline had more than her share of female intuition, but this was ridiculous. And worse yet, I didn't know how to feel about it. Part of me wanted to believe that she'd changed for real, that things were going to be better between us—between all of us. But the other half of me watched her stir the pan, eyeing the contents warily, as if chicken and vegetables might burst into flame at any moment.

"BJ," I hollered up toward the stairs. "Come set the table, sweetheart."

Within moments, the thunderous sound of her feet barreling down the stairs filled the air. "Mom's cooking?" She said as she looked at me with a puzzled expression, as if I had just told her the Dallas Cowboys had won the Super Bowl.

"Yes, she is." I glanced at her and mouthed the words: *Be nice.* "Can you put some drinks on the table? I'll grab the plates and silverware."

I couldn't believe that we were actually sitting at the table enjoying dinner together. It was such a normal feeling that I thought it might actually be one of those cruel jokes God has a knack of playing on people. I'd finally gotten an appointment with a divorce attorney, albeit a month away, and out of the blue we were acting like a family? The irony was overwhelming.

"Where's Honeysuckle?" I asked about halfway through the meal. "I can't believe the smell alone didn't have her right under your feet the whole time," I said, motioning across the table to Jacqueline with my fork.

"I'm sure she's here somewhere," Jaqueline said without looking up from her plate of food. "Maybe she's sleeping. All that cat does is sleep and eat," she said with a sigh. "Probably because she's old. Old cats are pretty much good for nothing," she sniffed, her tone bordering on disgust.

BJ looked at me and rolled her eyes. I just shook my head slightly, as if to say *don't take the bait.*

BJ and I cleaned up the kitchen after dinner. It was a rule we used to have in the house, whoever cooked got to skip the clean-up. I didn't mind though, it gave me a chance to catch up with BJ without listening to Jacqueline's endless commentary on everything that came out of our daughter's mouth.

"That athletic banquet's coming up soon, right? Do you know who you want to go with yet?" I nudged her playfully with my elbow before bending down to load a plate into the dishwasher, but instead of smiling and turning red like she usually would've, her face remained impassive. The athletic banquet was the highlight of the year, and girls who usually sport basketball shorts and ponytails get all dolled up in semi-formal dresses and high heels. And they always bring in La Freak, one of the best cover bands in Dallas.

"I decided not to go," she replied solemnly, her voice barely above a whisper.

I loaded the final dish and then turned to BJ, pushing the dishwasher shut with both hands. "What? No way," I said in disbelief. BJ's had scored the most baskets of any other player this year, which meant she might be up for an award. "Talk to me. I know you were looking forward to it."

There was a downtrodden look on her face as she stared at the floor. It took a few moments, but eventually she spoke. "Look, everyone is going to have a nice dress," she mumbled, almost as if the words themselves were an embarrassment. "I don't have anything to wear."

"Nonsense," I said as the rumble of the dishwasher filled the room with the sound of rushing water. "I'll buy you any dress you want. I know how important this is to you and I remember being your age. Seriously, pick one out and it's yours."

"I don't have a car."

"Nice try, BJ," I said with a chuckle, turning to wipe down the counters. "I'm good for the dress, but not a new car. Besides, you're too—"

She cut me off waving her hand in the air, "No, I mean, uh, duh. I don't have a car to go get a dress. And . . . " She stopped again, her face hesitant.

"And what?"

"And I don't have anyone to help me pick one out." She finally blurted out, her face flushing red, the way it always did when she was embarrassed or upset.

"What am I?" I said incredulously, which was met with the both of us answering back in unison, "Chopped liver?"

"You know that's gross, Dad. Whoever came up with that stupid saying anyway?" A small grin spread across her face. "Look, no offense, Dad but—"

"Offense taken," I replied with a grin.

"You're a dude. Dudes don't know anything about dresses."

"I know what looks good and what doesn't. I'll say that much."

"On old ladies, maybe," she said with a smile and a little chuckle as she placed a hand on her hip and shifted her weight, giving a bit of teenage attitude.

"Ok. I'll give you that." I stood there for a moment trying to find the words she needed to hear from me. "Well, the offer stands," I finally said. "You find someone to take you for that dress, someone you trust, and I'll foot the bill. Ok?"

"Ok," she said grudgingly. The tone of her response wasn't exactly filled with enthusiasm, but it did sound like there was a glimmer of hope in there somewhere.

I was driving to work the next morning when I realized that something was nagging at me, something I just couldn't shake. I had that weird feeling you get every so often when you know you've forgotten something important, but you can't figure out what. Something was off, and I couldn't quite place it, but deep down I felt it. The hair stood up on my arms. I reached for my wallet— check. Watch—check. Coffee—check.

I stepped past the glass doors to find the emergency room filled with cases. It looked like "Bring your family to the ER" day. Every patient had at least three relatives crammed around their bed. "Been like this all night," Roberts said as he brushed past me in a hurry.

Mary was logging some patient notes into the computer at the nurse's station. She peered up to look at me, dark circles rimming her blue eyes and said, "Where do you want to start? He's not going to brief you for a while, not until things slow down. She passed off a clipboard. "Here. Take the little girl in room three."

When I entered, I found a little girl lying on the bed with a big grin situated between two of the reddest cheeks imaginable. She couldn't have been any older than four or five and her curly blonde hair was in pigtails, with one being much higher than the other. Her mother's face was filled with worry as she held the little girl's hand and stroked her arm. She was a short blonde woman, wearing yoga pants and a hoodie. She either had the day off or appeared to be a stay-at-home mom. Beside the mother was another little girl about seven or so. I couldn't help but notice that all three had the same piercing blue eyes.

"Why, hello there," I said with a smile. I glanced down at the clipboard and said, "Rosie, well, that's quite a fitting name today, isn't it?"

Her mother didn't laugh. Instead she said worry written all across her face. "I don't know what happened. When she went to bed last night she was fine. No fever, happy, like nothing was wrong."

"Did she have a fever this morning?" I asked, placing my hand on her cool head.

"No, no fever," she replied as she reached in her purse and pulled out a piece of paper. "I looked it up. I think she might have Roseola, that slapped cheek syndrome."

"Thank God for Dr. Google," I said, a bit sarcastically, as I gestured that she could keep her printout. "No fever, no other symptoms?"

As I looked into Rosie's eyes and ears, I noticed her sister intently watching. "Want me to look in yours too?' The sister smiled, but shook her head no.

I stood there with my arms folded, looking at Rosie. She was cute, curious, and certainly didn't look sick at all. "I like your pigtails," I said.

"Thank you," she replied sitting up on the bed.

Her older sister chimed in with a little bit of attitude. "Thank *me*. I did them for you."

Rosie started moving her head from side to side, making her ponytails swing back and forth. When she did that I saw a small sparkle of what looked to be glitter.

"Oh, I see what we have here," I said with a chuckle. "Mom, we have your diagnosis. *Rouge Subitus*."

"Oh my gosh, that sounds serious," the mother said as she sat up straight.

"It just sounds serious. You know what rouge is and *subitus* is just Latin for "sudden." It looks like Rosie had a little help getting ready this morning. I walked over to the sink and dampened a paper towel with soapy water. Then I slowly removed the makeup from Rosie's chubby checks.

Both little girls started giggling hysterically. The mother didn't seem quite as amused, by the way she put her chin down and then looked up at them in disdain. Luckily, their laughter became infectious, breaking the mother's stare. She may have realized that the money she just spent on the ER visit, will eventually pay off in future. Stories like this were always great for dinner parties, weddings, and the like.

I guess that lesson Sergei gave me paid off. The answer wasn't always complicated, and it was usually staring you right in the face. As I was exiting the room it finally dawned on me why I'd been feeling so unsettled that morning. The cat. Honeysuckle never did come to the kitchen after I put her food out. I reached for my phone and tried to call BJ, but it went straight to voicemail, a sure sign that she was already at school. An hour or more went by before I could get Jacqueline to answer. "Can you look for Honeysuckle?" I asked, trying to ignore the sinking feeling in my gut. "I didn't see her this morning."

"I'm sure you're overreacting," she said, and I could practically see her rolling her wide blue eyes through the phone. "I'll take a look and call you back if there's anything to worry about," she said, as if I were being overdramatic. My stomach rolled and turned like a ship in rough seas, bringing with it a wave of nausea. *I should have looked for her the night before,* I admonished myself. Maybe it was because Jaqueline had acted like a relatively normal person the day before, but I truly believed she'd call me if there were anything to worry about, so I tried to put it out of my head.

The rest of the cases cleared out relatively quickly. Roberts and I finally made it into the lounge to shoot the breeze and make a few moves on the board before he headed out. "Ok, so what's the deal with you?" He asked, reaching for a cinnamon raisin bagel. As he shoved it in his mouth, he pointed over to the chessboard to show that he'd moved his bishop from c1 to g5. With his mouth full he mumbled, "that's a check."

"With me? What about me?" I said casually as I moved toward the board. "What do you want to know?"

He chewed for a while, swallowed and said, "Why we've never met Jaqueline. Why were you acting so nervous when the staff talked about bring her to the awards dinner?"

I picked up black bishop and moved it from d6 to e7, blocking his ability to capture my king. It was kind of funny how avoiding him on the chessboard mirrored my avoidance about Jaqueline. "Well," I finally said, choosing my words carefully, "she doesn't like that sort of thing."

By this time, Roberts was standing right next to me. "Nope. Sorry, that's a load of crap," he said bluntly. "Check. Again." He moved his knight from g6 to e6. He was moving in on me all right, and I was running out of places to go.

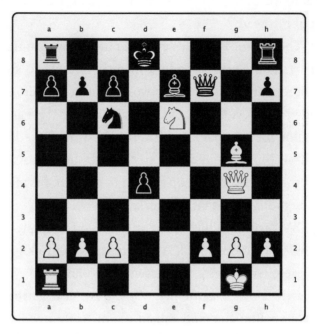

"It's complicated," I said, staring at the board.

He laughed at me sarcastically. "Oh, complicated. You don't say? Whose life isn't?"

Roberts had a point. This was the moment of truth. I was either going to have to trust him as a friend or I'd lose the opportunity to have someone to talk to. I took a deep breath and forced the words from my throat. They spilled out in a hurry, almost as if they were afraid I'd stuff them back in. "She's not the type of woman I want to bring around my friends. She's beautiful, but only on the outside. Inside she's terrible. She yells, she's unreasonable, unsupportive, and ninety-nine percent of the time I hate her with a passion. There," I said, finishing with a sigh. "Now you know."

"And the other one percent?" He asked curiously.

"Ok, maybe it's more like one half of one percent. Listen, every once in a while, she acts normal. Like last night. She made dinner, things seemed ok, I don't know." I didn't really want to make eye contact, so I kept studying the board.

"What about the kids?"

"Kid. It's just BJ now. We lost Jeremy a few years back." I swallowed hard. "Jeremy drowned. On her watch, not mine." As I said those words, I realized how much I'd been holding Jaqueline accountable. "But, it's my fault too. He came into my ER and I couldn't save him." Tears filled my eyes and I tried to swallow them back before they overflowed. "I've played that day over and over in my head. I couldn't—"

There was a moment of silence. Then Roberts reached forward and grasped my upper arm. "I didn't know," he said quietly. "I can't imagine."

I raised my gaze from the board and looked him in the eye. It was the first time since the funeral that I had cried, and it felt oddly good, like a cleansing.

"Was Jaqueline always like how you described her? I mean, before, was she like this before Jeremy died?"

"Trust me, she was like this before I married her," I laughed a bit through the tears. "It was the sex—the sex was so good that I couldn't see the real her."

"So, if she's so bad, why don't you leave?" He said with a shrug. "Sounds like abuse to me." His words were so matter of fact, not the reaction I would've expected. I always imagined that people would judge me harshly for wanting to get a divorce, Roberts among them.

"I have an upcoming meeting with an attorney. The same one Kipalski used." James Kipalski, the anesthesiologist, had been through a nasty divorce. He'd actually went through two other attorneys who couldn't seem to get the deal done. Finally, the last one, the one I intended to use, was able to get him some closure, and managed to do it without bankrupting him, too.

A few hours went by with scattered cases, nothing particularly of interest. Then the doors swooshed open and to my surprise, there stood BJ. She took few steps, wincing and hobbling alongside a teammate and her coach, each holding one of her elbows. "Dad!" she yelled across the empty emergency room.

I jogged over to her. "What happened?" I looked up at her coach, hoping for an explanation.

Her coach was the typical high school basketball coach, tall with an athletic build. Her brunette hair was cut short as a man's, but on her it looked more pixie-ish, delicate even. "It was a scrimmage," she said apologetically. "And let me first say that BJ here was playing her heart out. She went for a layup and just came down on it wrong." She pulled a bag of ice from her purse. "We cooled it down all the way here, but despite our efforts, it's pretty colorful and swollen."

"Dad, I wouldn't have bothered to come, but I can't walk on it. Not one step," she said as Jarrod helped get her up on the bed.

"Ouch," I said shaking my head and letting out a low whistle as I got the first glimpse of her ankle. It was pretty swollen and the blood from the forming bruise was giving it a purplish tint. "Well, you're pretty tough, BJ, an ankle like that is usually accompanied with tears and screams."

"Guess I take after you, Dad. I'm impervious to pain. Isn't that what you always say?" She smiled, but because of the pain it came out more like a grimace. A father knows his daughter and I knew that despite her good humor, she really did want to cry. I could see it in her eyes, they were slightly more moist than usual, and the lids had a pink tint to them.

Just then Elizabeth walked up. "What do we have here?" she asked.

"Oh, Elizabeth, this is my daughter, BJ. Her coach here tells me that she was smoking a scrimmage and her layup turned into a layout."

Elizabeth looked down at BJ's ankle and scrunched her face. "Oh boy, that's a good one. You really know how to do it, don't you?" Then she walked over to the computer in the room and put in the order for an x-ray. "Let's see if that puppy's broken."

"Broken?" Her teammate asked with a touch of desperation. Black strands of hair that had fallen from her ponytail and were stuck to the sides of her face with sweat. "You've only got two weeks to heal that up," she said looking at BJ.

"Big game coming up?" I asked.

"All games are big," the coach answered. "I think she's referring to the athletic banquet."

"Oh yes," I said winking at BJ. "The athletic banquet."

"Nice!" said Elizabeth brightly as typed the diagnosis into the medical record. "Well since heels will be out of the question, it will be all about that unforgettable dress. When I was—"

I quickly interrupted, "Elizabeth, can you give me a hand in room seven? Sorry, BJ, we just have to finish up with another patient real quick. X-ray will be here before you know it and we'll see if it's broken or just sprained." BJ was pretty calm, such a trooper. She just sat there quietly with her arms crossed like this whole injury was more of an annoyance than an injury. I reached over and kissed her on the salty forehead. I was almost positive it wasn't broken, but only an x-ray could confirm either way.

As if on cue, the mobile x-ray rolled in and the tech shooed us all out.

"Room seven?" she questioned as we entered the hall. "We don't have a patient waiting. As a matter of fact, we don't have a room seven either," she said drily.

"Yeah, well I need to give you the scoop. BJ is thinking of skipping that banquet."

"What? Why?"

"The dress. She refused to go with Jaqueline, she can't go with another lady she's close with because she was recently diagnosed with cancer, and she sure as hell doesn't want to go with me." It might've seemed strange that I was talking about dresses instead of my daughter's shattered ankle, but even though BJ's ankle was injured, I knew it would heal. At that moment, the idea that she would skip something that meant so much to her seemed equally, if not more, important. I knew if she didn't go, she'd regret it. I needed her to be with friends, to make happy memories that would distract her from what waited for her at home each and every afternoon.

"Oh." Elizabeth said as her closed lips moved to one side as if she were thinking. "I've got it!" she blurted out, her face lighting up with joy. "She can go with me! I have to get a dress anyway for the awards ceremony. I didn't have anyone to go with me either. It's perfect."

"That's nice of you," I said cautiously. "But I can't exactly offer that up. She'll know I told you. Look, I don't know why I'm telling you all this." I said with a shrug, feeling exasperated now. "I guess I just feel like a fish out of water here. Daughters are hard, I want to help her, but I have no idea—"

"Leave it to me. I've got this," she said authoritatively. Then she turned and walked over to the nurse's station, her red curls bouncing across her back.

A few minutes later the x-ray came up on the screen at the nurse's station. I took a good look and motioned for Elizabeth to follow me into the room. "Well, there's good and bad news. It's not broken."

"Whew," her classmate sighed, looking visibly relieved.

"Well, no surgery is required, but sprains like this can take some serious time to heal. You're going to have to stay off it for at least a week, BJ. Then baby it a bit. No sports for at least three weeks," I said looking first at my daughter and then at her coach.

"Three weeks?" BJ said in disbelief. Then the first tears arrived. Not playing was clearly far more painful to her than the sprain.

"He's right," said the coach, agreeing with me. "It's got to heal. Doctor's orders. Doctor and Dad orders, so it's doubly important. Got it kiddo?"

"Fine," she grumbled. It was the biggest pouty face I had seen since I'd told her five December's ago that she would *not* be getting a pony for Christmas because Santa developed an allergy to horses years ago and that's why he switched to reindeer.

"You can still go to the banquet," chimed her friend. "Just no heels, right?"

"That's right," piped up Elizabeth. "And, we got interrupted. Tell me about that dress."

"Oh, well," BJ hesitated. "I haven't gotten it yet," she said in a hurry, her cheeks flushing crimson.

"What? It's two weeks away," said Elizabeth. I glanced at her like she was crazy for saying that, but she returned the glance with a nod and a squint as if to say *trust me*. Then she continued. "Well, I can't believe I just said that. Look at me, the pot calling the kettle black. I still haven't gotten my dress for the awards ceremony!"

"Yeah, that's a bit hypocritical," said BJ rolling her eyes in a playful way. I could see exactly what Elizabeth was doing and it gave me a whole new appreciation for the sneakiness of women. It was like a talent, some kind of talent men just didn't have.

"I'd have a dress by now, but I hate shopping alone." Elizabeth continued nonchalantly as she wrapped a bandage around BJ's ankle. "I moved here not that long ago and I don't have anyone to go with. Dress shopping by yourself really stinks. I mean, I need someone to tell me if I look good or like a cow. It has to be someone I trust too. Don't you agree?"

"Totally," BJ replied. "You can't trust the salespeople. They lie because they want you to buy the first thing you try on."

"I know! Right?" said Elizabeth. I just stood back in awe. After she finished clipping the wrap in place she said, "Hey, I've got an idea? Do you think you could help me pick out a dress? I mean, if it's ok with your dad."

I chuckled as if on cue and then after learning from the master I answered, "Oh Elizabeth, no offense but I'm sure BJ wants to go with someone younger than you." Elizabeth pretended to be offended by putting her hands on her hips and rolling her eyes at me.

"If that's true BJ, its ok," she said.

"Dad! How rude. I'm sorry he just said that. Yes, that'd be cool." BJ looked at me for approval which I delivered in a slight nod. "That offer still stand, Dad?"

"Of course," I said jovially.

Elizabeth was buzzing around the emergency room the rest of the day with a huge smile on her face and I couldn't help watching her every move.

THIRTEEN

As I drove home from the hospital that night, I was starving as usual. Maybe Jacqueline had made salmon and rice, I thought hungrily, or my old favorite—spaghetti and meatballs. I imagined all of us eating around the television next to BJ, who would surely have her leg propped up on the couch. *Have we finally made it to the other side? Is my marriage salvageable?* I wondered with a feeling that hovered somewhere between hope and despair. At the same time, Elizabeth's face rose up in my vision, her red curls catching the light, a mischievous glint in her green eyes, making me feel almost bipolar. The way she'd handled the dress situation with BJ was nothing short of brilliant.

What if Elizabeth and I were together? I wondered tentatively. *She would have a daughter again and I could have a loving wife. Maybe even one who likes to laugh, cook, and take romantic trips together.* Those thoughts made me squirm in my seat, as if my body itself were trying to reject them entirely. I turned the corner onto our street and right then and there, I made a conscious decision to try and work things out with Jaqueline and bury my romantic thoughts of Elizabeth. If there was any glimmer of hope of saving my marriage and in the process, helping Jaqueline become a better mother, I knew I had to do it. As I pulled into the driveway, I had resigned myself to call off my meeting with the attorney. BJ deserved it. Hell, we all did, didn't we?

But when I entered the house, there was no smell of dinner to greet me, the only light coming from them the television and BJ's phone in the living room, a chilly, blue glow. I stopped at the edge of the brown leather sofa and reached under the lampshade to illuminate the room. BJ recoiled with a reflex-like squint and gave me a look of frustration that I had ruined her cave-like atmosphere. "Looks like you're planted here, huh?" I said to BJ who was on the sofa, her bandaged leg nestled on a stack of pillows, crutches propped up beside her. She was watching re-runs of *Sabrina the Teenage Witch*, something she did when she was depressed or upset about something. I patted the top of her head with one hand, just enough to toss her hair around. "You were a real trooper today. I'm proud of you," I said, but she didn't even look away from the screen. "Look, there's no research to support sulking in a dark room helps with the healing process."

"Proud of me for what? Screwing up my season in a crummy scrimmage?" She said sarcastically as she rolled her eyes. She was in full pout mode, and I knew from experience that when she got that way, there was no reply that could make her feel better. "Look, I finally got comfortable and realized my phone's on the kitchen table. No way was I going in there for it. *This*," she said, sprawling her arms out as if to showcase the dark room and pillows under her foot. "This is my life now, and it sucks. Big time." She folded her arms across her chest, sighing as if the world was ending. Which, for her, it probably was.

"Where's mom?" I asked, looking around, but the room was empty.

"Don't know. She wasn't home when I got here."

"She never called me back about Honeysuckle. I guess no news is good news." I shrugged, sitting down next to her, careful not to jostle her leg.

"What about Honeysuckle?" Alarmed, she shifted on the sofa to sit up a bit. "What are you talking about?"

"It's probably nothing. I just noticed she didn't come down this morning. I know I left a bit earlier than normal, but it's just not like her. Last night she wasn't around for dinner and then again this morning she wasn't there to wake me. You saw her though, right?"

BJ was scooching around trying to get up from the sofa and onto her crutches. "No, I haven't. That that freaks me out. We have to find her."

My heart sunk a bit. I was fully expecting BJ to tell me that Honeysuckle had been her own personal nurse since she got home. That cat has always had a sense that drew her to us when we were sick or injured. "Stay here, I'll look for her."

"Honey, Honeysuckle," I cried. I crawled down to look under the bed in the master, even checking the closets to be sure she hadn't been locked in by accident. When one by one, each hiding spot came up empty, the dread of finding her dead became stronger. My heart raced as I tried to stay calm. By the time I reached the top of the stairs, I was out of breath from the adrenaline rush.

I checked each room, under each bed, and inside every closet. Every room but one. As I stood outside Jeremy's bedroom door, I froze. I hadn't been in there for at least two years. The last time I dared to go in, I sobbed like a baby on his bed. Everything in that room had been left exactly as it was the day he died. The town made entirely out of Legos that we had so painstakingly created together each night before bed, even the colored pencils were sprawled out over the homemade card he was making for a friend. My hand touched the door, but it took all my strength to turn it, not because it was hard to turn, but because it was hard for *me* to turn. Opening the door was like picking a scab off a very deep wound.

With my heart pounding, I turned the handle and slowly pushed the door open. The lights were off, and I liked it that way. If Honey was in there, I knew she'd probably be under the bed, so I walked toward it and kneeled down, using the flashlight app on my phone to illuminate the space. There was dust, a few toy dinosaurs, and the tip of a furry white tail. "Honey, hey girl," I said in a subdued voice as to not scare her. There was a foul smell, a mixture between urine and feces. She let out a low, deep, but week growling sound. *Ah, she's alive*, I thought letting out a sigh of relief. But as I cleared the toys away and got a better look, I could see that things weren't good. My stomach rolled over in sudden nausea as I illuminated her white fur, which was covered in yellow urine. By the look and stench of the mess she'd made, it appeared she hadn't moved in quite a while.

"Dad, did you find her?" BJ yelled from the bottom of the stairs. "Dad?" she called out again. I didn't want to yell back. I didn't want to startle Honey. I remember from my Boy Scout days that injured animals can often act out, even attack uncharacteristically.

A towel, I thought. *Get a towel.* When I got back from the bathroom, I flipped on the light to Jeremy's room without even thinking. What I saw stopped me dead in my tracks. The whole room was packed up in boxes. No Lego town, no colored pencils on the desk. The only thing that hadn't been put away was the dust ruffle on the bed. I swallowed hard. *We never talked about this. We never agreed to just box everything up.* But, then I heard the sounds again from under the bed. After much coaxing, I was able to wrap Honey into the towel. Her back legs were ice cold and blue. The pupils of her eyes were so large that you could hardly see any gold at all.

As I came down the stairs, BJ was right there waiting. "Oh my gosh! What's wrong with her?" She asked as she immediately started to tear up.

"I'm not sure," I said as I rushed out the door to the emergency after hour veterinarian clinic a few blocks away. I had passed that clinic so many times, never guessing that someday I would need it.

Three hours later I headed back home, empty handed. As I walked through the door, I found BJ in the kitchen, on her crutches. She must have heard the garage door open and hobbled over as fast as she could. "No!" she cried. "Dad, no, no, no." Her crutches crashed to the floor, and there we were holding each other up, barely standing as sobs sent my daughter's strong, muscular body into a limp state, her knees buckling beneath her, leaving no choice but for her bad ankle to touch the floor.

Jaqueline must have heard the crash of the crutches or BJ's cries because she rushed in and flipped on all the lights. I don't know why, but I was expecting her to join in on the hug or at least offer some sort of condolence. But true form, the real Jaqueline showed up. She stood there in her red satin robe, rolling her eyes, one hand on her hip and said, "Is this all over that *cat*? Good grief, she couldn't live *forever*."

If it weren't for having to hold BJ up, I'd probably have decked her one, landing myself in jail, or worse yet, losing my medical license for spousal abuse. "You never even looked, did you?" I asked through clenched teeth and streaming tears. "I asked you to do one thing, one simple freaking thing—"

"Look, I didn't have time to go looking all over this house for that stupid cat. What do I look like, a pet sitter?"

Then, without even waiting for a response, she spun around and walked away, her robe flowing behind her like a red ribbon unfurling.

That night BJ took the sofa and I curled up in a fetal position on Jeremy's bed. Tears streamed from one eye over to the next and then down my cheek, soaking the mattress completely. The next morning, I showered upstairs. I let the water run over my back for what seemed like forever, unmotivated to face the day. I wiped a circle in the steamed-up mirror and saw a broken man looking back at me, eyes so swollen it looked as if he'd been in a boxing match. Never again would I let myself think that my marriage was salvageable. Never again would I try to convince BJ that there was something salvageable about her relationship with her mother either. Instead, I knew now that I would spend my days counting down each week, each day, each hour until my appointment with the divorce attorney.

FOURTEEN

Within a week, BJ was off the crutches, her ankle mostly back to its normal size and color. We didn't talk much about Honey, but I tried to spend as much time at home as possible so that I could help her with her calculus homework and prep her for the upcoming test. The last thing she needed was to heal her ankle and then get benched for her grades.

It was four days, five hours, and six minutes before my appointment with the divorce attorney. There I was, standing in the kitchen, reaching into the cabinet near the sink and pulling my travel mug, when Jaqueline appeared right next to me. "Crap," I yelled as I jerked in surprise. "What are you doing up so early?"

Her face was without expression, empty and eerie. I took a second look at her, thinking maybe she was sleep walking, something she did once early on in our marriage. She reached for the block of knives on the counter, running her fingers over each one slowly. Chills ran up and down my spine as I turned to face her, planting my feet firmly as if to prepare for battle.

Her hand slowly floated from the knives to the countertop. The light coming from under the counter was all that illuminated the kitchen, making her silky red nightgown glow across her bust, casting a pink hue upon her skin. But the light didn't reach as far as her face. It was as if her lips were speaking in the shadow of darkness as they softly said, "Bobby, do you remember my friend, Christie? Oh, I'm sure you do. Redhead. Her and her soon to be ex-husband live four doors down on our side of the street."

I knew exactly who she was taking about. That was the bimbo who tried to seduce me the night of drunco. "Can't say I remember her, why?"

"Well, did you hear what I said?" she asked a bit annoyed.

"Yes, and I answered you," I replied, trying to keep my tone calm and modulated.

"What I said *was*," she said, almost growling through her words as she stood up a bit taller. "Soon to be ex-husband."

"And?" I replied, as I moved her over a bit to place the pod in the Keurig. "This is important, why?"

She shook her head in disbelief and grabbed my arm, squeezing it just enough that her long, fake nails dug into my skin. She was close, close enough that I could see the indentions the pillow had made on her face, lines and indentations that looked, in that moment, like wrinkles marring her porcelain skin. As her blue eyes darted back and forth across my face, she said in the most terrifying tone, "If you ever think of leaving me, you will have hell to pay. Not just you, but BJ, too. After all I have sacrificed for her, for you, and for your career, you owe me. I will never, ever be like Christie. Forced to find a job, move in with her parents, and who knows what else. Do you hear me?"

She paused for a moment, letting go of my arm and standing back in front of the knives. She bent down, leaning her elbows on the counter, the light illuminating her face as she turned her head back toward me, looking me right in the eyes and whispered, "Hell to pay." Then without another word, she stood up and left the kitchen.

All the way to the emergency room my mind raced. *I have to get BJ out of that house. I have to get both of us out of that house and away from her. Or am I better off just staying to protect us both?* My heart racing and my thoughts all running together like a jumbled mess.

When I arrived at work, Roberts took one look at me and I could tell by his double take that he knew something was definitely amiss, "How about we grab a cup of coffee before things get too busy around here," he asked, his face creased with concern. Out of the corner of my eye I saw him nod to Mary, Elizabeth and Jennifer who were all standing there like a welcoming committee. When I walked up they were laughing and cutting up together. I could tell that my very presence had ruined the mood, but for some reason I didn't care or didn't have the mental bandwidth to snap out of the thoughts that swirled around my brain, like the eye of a hurricane.

When we walked into the lounge, Sergei was there. Roberts didn't want to make a scene, so he started making small talk about the chessboard. "Hey, Sergei, do you play chess? You're from Russia, isn't it in your blood?"

"I played a little in my time, you could say." Sergei said with a smile. "I've been following your game. I've watched Dr. Jackson get out of check a few times, giving you a run for your money. It's quite the match as you chase Dr. Jackson all over the board like a game of cat and mouse." He let out a chuckle, "Like how he recently moved his king from d8 to c8, but then you revealed a discovered check when you moved your white knight from e6 to c5."

"That damn white knight," I said before I knew the words had even left my mouth. I didn't even realize I'd been listening enough to have a say in that conversation. All the words had just seemed like background noise to the nightmare replaying in my head. At some point, I sat down on the ratty blue couch, and listened half-heartedly they finished their chess talk and Sergei left the lounge.

"You look completely rattled, my friend," Roberts said as he came over and put one hand on my shoulder before sitting down beside me. "How can I help? Talk to me."

"I can't do it." I mumbled, staring into space, afraid to meet his gaze. "There is no way I can go through with the divorce." My voice was almost a whisper, as if I were afraid to say the words out loud.

"You two have worked things out?"

"Not exactly," I said as my voice broke. We sat there for a few minutes, the only sound in the room the tick, tick, ticking of the clock overhead, as I fought back the wave of despair that bubbled up in my chest. After I got up the courage, I told him everything that had happened that morning in the kitchen, how terrified I was, and how trapped I felt.

"Well, I have some good news for you," he finally said, breaking the silence that had settled over the room. "First of all, you don't have to figure this all out today. Second, I'm going to help you. Don't know how, but I will think about it and help you find a solution. Jackson, I spent years trapped in my own nightmare, terrified by the threats of a woman. Now, my nightmare is finally over and I can breathe again. You deserve better than this. You're young, you have a beautiful daughter and the two of you deserve a better life. I don't have a solution yet, but I have faith that God hears your pain and will help you two.

Roberts and I never had a conversation about religion before, and not after. I had no idea what his particular beliefs were, but, somehow, there was comfort in his words, words that seemed to echo the sentiments of my mother. Whenever I'd felt frustrated, afraid, or sad, Mom would always assure me that God had a way of helping us out when the world became too complicated for our little, mortal brains. Of course, being the arrogant know-it-all, I didn't see the wisdom in her words at the time and took offence to the fact that she had essentially referred to my brain little and mortal.

The day was steady with usual cases and the nurses seemed to be trying to keep the mood light in the ER. Nobody asked what was troubling me but seemed to take extra care not to stir up drama, especially Mary and Elizabeth.

"Hey, Elizabeth," Mary said. "What's your take on the girl in three? Don't you think something seems off?"

Hold up. Mary was actually interested in what Elizabeth thought? The very idea of it peaked my interest. "OK," I said, wandering over to where the two of them stood at the nurse's station. "I'll bite. What do you girls think is off?"

"I don't know, "Elizabeth replied. "It's the stepmom. She is insistent that something's seriously wrong with the girl. I mean, heavy periods at twelve is a little unusual but it's not excessively abnormal, by any means."

Mary chimed in, "It's something about their inter-action, and it's unnatural. The woman has mentioned several times how upset she is that her husband travels all the time and she's burdened with all of the daughter's heath issues."

"Issues? So there's more than one thing going on?" I inquired, seeing the confirmation on their faces immediately. "Let's get the girl alone and see what she has to say."

After much coaxing, we finally had our chance to talk to the shy, hefty girl without the stepmom. "Meredith, your mom—"

"She's not my mom, she's my dad's wife," she said, looking down at the covers while she swiped away a tear she was trying to hide.

"Ok, your dad's wife," I said very matter-of-factly, but looking back at Elizabeth to make sure she caught it. "She mentioned you have quite a few health issues. Want to tell me about them?"

"I didn't used to have all these issues. Back when I played softball and ran track," she said a bit angrily as she twisted the covers around in her hand and refused to make eye contact.

Elizabeth looked at me with a glance of confusion. I too was confused. Meredith didn't look like the type of girl who could run track. Her breasts were large, probably the largest I'd seen on a twelve-year-old, maybe ever. She was a bit chubby around the middle, and didn't look all that healthy, let alone athletic. "Why did you stop playing sports?" I asked.

"When all this happened," she said, holding her arms out in front of her. "I blew up. Everywhere. Then the headaches, anxiety, you name it, everything happened to me all at once." Without warning, her face crumpled all at once, and she started to sob.

Elizabeth came over with an understanding smile and took her hand. In a soothing, motherly tone she said, "Growing up is hard, I know. I was a bit awkward at puberty, developing faster than the other girls, but eventually everyone caught up and it all worked out."

I knew that Elizabeth meant well, but Meredith jerked her hand away from Elizabeth's and let out a huff. I could see that nothing we could say was going to console her.

Then, Meredith said something that struck us both as odd. "Once he married Andrea everything got worse. The school nurse talked to Andrea and without my permission, told her I was feeling sad. She didn't have the right to do that," she said, finally making eye contact with both of us. "I know Andrea thinks those vitamins are helping, but they're not. Since I've been on them, I got my period, my head hurts, and I feel so angry all the time."

"What vitamin? Can you describe it?" I asked, trying not to sound suspicious.

"I don't remember what it's called, but its small, blue and kinda oblong," she said. "Please don't tell her I told you about it. She said that Dad could get in trouble if people knew he was bringing it back from his trips to Europe."

Elizabeth looked at me with wide eyes. The girls were right, something was off about this case. "Hormone panel," I said to Elizabeth. Then I looked at Meredith with a smile and said, "I think we may be able to help you with all this."

"Really?" she asked with a big smile. "I just want to be normal again."

When the results came back, just as I suspected, the "vitamin" was actually estrogen. The stepmother was giving that poor girl her own hormone replacement pills. I called social services to come down and together we explained to Meredith that she wasn't crazy and that it would take some time, but her moods would stabilize, her weight would most likely go down, and that social services would have to step in and contact her dad about all this.

"Munchhausen's by proxy," said Mary. "You rarely see a parent who wants something to be wrong with a child, but when you do, it's heartbreaking." Mary's head shook from side to side, as she leaned in toward Elizabeth. "Wow. We nailed it," she added giving a high five to Elizabeth. I couldn't believe what I was seeing, the two type A's had finally bonded.

Everyone was on a bit of an emotional high for the next few hours, even I was able to forget about Jacqueline for a short while. Then, just before the shift ended, Roberts came in a few minutes early. "How are things?" he asked a bit surprised to see my mood lifted. "Good. We had a little Sherlock Holmes case playing out, and these girls," I said pointing at Mary and Elizabeth. "They are quite the detectives."

"Well, I'm leaving for my vacation in just two days. I refuse to be this close to a win and lose my momentum. After you," he said motioning toward the lounge.

"Do you have a plan yet?" I asked with a smile as I picked up my king and moved it to b8.

"Geez, it's only been twelve hours, Jackson," he said with a chuckle as he moved his white knight from c5 to d7. "Check."

"This is not helping," I grumbled as I moved my king to c8. Sergei was right, this was a game of cat and mouse.

He moved his white knight to b6 for another check.

"Damn it Roberts, can't you give a guy a break?" I moved my king from c8 to b8. Then I looked at the board, knowing I still had a chance to win. He might have made all these checks, but there was clearly no real strategy behind them. I just needed time to think.

Just then, as if on cue, Mary popped her head in and asked, "Which one of you wants to take this case?"

"Well, that depends," I said with a smile as I winked at Roberts and headed toward the door.

Mary led me toward the patient, a Middle Eastern looking young man in his twenties. "I don't know what's wrong with him," said a rather plump guy with dark rimmed glasses. "We were at work and he was fine. When we went to lunch he started talking really fast and crazy, not making much sense. I told him I was going to call an ambulance and he yelled at me." The young man talking had brown curly hair and was wearing blue jeans and a black hoodie. I could have guessed that they worked in software development had he not told me. "I basically drove him here without telling him where we were going."

"Abdul," I said, shining the light into his eyes. His pupils were dilated, and he turned his head quickly as to avoid the brightness of the ophthalmoscope. "Do you remember having lunch?"

He was fidgety and paranoid as he flinched every time I touched him. He stared at the doorway without blinking as if someone was standing there watching him. I turned to look several times, but I couldn't quite figure out his fascination with the door. "Can you tell me what's going on?" I asked as I examined the rest of his body. "Did you happen to take something today? Nobody's going to arrest you, we just want to help you. You can tell us." Just about that time I turned over his hands and noticed some burn marks on the tips of his fingers. I made eye contact with Mary and she nodded in return, her way of confirming she was making a note in the chart.

I turned to the man who brought him in. "Didn't you say you're both in software?"

"Yep, just down the street."

I looked up at Abdul, trying to make eye contact, trying to break his stare, but he avoided me at every move. "Hmm," I said as I stood back and crossed my arms. I thought if I waited long enough, he would offer up some clues, but no luck. "What happened here?" I asked as I pointed to some small burns on his fingers, but before he could answer, he jumped off the table and ran out of the emergency room, his co-worker chasing after him. He pushed past Roberts on the way out the door.

"You sure know how to clear an emergency room, Jackson," Roberts laughed.

We all chalked that case up to methamphetamines. The paranoia and the dilated eyes were a dead give-away. It was a problem that we saw way too much of these days. I never got to the bottom of his burnt fingertips. Later, as we ended the shift, we all imagined what took place after he and his co-worker left, telling our own versions. All of us agreed that the incident was probably the most exciting thing that had happened at that big software company in a long time.

As I was leaving, Elizabeth ran toward me with a big grin on her face. She stopped and planted her feet in that famous wide stance of hers. Holding each side of the stethoscope around her neck, she shifted from her heels to her toes and said in a sweet, yet sassy voice, "Guess where I'm going three days from now?" She slid her tongue along inside her lower lip as she raised her eyebrows. Before I could venture a guess, she added, "Dress shopping with BJ. Yep, she called me." With a little tap to my shoulder she professed, "It's a date."

I couldn't help myself, I reached out with both my arms and hugged her, right there in front of the sliding doors, for all to see. As I grabbed her shoulders and pushed her back just far enough to glance into those emerald eyes, I smiled and with deep feelings of gratitude and whispered, "Thank you."

I nestled into the leather seat in my car. It was warm and it felt like a hug wrapping around my back. My smile over Elizabeth's news faded as I remembered the sight of Jacqueline standing over the knives. Chills came over my body as I reached in my pocket and grabbed my phone. The last thing I wanted to do was to go home. "BJ, how'd you do on that test today?"

"88," she said proudly, "and I couldn't have done it without you. Can we grab a burger?" It was as if she was reading my mind.

"Honey, after the day I had, nothing sounds better than grabbing a burger with my baby girl." I hung the phone up and dropped it into cup holder. As I drove home I had visions of sharing a burger with both BJ and Elizabeth. I could just about taste it, hear our laughter, and see me dabbing ketchup away from the corner of Elizabeth's mouth. The visions seemed so real, almost as if they were a memory, not a dream.

FIFTEEN

True to the form of any psychopath, when I arrived home that evening, Jacqueline acted like nothing had ever happened. When I stepped inside, she asked with an expressionless face, "Have a good shift?" But, before I could answer she had turned and walked away. I daydreamed, or should I say, more like nightmares all day that she might be standing in the kitchen, knife in hand just waiting for me. But luckily, those visions fell flat as soon as I walked through the door. It was as if the whole kitchen incident had been a hallucination. Only, I knew it was true and I knew she meant it, but I didn't dare bring it up. I even checked to see that the divorce attorney's card was still in the glovebox of my car. Just to be darn sure she wouldn't see it, I tucked it inside the owner's manual, where I knew she would never go looking. As far as I was concerned, I was just buying time. Time to come up with an exit strategy.

My blank stare and deep thought was broken by BJ's footsteps barreling down the stairs, sounding like rolling thunder. "You're never going to believe it Dad," she said, her eyes all aglow as she slid her shoes on and looked around to be sure Jaqueline wasn't within earshot.

"Try me." I cocked my head a bit to one side trying to hide that I knew exactly what she was going to say. Elizabeth had already told me they had plans, but I was trying to seem surprised.

"Darren asked me. He asked me to go to the athletic banquet!" She started to bounce back and forth on her toes.

"Hey, hey, be careful on that ankle, baby girl. You know you're not supposed to even be putting weight on it." She gave me that look, the one teenager's give when they think you aren't listening.

I straightened up tall and looked her square in the eyes. "Wow," I said with a big smile. *Darren, who's Darren?* I thought. "That's great honey. And the dress?"

"Oh, I've got that covered. I called Elizabeth. We were on the phone for like an hour. Oh and she said I can call her Lizzy. Dad, she's so nice." Her voice grew higher and her smile wider. "I'm so excited."

An hour? I thought. I didn't dare ask what they could have possibly talked about for an hour. It felt so good to see BJ so happy, truly happy. I honestly don't think I had ever heard her mention a boy before, let alone bounce around about one. "This Darren must be something special. Look at you, all grins and giggles." I opened the garage door and waved her to go ahead of me.

"Oh, he is. He's smart, athletic, and everyone is so jealous." She opened the car door, but stopped before climbing in. Over the roof of the car she looked at me and clarified, "Not that I want to make people jealous. I'm not mean like that or anything. It's just—"

"It's just that you deserve a win," I finished as we climbed in.

We sat down to eat and I noticed that BJ was wearing makeup, not a lot, but enough to make her look grown up. As she carried on chattering ninety-to-nothing, I just smiled and nodded. Nothing can bond a dad and his daughter like a greasy burger and salty French fries, but for the first time ever, she didn't finish either of them. I couldn't even tell you what all she said but knew she hadn't talked that much or that fast since she was around ten years old.

I'm not sure how I managed to stay out of Jaqueline's way for twenty four hours, but my day off seemed to fly by and before I knew it I was back at the emergency room again, only this time Roberts wasn't there to hand off his shift. "Vacation," I said to Jarrod with a smirk. "Since when do we let Roberts go on vacation?"

Jarrod smiled that big pearly white smile he's so known for. "You know, I don't ever remember Dr. Roberts ever taking vacation before. Shoot, with all the work he does here and around his house, that man deserves it." Jarrod leaned across the nurse's station and said in a low, almost whispering voice, "I heard Dr. Elohssa took his shift, but I haven't seen him yet." I always find it funny when a big guy like Jarrod whispers, it just seems wrong. All that manly muscle and dark skin deserves such a louder, more boisterous sound coming from it.

Dr. Elohssa wasn't his real name. The nurses just called him that after he chewed a few of them out. I guess they took another play from that practical joke about the Nodrah drug I told them about. Spelling things backwards became a thing, sort of our secret code. His real name was Brent Birchfield and he moonlights at a few hospitals across town. He was a good looking fellow, tall, muscular and blue-eyed, but his arrogant attitude over the years had earned him quite the reputation, thus the name Dr. Elohssa.

"Dr. Jackson," he said swiftly, as if he were my commander, as he rounded the corner and approached me. "You have a few patients to take over, nothing I'm sure you can't handle."

I can't handle. What the hell is that supposed to mean, I thought in annoyance. "Well, Dr. Birchfield, I'm sure you're right. I'll do my best to not screw them up," I said with a bit of sarcasm as I walked away.

There was an audible chuckle that came from Elizabeth and Jennifer who happened to have walked up during the exchange. Jarrod was standing behind Elohssa shaking his head and rolling his eyes so hard they fluttered within the socket. The comradery among my team warmed my heart. It was good to have a place to go where I felt loved and appreciated. Work was a great escape, probably the thing that was holding me together. Work and BJ, that is. Oh, and that green-eyed redhead that I couldn't get out of my thoughts.

I pushed the lounge door open, wishing I would find Roberts on the other side, but instead it was just the usual spread of continental breakfast. Only this time, the cream cheese had not been disturbed and all the bagels still had both sides. I admit, I was missing Roberts, our talks, and our chess game.

The day was busy, not hectic, but steady with all the usual type cases. "Last one," I said to Jarrod as I placed the clipboard at the nurse's station. The day's cases were all so routine that it made Dr. Birchfield's comment even that much more disturbing.

"Damn," I said as I looked over at the board before heading home. Roberts must have come in and made one last move. His white queen was now on c8. I could almost hear Roberts say, "Check!" I stared at the board almost in disbelief. *How could he do me like that? Leave and put me in check at the same time. Then again, I had the advantage of time. Time to work this out and find my best move.*

About that time, Elizabeth popped her head in. She glanced over at the board and raised her eyebrows. I wasn't sure if she knew anything about chess, but I was hoping she didn't. Especially since I was about lose. "Hey there, looks like the boy in bay three is going to need quite a few sutures. I've set it all up." She tilted her head to once side, as if to say *please*. The shine of her red curly hair was almost begging me to follow her out of the lounge.

I'd hardly call the patient in bay three a boy. He was over six feet tall and made of solid muscle. His head was sweaty, with a few small pimples along his hair line, and he smelled like a gym locker. Next to him was a slender man about in his thirties with short strawberry blonde hair. The man was not quite old enough to be this kid's dad. I looked at the boy's arm, all gaped open and bleeding, and then asked the usual first question, "So, Sport, how'd this happen?"

The slice had to have been six or more inches long. Luckily it missed a large vein that was bulging right beside the cut. The boy looked at me completely unimpressed with the cut or the amount of blood and said, "We were just running drills at school and something sharp somehow got on the field. I slid right over it. I think it was part of a can or something."

I nodded at the boy to acknowledge that I heard him, and then I glanced at the man beside the bed. "So, you must be a trainer?" He was obviously too young and subdued to be a couch. Coaches usually do all the talking, but not this guy. He more or less stood there like he had no idea what to do. The faint freckles on his face made him look incredibly young and innocent. And, if I didn't know better, I would say he didn't like the sight of blood either.

"I am," he answered nervously. It's my first year at this school. Well, first year at a high school, actually." He chuckled a bit and his hands were a little shaky. "High school's a different ball game. A lot of the kids, like this one, are bigger than the coaches."

"True," I said as I looked at the patient who had muscled on muscles, "and the doctors."

The boy watched as I numbed his arm and started to stitch. "That's cool," he said with a sense of wonderment. "Good thing it's the end of the year. This thing will be healed up in plenty of time for next season. Right doc?"

Before I could answer him, the door popped open. "Dr. Jackson," Elizabeth said. "Do you want me—"

"Wait, you're Dr. Jackson?" said the boy as he tried to sit up a little taller. "No way," he added drawing out the word no and extra beat or two.

"Way," I replied without taking my eyes off the suturing. "Now, try to stay still," I added as I touched his upper arm.

"Yes, sir," he replied in an apologetic fashion.

"Wow," said Elizabeth smugly. "You're reputation has gotten all the way back to the local high schools. Impressive." She drug out the word impressive in such a cute way, like she was adapting to the dialect of the teen.

The trainer piped up, "That's good luck on our part. We were hoping for you. The basketball coach told us to come here. She said Dr. Jackson took great care of BJ and her ankle's almost as good as new."

I smiled as if to accept the compliment graciously. "BJ's actually my—"

"I'm Darren," the boy blurted out as he extended his good arm out to shake my hand.

Before I could, Elizabeth burst out with, "Wait, *you're* Darren?"

The trainer said with a chuckle, "Look, Darren, your reputation as a star has made it all the way to the local hospital too."

I stopped stitching and looked up at Darren. I saw him completely different now. I saw him as a young man, not a kid, but a strapping young man that would have my daughter in his car a week from now. I swallowed hard at the thought. Then I had another thought, the kind dads have, the thought of stitching something else, like his fly shut.

I gathered that he was a bit nervous too by the way he tried again to sit up a little straighter in the bed. "I'm not sure if BJ told you," he started to say with a quiver in his voice. *Look who's intimidated now,* I thought holding the needle driver.

"She did," Elizabeth blurted out. "She told us."

Us, I thought. I liked the sound of that. Looks like I now know what her and BJ were talking about for an hour. "Yes," I said looking him in the eye. "You better be a gentleman with my daughter. As a matter of fact, I don't think you should put this arm here around anyone for at least ten days, until the stitches come out."

I heard Elizabeth snicker under her breath. Darren didn't crack a smile though. He just very solemnly said, "Yes, sir." It was typical polite, Texas-boy charm. Although, I've rarely seen anyone argue with a doctor who has a needle in his hand.

"Unless you're slow dancing," Elizabeth added. I turned and gave her a stony expression. She cleared her throat and promptly added, "With plenty of distance that is."

A few minutes later, Darren stood up and shook my hand to thank me. He was about an inch taller than me and what felt like a foot wider. I swallowed hard and said, "Ok now, remember what I said."

"Don't put my arm around anyone," he replied with a serious nod of understanding.

"Yes, exactly," I replied trying not to smile. "And . . ." I stopped like I was leading the witness, "keep it clean and no working out until after the sutures are out."

We walked them out of the room and as Elizabeth stopped right in front of the nurse's station. As they started to walk away, Elizabeth said sternly, "Oh, and Darren, we have to take them out. Remember, you will be forced to see us after that banquet, so behave yourself." She smiled and gave a chuckle, looking Darren right in the eye. Then she turned and winked at me. I looked back at her, locking eyes with a smile that lasted a bit too long. Long enough for anyone who was watching to notice. And they were all watching.

SIXTEEN

They say three days can change your life. Historically, we know that to be true, even biblically three days changed so much, as my mom quite frequently reminded me. She used to say that if you don't like the circumstances you're in, just wait three days and that the opposite was true too. If things were going great and the stars were aligned, there was generally a seventy-two hour expiration date attached to it. I always took that advice to heart. When I decided to go to medical school, I filled all the applications out and then waited three days to apply. Just in case.

Two of the three days leading up to the infamous dress shopping were up, and I was secretly hoping for something on day three. I didn't know exactly what, but my imagination was running away with ideas of bliss, love, and happily ever after. Then I would catch myself and wonder why I was allowing myself to carry on with this narrative that was playing out like a story book ending where there was no chance of it actually coming true.

As I left the house BJ gave me a kiss on the cheek, her eyes all aglow and said, "Thanks for introducing me to Lizzy. I looked her up on social media, and she's got great taste."

I stopped for a moment and wondered. *Social media? Ok, I just found a reason to get Facebook.* "Hey, she continued, just one more day, Dad. One more day before your baby girl finds her perfect dress." Then she giggled in a way that was wholly new. My tomboy, athlete, tough as nails baby girl was giddy, nearly stumbling over her own feet as she danced toward the refrigerator.

Walking into the emergency room, I found Elizabeth all smiles. I couldn't help but smile back, our eyes meeting a bit longer than they should've, but luckily nobody seemed to notice. "Hey, do you think you can swipe a bagel for me from the doctor's lounge?" She asked as she tilted her head and flashed me a cute little smile. "I ran off without breakfast."

"Well, you my dear, have made my baby girl so happy. It's the least I can do." I was headed in there anyway. I had thought about that chess game all night and couldn't wait to take his queen with my rook. Normally, I would look at the board one last time before moving my piece, but that lady in waiting was waiting for a bagel. I stood over the bagels. *Plain or onion? Cream cheese or no cream cheese? If I guess am I presumptuous? If I go ask am I indecisive?*

"Here you are. One plain bagel, toasted, and with cream cheese lightly spread to help it slide down easier," I said as much confidence as I could fake.

"Wow. Perfect! Exactly how I like it." Then she scurried off to eat it in private. I guessed she didn't want anyone to see her mooching off the doctor's lounge food. Not that it would have mattered.

A few minutes later I was met at the nurse's station by Mary. As always, her scrubs were perfectly pressed and each hair of her bob was in place. She said in the most professional way, "Looks like they had a sleeper kind of night, very few cases." Then, she shrugged her shoulders as if she needed to find something to busy herself with.

"Nothing to report," said Dr. Elohssa as he brushed past us without even making eye contact. The arms of his scrubs were rolled up as if to show off his biceps. Not that they were much to brag about. No matter how much he worked out and ate clean, that attitude of his turned everyone off, nearly 100 percent of the time. Mary didn't realize it, but I caught a slight roll of her eyes as he passed. *Look at that*, I thought. *Even Mother Mary can't stomach that guy.*

The emergency room was steady, just the usual softball cases, like stitches, dehydration, sprains and strains. It was nice to have a break, but at the same time, it gave me way too much time to think. I thought about the girls going dress shopping. I thought about Elizabeth and the way she asked me so sweetly for that bagel. I thought about her green eyes and her red hair. Then I thought about how bad I felt for thinking about her so much.

"Jackson? Hey there, hello?" Jarrod said as he waved his hand in front of my face. I actually heard him, but it took me a second to snap out of my thought. Of course, I was thinking about Elizabeth again. "Want to drill me?" He asked, as he handed me a stack of flash cards.

"Absolutely," I replied. "I love being on this end. Besides, you've got the answers on the back, right?"

"It's anatomy and physiology. Not like you couldn't do this stuff in your sleep," he said, shaking his head. He started off a bit shy, as if he was embarrassed to be doing something I may think as trivial. But then, as he got more right, his stance grew taller, mimicking his confidence.

"Scapula," I said, trying not to give any visual cues. I really wanted to point him in the right direction, but resisted the urge. After a few seconds of silence I gave him some advice that my old A&P teacher gave me. "Just visualize it. Think of words that look or sound like it so you can jog your memory easily. Ok, this is a flat bone so think *spatula*. Scapula is often called the shoulder blade. So scapula sounds like spatula, which is flat. The shoulder blade is a flat bone. Got it?"

"Ok. Cool. Yeah, got it," Jarod smiled real big as if he appreciated the tip. "Well, maybe you've got one for those for the little bones in the ear. I never can remember those," he said hanging his head and shaking it as if ashamed.

"Well my friend, that's where my mom's advice to take Latin paid off. The bones in the middle ear are called the malleus, incus, and stapes. In Latin, that's hammer, anvil, and stirrup."

"Yeah. No, that does not help," he laughed.

The flash cards went on for well over an hour and Jarrod did pretty well, about eighty percent or more correct. "Not bad," I said. "Besides, you still had two days before the big final exam." I watched as he divided the cards up carefully, being sure to take the cards he'd had trouble with and placed them in the chest pocket of his scrubs.

Elizabeth happened to walk by. I didn't see her at first, but I smelled the hints of jasmine from her perfume. My eyes followed her, looking her over from head to toe as she passed. Then, as I brought my glance back to Jarred, it was obvious. He didn't say anything out loud, just a sideways smile and an almost inaudible *"Hmmm. Ok."* Under his breath.

I broke away as soon as I could to avoid any sort of acknowledgement. Turning my body a slightly different direction, I looked up over the nurse's station and asked, "What's up with you, Mary?" We rarely get a chance to shoot the breeze and catch up, so this quiet time was a welcome visitor. That is, as long as I could keep my attention off of Elizabeth.

"Not much. Things are good. Can't complain. My daughter's going to have her baby soon, so I'm trying to get used to the sound of Grandma or Nana or Mimi—whichever they decide to call me."

"Nope," Elizabeth said as she walked up sipped a cup of coffee. "They don't get to choose. I read somewhere that *you* choose what to be called. It's a thing."

"It's not a thing," said Mary, looking a bit annoyed that Elizabeth was doling out grandmotherly advice.

"Yep, it's right here," said Elizabeth staring at her phone. "Picking what you want your kid's kids to call you is a rite-of-passage. Not all names are created equal. Nanas are generally more engaged with their grandchildren, while Grandmother is generally reserved for those wishing to keep the kids at more of a distance with less sleepovers or field trips."

"That's ridiculous," Jennifer said as she bit down on a bagel so smothered with cream cheese that it oozed out around her mouth.

"You and Roberts," I said as I shook my head from side to side. "Want a little bagel with that cream cheese? Besides, where'd you get that?"

As she wiped the smear from her lips she pointed at Elizabeth and with a mouthful said, "Caught her with one and asked her to sneak in and grab one for me."

Mary had a stoic face, as if she could not believe the disrespect these two girls were displaying. Mary was always so old-school. Her professional demeanor may not have made her any fun to be around, but it certainly made her a great nurse.

"Wait, what did you do, pick the lock?" I said a bit confused. They all know the doctor's lounge was locked and required a key or badge to get in.

"Nope," said Elizabeth holding up my name badge. Her sly grin caused everyone to break into peals of laughter, even Mary.

"Add B&E to your rap sheet," said Sergei who was just a few steps away mopping up an already clean floor.

"And ninja to yours," I said looking a bit surprised that Sergei once again appeared out of nowhere.

If the emergency room was a pressure cooker, its days like this that let just enough steam out to keep us from blowing up. Even adrenalin junkies like us need a down day every once in a while. I ended the perfect day with stop by the chessboard before heading out.

That night when I arrived home, I was met at the back door by BJ. With phone in hand, she asked me a question, the question every dad dreads. She asked, "Do you want to see a picture of him?"

Very unconvincingly I played dumb. "Picture of who?"

"Daddddd," she wined. "*Darren. The boy I'm going to the banquet with.*"

At that moment I realized I never told her about him coming in. Well, it's not like I could have, after all HIPAA regulations keep me from discussing patients. *Yep, that's him,* I thought. *Dang, looks even bigger with all that padding on.* "Football, huh?"

"He's a triple threat," she said proudly. "Football, baseball, *and* wrestling."

"Good, then certainly he'll get a scholarship to college and avoid all that debt. Don't marry a guy with too much debt." My words were a bit hypocritical, but she didn't need to know that. Inside I was thinking of all the ways this guy could probably take me if there was ever a physical fight. Not that there would be one, but I would guess that every dad plays the scenario out in their head, just in case.

"Dad," she said seriously. The most serious she'd been in days. "It's a banquet, not an engagement."

That was music to my ears. I certainly didn't want her rushing into anything. Because of my own failed marriage, I knew how important it was to heavily vet any potential mates she might someday consider. *Mates? Am I really thinking about my daughter and her wedding day?* I looked at BJ and had to wonder where all the years went. How she grew up so fast. I was grateful for her innocence, her determination, and all the things that made her so incredibly unique. She may have seen it as a banquet, but I saw it as one step closer to walking her down the aisle, giving her away, and someday having to let go of the one thing that kept me sane all these years.

SEVENTEEN

After all the years of being gently awoken by Honey, the sound of the alarm clock was an unwelcomed siren that breaking the early morning silence. As I blinked my eyes open, I remembered almost instantly that today was BJ and Elizabeth's shopping trip. As I laid in the bed, one hand behind my head, I stared at ceiling, trying to bring the fan into focus in the darkness. I saw images of Elizabeth, her curly, shiny red hair bouncing around in the sunlight. I saw BJ smiling and giggling. It seemed so happy and so real that I smiled to myself right there in bed. A smile that stayed with me as I showered and dressed.

"Well, hello there, princess," I said with a smile. BJ was already awake and standing by the kitchen island with my coffee already made and ready to go. "Thank you," I said with a whisper, remembering Jacqueline was passed out on the sofa after another night of drinking with her friends.

"No need to whisper, Dad. Mom didn't get home until after 2 a.m. I doubt she moves before noon."

I looked at BJ with sad eyes and tight lips, as if to apologize she had to witness that. "You know, I am so sorry—"

"Shhh," she said, pressing her first finger against her lips to hush me. "Nope. Don't worry about that, Dad, this is going to be a great day. I'm going to find the perfect dress. And *nobody* is going to ruin it." Then she leaned forward and kissed my cheek. "I love you, Daddy," she said.

Daddy? I was so touched. She hadn't called me that for years. It melted my heart in a way that only another dad could understand. That daddy comment was like a deposit of a million dollars to my emotional bank account. I stood there looking at BJ for just a moment longer, smiling at her. "I love you too. Have a blast today. Oh, and here," I said handing her the Visa card from my wallet. "Nothing's too good for my daughter. Well, maybe Armani?"

"Who?"

"That's a—" Then I stopped myself, remembering that a little makeup doesn't make my tomboy baby girl a fashion expert. "Never mind. Find the perfect dress." With one hand on the door and the other holding my coffee, I looked back at her and winked. "You deserve it."

"Well, the troops are all here," I said as I approached the nurse's station and found Mary, Jarrod, Jennifer, and Sergei. Sergei with his briefcase full of cases to study, Jennifer with unruly blonde hair, controlled by a rainbow scrunchy, Jarrod looking tired from studying, but still smiling and happy, and Mary standing there stoic and ready to work.

Jarrod looked at me with a slight grin and said, "Not *everybody*." I knew he was referring to Elizabeth.

"Oh, you're right. I'm sure Dr. Elohssa's here somewhere," I replied with a wink.

Then a loud and abrupt voice blurted out. "Dr. Elohssa? Why the hell do you all keep calling me that?" We all looked at one another, panic stricken. Nobody had seen him walk up and nobody wanted to answer *that* question.

"Me," Jarrod said quickly. He walked toward Dr. Elohssa and placed one hand on his shoulder and gave it small shake. "You, my friend, remind me of this professor I had a few semesters ago. Oh yes, Professor Elohssa was quite memorable. Unforgettable, actually."

"Well, just in case you have forgotten, my name is Brent Birchfield. Dr. Birchfield to all of you," he said pointing to everyone but me. I wasn't sure if that meant I could call him Brent or if he just left me off his hit list out of quasi respect.

Jarrod never expanded on why this fictitious professor was so unforgettable, but Dr. Elohssa was a true narcissist, so he assumed it was a compliment and had replied in a boasting voice with, "Of course. All the good ones are unforgettable."

Jennifer, stood there, unable to control her urge to add to the conversation said, "Well, some people don't faze you, while others never seem to leave your memory." A comment that was met with a smile from Dr. Elohssa, until Jennifer added, "That includes both good and bad memories." The room got awkwardly silent for about a minute. Then Jarrod changed the subject, naturally, as if he hadn't heard or understood what Jennifer was driving at. Of course, we all knew he'd heard it loud and clear and we all agreed that Jarrod deserved an Academy Award for his performance.

That morning's cases were pretty routine. Food poisoning, a landscaper who'd weed-whacked himself to the tune of seven stiches, and a baby with a fever. Around eleven o'clock my phone dinged in my pocket. To my surprise it was BJ sending a selfie of her and Elizabeth. The two of them looked so beautiful, leaning their heads together for the shot. They didn't look like two people who had only met once, but more like friends who had a history together. The text read: "Lunch first and then the HUNT!"

I didn't quite know how to respond and I was sure whatever I typed would immediately be shared with Elizabeth. So, I took the safe route and texted a very dad-like comment: "Stay safe and have fun." After I hit send I thought, *Stay safe? Seriously?* I stood there pondering the idea of sending a second message, but before I could think of a good save, BJ had already replied.

"Dad. It's the mall."

I looked at my phone, started to type. Then erased it. Looked instead for a GIF that might make them laugh but couldn't find one that seemed right. A cartoon hug would have been too childish. Carlton from *Fresh Prince* was funny, but only Elizabeth would have understood how funny. So, I just gave up and put the phone in my pocket, deciding to just leave well enough alone.

Mary approached me with a puzzled look on her face. "I think this is the most I have ever seen you on your phone at work. Save that bad habit for the millennials. We've got a case in you may be interested in right over there," she said pointing toward a little girl.

"Hello, Dad," I said as I pulled my stool up alongside the bed. The little girl couldn't have been more than five years old. She had on a cute little summer dress and white sandals. Her hair was a bit unruly and looked as if it needed a good brushing. "What brings you and your princess in today?" I could tell the little girl liked me calling her princess, by the way she gave a shy smile at me and then looked down. She was twisting her arms around each other and grasping her hands as if she didn't quite know what to do, or how to act.

"This here is Rebecca," he said, stroking her hair back as if he was trying to fix it. "I thought it was just allergies—"

"Dog," the little girl said. "I have a dog in my nose."

"Oh, a dog," I replied with a smile.

"I guess she thinks she's allergic to the dog," said the dad. He had one hand rested on top of her head, and the other in the pocket of his khaki shorts. The tattoo that covered his arm made it clear that he was or had been a marine.

"She might be right," I said, smiling at the little girl as if to justify her diagnosis.

"I am," she said proudly. Her dad and I both chuckled, but she kept a safe and serious face, as if she were surprised that we found her confidence so amusing.

"Marines, huh?" I said as I looked up the little girl's nose. "Oh, this is pretty infected."

"Served a few tours in Iraq. Medical actually."

I looked up at him knowing he had seen probably more carnage than I would ever see in my career. I stood up straight, looked him in the eye, out-stretched my hand to shake his, and said, "Thank you. Thank you for serving." It was a touching moment, one where I felt as if I truly in the presence of a hero, someone who gave freely to my country. I even had a small moment of guilt, wondering why I never thought about the service.

"Does this hurt?" I asked the little girl as I pushed on her sinuses. She didn't have to answer. I could tell by her grimace that her face was tender.

"Sinus series," I said to Mary who typed the x-ray order into the chart. Then I looked at the little girl and said, "Rebecca, we're going to take a picture of your face, but with a very special camera, a big camera. Ok?"

The little girl smiled and held her arms out on both sides. "Like this big?"

"Even bigger," I said with a big smile as I jiggled her little foot. She was so petite that she hardly took up any room on the bed. She reminded me of my own little princess who grew up all too fast.

"Are you going to take the dog out?" She asked. Her dad looking at her quite puzzled.

"Well, we're probably going to give you medicine to take that dog allergy out of your nose." Then I turned to the dad and said, "Sometimes allergies can turn into infections. If you have a dog, maybe you can visit with an allergist to help manage her symptoms."

"No dog," said the dad. "I don't know why she insists this is from a dog."

"It's a dog," she insisted, as she crossed her arms and started to pout.

About thirty minutes later I came back in the room. "Sir, your daughter is a master diagnostician."

"Yes I am," she said so proudly, her nose a bit turned up in the air.

"Oh, you are so smart!" I said as I bent over and looked her right in her little blue eyes. "You know what a diagnostician is?"

She smiled and just as proud as before she said, "Nope."

The room filled with chuckles. I don't know what was cuter, her confidence or her innocence. I turned the computer monitor toward little Rebecca and her dad.

"This," I said, pointing to a perfect outline on the x-ray, an outline that lit up like a bulb on a Christmas tree. "This right here is—"

Then in unison, Mary, little Rebecca, her dad, and I all said, "A dog!"

The sweet little shy girl had managed to put a little Monopoly piece up her nose. "Rebecca, you just earned yourself a visit to my friend, the ENT. He can get that dog out for you. In the meantime, you'll also need to take some medicine for the infection. Dogs do not belong in little noses," I said as I put my first finger on the tip of her tiny nose.

Her giggle was infectious. It was almost as if she was proud of her little accomplishment. She smiled a big smile, and with the most confidence of any kindergartener I had ever met, she looked at her dad and said, "See, Daddy, I told you!"

Daddy. Oh how I loved the sound of that. That big marine, with all his muscles and tattooed arms loved it too. He seemed to melt right before my eyes as he got down on one knee and kissed his little girl's hand and said, "Yes. Yes you did, baby."

Mary started working on the referral, and as I waved bye to the little girl, I heard my phone ding in my pocket. My heart skipped a beat, as I was anticipating another picture from BJ. Instead, I found a text that read: *Call me.* I didn't recognize the number so I slid the phone back in my pocket. Then it dinged with a text again: *This is Ariana from your house the other night. Please call me.*

469-960-6950. The women who'd stood in my doorway trying to seduce me with her large breasts and low-cut top?

I texted back: *Sorry not a chance.*

A few minutes later, my phone dinged again. At this point I was a bit irritated. I was prepared to shoot off a longer text, asking how she got my number and instructing her to delete it from my contacts, but oddly it was Carol, another friend of Jaqueline's. As soon as I saw who it was, I immediately assumed she was going to give me bad news about Jeanie. But instead, it read: *Bobby, sorry to bother you at work. When is the last time you spoke to Jaqueline?*

I had no idea where she was going with this question and I wasn't quite sure how to answer her. *Should I tell her that the last I saw Jaqueline she was passed out on the sofa?* I wasn't quite sure how much Carol knew about Jaqueline's continuous spiral down or the demise of our marriage. The last thing I wanted to do was tip any of her friends off that I would be leaving her soon. So, I simply texted: *No, she was asleep when I left. Haven't talked to her since my shift started.*

Her next text read: *She said she was going to the mall today.*

The mall! I thought *Oh crap! She's going to ruin BJ's day.*

It still didn't make sense. Why would Carol tell me this? There was no way she could know about Elizabeth and BJ, or the big dress shopping event. In an effort to play it cool, I just texted, *Ok. Well, I don't know. Just try calling her back.*

I placed my phone back in my front shirt pocket, but no sooner had I reached the nurses station had it rang. I let out a sigh and felt my eyes roll in my head a bit as I sent Carol to voicemail. The last thing I wanted to do was have a conversation about how Jaqueline was going to spend her day or worse, show any uneasiness about her trip to the mall.

My phone dinged again and the next text changed my life. It was the kind of text that no parent ever wanted to receive. A nightmare of all nightmare texts that was the preview to the horror that was about to fill my emergency room.

Bobby, please pick up the phone! You don't know what happened at the mall yet, do you? Please call me ASAP!!

EIGHTEEN

No sooner had that text come over my phone that all hell broke loose in the emergency room. Calls were coming in one after another, the sound of ambulance sirens filled the halls as stretcher after stretcher rolled through the door. "Call Dr. Elohssa. Get him up here," I said to Mary. "Then call Roberts and see if he's anywhere nearby. If he can make it in the next three to four hours, he has to come in."

I looked at each stretcher as they rolled in, terrified that the next one would be my daughter. The smell of burning flesh mixed with the metallic stench of iron rich blood filled the air. I frantically tried calling BJ. I was holding the phone to my ear with my shoulder as I started to take inventory of the cases that lined up in front of me like a battlefield war scene. No answer. I dialed again. No answer. "Somebody call Elizabeth!" I yelled.

"I don't think she can come in, Dr. Jackson. She said something about having to take the day off today. It was something important," answered Jennifer as she was cutting the pant legs off the young boy on a stretcher.

"Call her. Damn it!" I yelled back at anyone who was willing to listen. Nobody in the emergency room had ever heard me yell or curse quite like that before. I looked up and everyone was tending the patients before then, seemingly uninterested in my plea. "She was with my daughter!" I yelled, looking around the room hoping for some eye contact. My eyes caught Jennifer's. I lowered my tone and added, "At the mall."

Jennifer's face fell, and she grabbed her phone from her pocket and began hitting the screen quickly, then raised the phone to her ear and waited. After a moment she looked over and swallowed hard. "Sorry, no answer," she said, her fingers trembling. Tears started to well in her eyes, but none came out. "I'll text her too."

A paramedic I hadn't seen before, but couldn't have been more than twenty-five, came rushing in with another victim, a child. "Suicide bomber." His eyes were widened and his pupils so large that they seemed to fill his eyes. It was the look of fear, shear horror that came across his face. "Half the Galleria is missing. The guy had enough explosives—"

"Stop!" I yelled. "Spare me the details unless they're pertinent to the individual patient." I could feel panic flowing through my veins as sweat filled my brow. My heart was pounding so hard that I felt a choking sensation in my throat. At one point I thought I would succumb to the stress of the unknown. *Maybe they were still eating,* I rationalized. *Or, they'd already found the dress and left the mall.* The internal struggle between being a doctor with patients to care for and being a father who wanted nothing more than to know his daughter was alive, was simply too much. Too much for me, too much for any man.

Then, as if on cue, I noticed the marine in my peripheral vision. He was caring for patients, assisting Mary and Jennifer, and triaging the victims as if he were one of the team. It was the first time I felt helpless, like I was watching everything unfold in front of my eyes in slow motion, while the rest of the crew moved quickly and systematically. The only other time I had felt like this was the day Jeremy had died. It was a feeling I never forgot and one I never wanted to feel again.

I looked over at a chair in the waiting room and there sat little Rebecca. She was swinging her legs back and forth and entertained by the events as if she were watching a movie. I saw her look at her dad. Her eyes sparkled in amazement, like she was watching a superhero on TV. There was a faint smile on her face, but she watched his movements carefully, hardly blinking at all.

I had no idea how much time had passed, but it felt like forever before Dr. Elohssa came running through the door, ready for action. "Bradford?" He said, a look of confusion washing over his face as he looked inquisitively at the Marine. "What're you? I mean how—"

Wait, Elohssa knows this guy? I thought. *Oh great, I have a non-employee medic pitching in. Could I look any worse right now?*

"It's a long story Sergeant Birchfield. No disrespect, but it will have to wait," said the Marine.

Sergeant? I looked at Elohssa and suddenly felt a bit guilty for calling him that. "Look, Dr. Birchfield. He was just here. I know it's not protocol, but we need all the—"

"Screw protocol. I'll have Bradford on my team any day," he said in a very militaristic voice. I caught the glance that passed between the two men, a solid two-beat stare with a slight nod—a nod of admiration, appreciation, and deep respect.

I wanted to alert dispatch that we were at capacity, but there was no way I was going to take the chance of BJ and Elizabeth being rerouted to another hospital. I had to know what was going on and it would be impossible to focus on patients here, knowing she was somewhere I couldn't go. There simply was no possible way I could stop and try and call again. Things were just moving too fast and the patients were too critical.

Just then, the doors opened again. Alongside the patient, Roberts entered, "Jackson, this is one of ours. I'll take care of her." I looked over at the gurney and sure enough, red hair with dried blood matting the strands, spread out over the top of gurney. Her hair was filled with bits of glass that seemed to shimmer as the overhead lights bounced off the glass like glitter. The sight of blood had never made me feel like vomiting until that moment.

I stood in my emergency room, feet planted firmly in place, and the room spun around me as if I were on a merry-go-round.

Sergei walked up and grabbed my arm, looking me in the eye. "I can help. Please let me help," he said. His voice was so calming and grounded that I immediately came back to myself. The room stopped spinning, and suddenly my mind was back in the game. My eyes looked into his, and I nodded an affirmation, and I watched as he immediately approached Elizabeth's lifeless body.

I started to follow, but a cry of "Daddy!" coming from the entrance stopped me dead in my tracks. It was BJ, covered in blood and streaked with grime, her hair wet with tears, but running toward me. I grabbed her and hugged her, embracing her tightly as her whole body shook.

"Honey, you're bleeding," I said as I pulled away after what seemed like forever. "No, Dad, it's not my blood. It's Elizabeth's. Where is she?" Her lips quivered as she spoke and her words were broken and shaky.

"She's over there with Dr. Roberts," I said. "I—" I stopped, looked at her again, my eyes filled with happy tears that she was alive and seemed ok. "I was just headed to her when you came in. Are you sure you're all right?"

"I'm sure," she said motioning for me to go. "Go save her Dad. She saved my life."

I could hear BJ's sobs as I ran toward Elizabeth, my shoes leaving a path of bloody prints on the floor behind me. The once white emergency room floor was now covered in blood. There was a little from each patient that was wheeled in, and a lot from a select few, like Elizabeth. I stood by the bed for a split second to hear Dr. Roberts and Sergei. "Wounds to the back, sides, and back of the head," Sergei yelled out. "Looks like the front, with the exception of her face, was spared."

"Call dispatch," I yelled out to Jarrod, who was running between patients. "Tell them to cut us off. Reroute all patients for at least the next two hours." Jarrod looked at me and nodded, then ran off. But as he rounded the nurse's station, his shoes lost traction. The blood on the floor was like a river of gooey scarlet slime. He grabbed the ledge of the nurse's station just fast enough to get his legs back under him before crashing to the ground.

Sergei looked at me as if he were a bit conflicted. He didn't say it, but I could tell he couldn't stand all the mess. After all, that was his job. So, I looked him straight in the eyes and said, "Not today. Not right now. This is where you belong." He nodded stoically and then looked back down at Elizabeth, at the task before us.

Elizabeth's wounds were deep. As I stood over her, assessing her injuries, I could see exactly what happened. She used her body as a shield to protect BJ. That's why BJ was covered in her blood and why Elizabeth's front side didn't look too bad. I looked closely at her face, noticing a slash to her lip and another across her right eyebrow. Her clothes had been cut off and just a sheet covered her chest. Sergei and I rolled her over to assess her back. I removed her emerald necklace, careful not to break the chain as

I maneuvered it around her neck brace. Then I hollered out to BJ, who came running over almost instantly. "Take this," I said. "Don't lose it. Oh, and see that little girl? Her name's Rebecca. I need you to keep an eye on her." Elizabeth's wounds nothing in comparison to how deep my feelings had grown for her.

BJ looked at Elizabeth's back. She stared for a second, her eyes wide, then she broke her trance, looked up at me, and in a brave voice said, "You got it, Dad." She took the bloodied necklace in her hand, and her brave face turned to sad eyes before she sheepishly asked, "Do you think she'll make it? If it weren't for her—"

"I hope so, sweet pea. We're going to do everything we can. Now go sit with that little girl." Then, without another word, BJ did exactly as I asked.

Roberts had moved on to tend to another patient, as Sergei and I worked on Elizabeth for what seemed like forever. I was conscious of the fact that I was distancing myself emotionally so I could rely solely on my medical training. A professor once told me that emotionally involved trauma doctors have a higher patient mortality rate. It helped that I was working on the back of Elizabeth, that I couldn't see her face.

"Dr. Jackson," Sergei said as he looked down at Elizabeth's face and up at me again. He whispered, "She's coming to."

I quickly scooted around to see for myself while Sergei held on tightly to keep her on her side. "Well, hello there, beautiful," I said with a smile. My heart was pounding. I didn't want my face or words to relay my fears of her condition.

As her eye's opened, they darted around. The brace around her neck kept her from moving it, so she forced her eyes as far as they would go in each direction to catch a glimpse of what was happening. "BJ. Where's BJ?" she managed to get out as tears filled her eyes.

"BJ is fine," I assured her as I started to cry. I knew I wasn't supposed to get emotional, but damn it, I was human after all. "You saved her. You saved my baby girl," I said as I picked shards of glass from her hair. Then I reached over and kissed her bloody forehead. Sergei didn't say a word, but when I looked up at him, I could see a smile peeking through his otherwise stoic expression. I was torn. As much as I wanted to stay at her back before, I couldn't bear to leave her sight now.

"Here," Sergei said as if he knew what I was thinking. "You hold her. My arms are tired. If you trust me, I can take over on the back. If you feel better about it, you can call out orders."

I was holding Elizabeth toward me, trying to say comforting words and instruct Sergei at the same time. After a few minutes, I realized he was doing exactly what needed to be done prior to my instruction. His previous medical experience was shining through. "You know," he said as he pulled a piece of glass a few inches long out from around her shoulder blade. "We didn't have any bells and whistles in our emergency rooms like you do in the states. But, the war, well, it gave us enough of this kind of experience to last me a lifetime."

No sooner had we gotten into a routine than the doors swished open again. "What the—" I said exacerbated. "I said no more—"

Roberts looked at me. We made eye contact that lasted a bit longer than usual. It was as if we had some sort of brotherly code. "I'm almost done here," he said from the bedside of a patient that was sitting up all bandaged, but alert. "I'll take that one," he said. I couldn't see much, but the patient seemed to be in pretty bad shape.

"Dad," a voice said. It was BJ. Her face was ashen and she was standing half way between Elizabeth and the new patient. She didn't motion for me or anything, but something told me I needed to go to her side.

Sergei looked at me. Then he called to Jarrod to give him a hand. The two of them held on to Elizabeth while I walked over to BJ. "I know, honey, it's a lot to take in. Good news, though, Elizabeth's awake. She asked about you." I thought that would make her smile, but instead, she looked over at the other patient and then again at me. Her eyes begged mine to follow hers. That's when I saw her. It was Jacqueline. Roberts looked up at me and in that moment, I knew he'd figured it out. I started to walk toward Jaqueline, but then I turned to look back at Elizabeth.

Almost instantly, the alarms started chiming. Elizabeth's blood pressure was tanking. I stood there, looking at one and then the other, and then at Roberts and then at BJ. Roberts nodded his head forward, towards Elizabeth, as if to say, "Go to her." I stood there frozen. Then BJ tugged my arm. She looked at me, and without a word, she motioned with a head tilt toward Elizabeth.

Moments later, I was standing at the bed of Elizabeth, and she was once again stable. I could see Roberts out of the corner of my eye. He had been working on Jaqueline, but not with any sense of urgency, and he never asked for assistance. It all seemed like a dream, a bad nightmare to be exact. Often during those moments, I felt like someone else. Someone who was just watching it all take place. The brain's a funny thing when it hits overload.

Off in the distance I heard BJ tell Rebecca, "My mom just died." She said it so matter of fact, so calmly and emotionless. I wanted to go comfort her, but there were still more patients to tend to.

Little Rebecca just sat there, still swinging her legs. She looked at BJ, placed her little hand on BJ's knee. "It's ok. My mommy died, too. But I still have my Daddy," she said as she pointed over at the marine who was busy working with Dr. Birchfield. "That's him." The man right next to Dr. Birchfield, the man I would never refer to as Dr. Elohssa ever again.

At the end of about twelve hours, things finally calmed down. Dr. Roberts put his hand on my shoulder, turned me toward him for a hug. Our bloody scrubs meshed together like we were becoming blood brothers.

In a way, we were. He whispered in my ear, low enough that nobody else could possibly hear. "It's over. Your nightmare is over."

NINETEEN

The days that followed were filled with casseroles, cards, and well wishes. Most of it came from neighbors, many of which I had never seen without a glass of wine in their hand. Nonetheless, it was somewhat comforting. Three days after the bombing, I was sitting in front of the television eating a plate of someone's spaghetti when a special alert came on, with a headline that read:

UP NEXT: Suspect Identified in Galleria Bombing.

I immediately put my plate down on the coffee table. I felt my palms beginning to sweat and my chest muscles tightened. I sat there through what seemed to be the longest commercial break ever. I could've cared less about saving ten percent on car insurance or buying a new pillow for a better night's rest. All I wanted was to know was who was responsible for this awful thing and why they did it. I was frozen in anxious anticipation.

The picture went up, and I spit or rather vomited my spaghetti back onto my plate. It was him, Abdul, the crazy guy from the emergency room. The one with the burnt fingertips. "God, how could I have missed that?" I yelled as I threw my plate across the room, where it shattered against the opposite wall.

"Dad!" BJ yelled as her feet trampled down the stairs, probably to see what all the commotion was about. "Dad?" she repeated more quietly as she came toward me, her eyes filled with questions I didn't want to answer.

I quickly turned the television off. I didn't want her to see the news, didn't want anything to remind her of her that terrible day. Her eyes were red rimmed and swollen, as if she had been crying all afternoon. "Oh honey, are you ok?" I asked as I reached out and pulled her against me for a hug. I held her for a long time while she cried, her chest heaving with sobs. And hearing her let go in my arms, I cried, too. I didn't know if we were crying for Elizabeth, for Jacqueline or just from the waste and horror of it all. "I know it's hard. Losing your mom." And I did know. It hadn't been that many years since I'd lost mine, and Jacqueline's death had brought all those buried feelings back to the surface.

"Dad," she said as she pulled away slightly to look at me. "It's not that I miss Mom, it's that I miss having the idea of *having* a mom." Her eyes filled again with tears that fell down her cheeks one after another, drenching her pajama top. Then she added, "A mom like other moms, you know? A mom that loved me. The mom I always *hoped* she'd be one day."

I didn't know what to say. I just pulled her close again and held her tight. We both cried, hard, deep sobs. I understood, probably more than anyone just how complicated this loss was for her. And for the next few hours I pondered many questions that I would never have the answers to. *Was Jaqueline worse after Jeremy died? Should I have gotten her help for her drinking and anger issues? Did she really hate us that much and if so, could I have done anything to change that?* Much like BJ, I wasn't really mourning the loss of Jaqueline, I was mourning the loss of a wife that had never once lived up to the meaning of the word. I was mourning a failed marriage and a child whose deep emotional wounds I could never erase.

TWENTY

"You sure you're up for this?" I asked as I dropped BJ off at school that Friday, the car idling at the curb as we stared out at the red brick exterior, the kids swarming around the entrance like bees. "You probably already know that people are going to be weird. That's just because they don't know what to say, or if they should say anything at all. So, just be polite and thank them for trying."

"I know, Dad," she said, looking over at the school and then back at me with a determined gaze. Then she inhaled and with a smile proclaimed, "I've got this. Besides, the athletics banquet is tonight and don't forget—*your* big night is Saturday."

"Honey, about that," said slowly, reaching out for her hand. "You don't—"

She pulled her hand away, rejecting the gesture. "Are you kidding?" She asked incredulously. "Don't go there,

Dad," she lectured. "We can't stop living because some freak blew our world up. He can't *win*."

I sat there for a moment looking at how stoically she sat there, crossing her arms over her chest now in defiance. She was right. We couldn't let him win. "BJ, you're so strong," I said, unable to keep the admiration I felt for her from my voice. "And you know what? You're absolutely right."

She looked over at me in surprise, her eyes widening, and when, after a long moment, I winked at her, she winked right back. I watched as she opened the car door, got out, and walked away, her shoulders straight and her head held high as she approached the sea of teenagers. I sat there with the window down and watched her walk all the way to the door and go in, just as I did when she was in elementary school. At that moment, I knew beyond a shadow of a doubt that my daughter was unnaturally and wonderfully strong-willed—much like my mother had been.

As I exited the freeway and the hospital came into sight, I felt my heart begin to race. Not only was it beating faster, but it was also skipping around inside my chest. *Palpitations*, I thought. My palms grew sweaty. *Diaphoretic.* As I checked off each symptom, assessing myself, I learned for the first time what it felt like to have a panic attack. And it felt bad, jumping out of your own skin bad. For years, I heard patients describe what it felt like, but I honestly couldn't relate to their seemingly endless litany of complaints or their sense of dread and anxiety, until that moment. *PTSD.* I thought to myself, my hands gripping the steering wheel so tightly that my fingers became bloodless. *Holy crap, I have PTSD.*

My breaths grew shallower and faster as I neared the doors, which swooshed open as I stepped inside. I closed my eyes for a moment as if to convince myself that it had all been a dream, the shortness of breath, the sense of overwhelming anxiety. When I opened them and looked around, everything was different than how I last saw it. The ER was clean, organized, and appeared as if nothing bad had ever happened there.

Mary was standing at the nurse's station. As usual, her brown bob was heavily sprayed so that each hair was steadfastly in place. She smiled at me as if she didn't quite know what to say, so I simply smiled and nodded back. It was the first time I didn't really feel like talking or smiling for that matter, but I fought my instincts to shut down, to run and hide. I had a job to do, a life to live, and BJ was right—we couldn't let him win.

"Roberts," I said with as much energy as I could muster as I spied his familiar face seated behind the desk at the nurse's station. "Boy, am I glad to see you, my friend. Sorry, we crashed your vacation plans, but we couldn't have made it—"

"Bagel?" He asked, as if it were an ordinary Monday morning. I watched as he walked around the nurse's station, and without another word I followed him into the lounge.

As soon as we entered the room, I looked over at the chessboard warily eyeing it as if it would rear up and strike me without warning. I didn't really feel like playing chess. I didn't feel like doing anything, really. "Nice move," I said in a low voice, pointing at his white queen that had been moved from g4 to c8.

"Not my move." He squinted and tilted his head to one side.

"Yeah, right," I replied sarcastically. Obviously, he was playing more games than just chess with me. I took my black rook off h8 and captured his queen on c8. "Nice, but not nice enough," I said a bit cockily, trying to sound tough, like someone who lets stress, death, and destruction roll off their back like water on a duck.

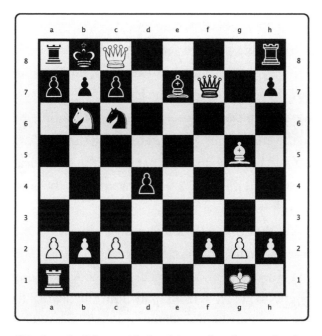

"Seriously," he said, looking closely at the board. "Maybe it was Sergei. He plays too, you know."

Not a chance, I scoffed. If it were Sergei, surely he would have mentioned that he played at some point. Roberts kept asserting that it wasn't him who made the move, but I knew better. *Sore loser,* I thought as I walked away from the board and toward the bagels, assuring myself that I had just foiled his game.

"Cream cheese?" he said sarcastically as he watched me make a move I never make- smear my bagel. "What about that five pounds you keep talking about?" I could tell that he was willing to talk about anything, anything at all that didn't have to do with the bombing. "Besides," he continued, "aren't you off today? I heard you're not on the schedule again until *next* Monday."

"BJ wanted to go to school, so what was I supposed to do? Stay home and go out of my mind?" I retorted, smearing cream cheese on one half of my bagel. "Actually, I have to stop by the funeral home to sign some papers for. . . the cremation." With that word, a silence that grew descended between us, one that grew almost unbearably before I ended it with, "Besides, I wanted to check on our patient upstairs."

"Elizabeth?" Roberts said with a chuckle. "Oh, well you're a day late. That girl busted out of here yesterday. I don't think any of us expected to recover so quickly. She's got to be in serious pain, but according to the nurses upstairs, she was adamant that she could handle it. A tough cookie, that one." Roberts walked to the door, opened it, and said, "Now, time for us *both* to exit this place for a few days. Doctor's orders! He said with a smile, and without another word, I followed him out."

That night, when Darren came to the door wearing khaki pants and sports jacket with a tie to pick up BJ for the dance, he seemed even bigger and stronger than that day we'd first met in the emergency room. His face bore a nervous smile and his rather large handheld a corsage inside a clear plastic box. "Sir," he said, clearing his throat. "I was wondering if I have your permission for BJ to accompany me to the banquet tonight?"

I avoided the urge to snicker at his formal request, but I did wonder how many times he had rehearsed that line. There was some comfort in watching this jock melt into a humble and nervous child right before my eyes. "Well, Darren," I said. "Thank you for asking. And absolutely."

No sooner had I uttered those words that BJ walked up behind me. The sound of her heels clicking against the wooden floor sent chills up my spine. Normally, that sound was reserved for Jaqueline, but this time, for the first time, there stood BJ in her own set of high heels. "Wow!" I said as I took one look at her, so elegant, so lady like that I had to shake my head and do a double take.

Her hair was curled and atop her head, in a way I'd never seen her wear it before. She was holding a bouton-niere: a single red rose with a spray of baby's breath behind it. As she pinned the flower carefully on his jacket she said, "A very good friend of mine helped me with this today. Both the boutonniere and my hair."

Good friend? I thought. I didn't want to appear rude, or worse yet out of the loop, so instead of asking out loud, I just caught BJ's eyes and gave her an inquisitive look.

"Yeah, she left the hospital a day early just to help me," she continued as she winked at me.

Elizabeth? Wow. Wait, she was here? I opened the front door and watched BJ and Darren walk out together, notic-ing BJ had a little pep back in her step. That wasn't all I noticed. *Truck*, I said to myself as I looked at his big black Ford with shiny chrome detail. *Nice. No back seat*, I thought with a sense of relief. I watched as he opened the passenger's door for her. *Good move, dude.*

I smiled and waved as he opened his door. But before climbing inside, he looked up over the roof of his truck and said, "Don't worry, Dr. Jackson. I'll take care of my stitches tonight."

Ok, he's not so bad, I thought, chuckling to myself. *Glad he remembered my advice.*

Then BJ rolled down the window and hollered out to me, "Dad, one more thing. That friend is really looking forward to your awards ceremony tomorrow." She smiled a big smile, a happy smile, and rolled the window up as they drove away. In the living room, a small box, wrapped in bright white paper and tied with a white bow was sitting on the coffee table with a note that read:

Dad,

Nothing can replace our sweet Honey, but we talked it over on our shopping trip and thought you might need one of these.

 BJ

To my surprise, they had bought me an alarm clock.

The next day I didn't want to ask too many questions, even though I really did want the details of the banquet, of Darren, of how BJ was feeling inside after all of it. But, I remembered that my mom had always made herself available, but didn't pry. Even that time that I stayed in my room crying into my pillow for hours. She knew I had a broken heart, but she waited until my sixteen-year-old self was ready to tell her that my life was over because Sandy, an outgoing cheerleader I'd been dating, had decided to go to a college four states away. We guys think we aren't supposed to talk about things like broken hearts or feelings, so Mom never asked, she just baked brownies. When the smell drew me into the kitchen, there were two glasses of milk and two plates set out on the table. Between bites, I poured my heart out to her. That day, Mom, the milk, the brownies, melted all the pain away. Moms were magical like that. *But, are Dad's too*, I wondered.

I heard BJ's steps on the stairs. They were light and slow, not at all like her signature quick barreling that resembled rolling thunder. "I hung it right up when I got home," she said looking down at her silky blue dress. "And I thought I would wear this with it, what do you think?" In her hand was a silver shrug that shimmered with metallic thread. "I thought it might be cold in there."

"I think it looks fabulous. Was it cold last night?"

"No, not really." She paused for a moment, realizing what I was getting at. "Ok, Dad. The truth is that I thought covering my shoulders with this would be a little more daddy-daughter appropriate for big awards ceremony. More professional and grown up, well, you know."

I chuckled a bit as I smiled at her. Standing there in my tuxedo I looked at her with a faint smile, patting down my pockets as if to check for both my keys and my wallet. Then, I took in a deep breath and swallowed hard. *How could I accept this award?* I wondered. *I witnessed heroes in my ER daily, docs that were way better than me. Even Dr. Birchfield was more deserving.* But knowing that I could never let BJ down, I extended my elbow, "Shall we?"

"We shall," she said with a beaming smile.

When we arrived, the hotel ballroom was decked out with no expense spared. The tables were filled with frosted glass centerpieces, filled with white flowers of all kinds and tall sticks pointing out in all directions. They had to be four feet tall, each arrangement hundreds of dollars each. Dozens of candles shimmered, filling the room with an almost dream-state flicker. On the back half of the stage, a rather large jazz band played the tunes of some of the greats, Duke Ellington and Count Basie. My parents had both loved jazz, so the notes wrapped around my jangling nerves, injecting them with a sense of nostalgic comfort, the kind that only music and memories can provide.

I scanned the room of both familiar and unfamiliar faces. BJ caught my eyes searching the crowd and said, "Don't worry. She's coming."

"BJ, I wasn't—"

"Yes you were," she said with a telling grin. "And, I promise she will be here. She said she would never miss this." She wrapped her arm through mine and gave it a squeeze. "Man, this makes our banquet look so . . . so . . . high school-ish."

"Honey, I'm pretty sure your high school doesn't have one hundredth of the budget these guys do."

"Dr. Jackson," Dr. Birchfield said as he came over to shake my hand. Then, he pulled me in and gave me a bro hug. I was so stunned and surprised. Happily surprised.

"Dr. Birchfield," I replied with just as much enthusiasm. "This is my daughter. BJ, meet Dr. Birchfield. Dr. Birchfield, this is BJ, my one and only princess."

"Dr. Birchfield. What? No more Dr. Elohssa?" He said with a chuckle.

At that moment, I felt my face flush with embarrassment. Luckily, he never knew why we actually called him that. "Oh, that guy. No way, I saw you in action and I can assure you that Elohssa has nothing on you, Birchfield." I gave him a big smile and patted him on the back. "Matter of fact, I'll go to war with you anytime."

"Good to hear," Roberts, who had walked up at the end of that conversation, said jovially. "Because Dr. Birchfield has just accepted a job with us. Matter of fact, he's in line to take my shift when I retire next year."

"Retire?" I said shocked and a bit disappointed.

"Dad." BJ tugged on my arm and pulled me down as if she needed to whisper something in my ear. "Look who's here. I can't believe she made it." She pointed in a bit of a secretive fashion as not to get the attention of the others in our circle. Then under her breath I heard her say exactly what I was thinking, "Wow, she's beautiful."

There she stood. Elizabeth. Her red hair was piled atop her head, making her a few inches taller than usual, a single ringlet on either side framing her high cheekbones, her green eyes a perfect match to the emerald satin dress she wore. She was so beautiful, bruises, stitches, and all. Perhaps the most beautiful woman I'd ever laid eyes on.

"Well," BJ nudged me. "Don't just stand here with me. Go to her, Dad."

As I walked toward her, all the bodies parted like the red sea, and the noise of the conversations in the room seemed to fade away. At the end of that parted sea was a shimmering angel, dressed in the color of jewels. It was as if the band was playing a tune just for us. As I approached her the first words out of her mouth were, "In Your Own Sweet Way."

I stopped dead in my tracks. "Wait, you know this tune?"

"Of course, it's written by Dave Brubeck, but nobody plays it like Miles Davis. I grew up on this stuff," she said with a smile, followed by a sharp grimace as she shifted her weight. it was obvious that she was fighting back the pain, just standing there.

A bit presumptuously, I extended my elbow. "May I?"

Without missing a beat, she took my arm and I led her to a table at the front which was reserved for our group. "I'll be right back," I said as I got her settled into a chair. "Roberts," I said. "Where is he?"

"He's coming," Elizabeth said, her eyes scanning the room. "Mary asked him to come as her plus one. Don't worry, nobody told him anything," she finished, a knowing smile on her lips.

The beginning of the awards ceremony was your usual boring stuff. All the thank-yous, sponsor recognitions, and so forth. I sat there looking around the table, thinking about how strong the people seated around me were. Then they called it out, "And tonight, we're here to honor a special man, a doctor that . . ."

I couldn't remember a thing they said after that. My heart was pounding and all of a sudden, I was nervous about what was about to happen. While it had never been done before, I'd jumped through all the necessary hoops to be sure that my actions wouldn't be met with any resistance. I stood up, ran my hands down the front of my tuxedo jacket, took a deep breath and started to walk towards the stage.

Everyone was clapping, and the staff from both the St. Mary's, my current hospital, and Methodist, my former hospital, were standing and cheering. As the crowd settled down, I could hear the sound of a few whispers. While I couldn't hear what they were saying, I could only imagine. *What's he doing up there? He's nothing special. Besides, didn't his wife just die? Why is he even here? After all, he had the terrorist right in front of him and missed all the clues.*

I blinked the thoughts away, swallowed hard, and reached in my pocket for my speech. While I knew what I wanted to say, I'd actually written it all out while BJ was at the banquet. With humility in my heart and a healthy dose of fear of public speaking I began . . .

"Ladies and gentleman, I stand before you in both humility and gratitude. As everyone in this room knows, the emergency room is a special place. A place where tragic endings are often overshadowed by the ongoing miracles that tend to take permanent residency within our memories. The last few days," I continued, "have taught us that we must be vigilant. That any normal shift can quickly turn into your worst nightmare." The room had filled with a few glassy eyes, some holding back the tears, while others letting them flow freely.

"But it's within those nightmares that we often find out who we really are, and what our department is made of. People can surprise you beyond your wildest dreams. Some are like sponges, they absorb it all. They see each case as a challenge for learning and expanding upon that knowledge. Then, when we all least expect it, that sponge is squeezed, and the knowledge freely flows. It's been stored within the sponge so long and so well, that it flows out without any second guesses, without nerves, and with pure confidence. I dare say that this type of personality is so rare that it's often missed. Why? Because the sponge doesn't need any recognition. They're not there to shine like a star. Instead, they're happy just being who they were designed to be, the clean-up crew, the absorber, the person who's so dependable that at times they are often taken for granted."

I looked over at BJ and Elizabeth. BJ's hand was delicately pressed against her mouth as if she were holding back the tears, and Elizabeth met my eyes, giving me an encouraging smile as if to say, *Go on.* `

"Many of you know that this award comes with a monetary prize of $100,000. Tonight, it is my privilege to pass this award on to the biggest sponge I know, a future recipient of this award." I caught Mary and Jennifer looking at each other with wide eyes and then back at me. They seemed to be hanging on my every word. "This sponge may not have his American Boards yet, but I have no doubt that this money, along with the agreement from UT Southwestern to accept him into their medical program, will help propel my friend and colleague, Sergei Molonkov."

I outstretched one arm as if to announce him to the world, and I couldn't help noticing the tears of surprise and gratitude in Sergei's eyes. Everyone in the room was on their feet, cheering him on, but he was overcome with excitement and as a result, had trouble standing. But Jarrod ran over and lifted him out of the chair and into a giant bear hug. I was half expecting Jarrod to put him up on his shoulder. Mary pointed toward the stage, poking the air, again and again, encouraging Sergei to come shake my hand. As he approached me, he outstretched his arm towards mine and embraced me in a strong and lasting hug.

After a little encouragement, Sergei approached the microphone. "Sponge, huh?" He said, gaining a laugh from the audience, who also appreciated the metaphor. "Well, Dr. Jackson, there is nobody I would rather soak up knowledge from."

Then the crowd roared again.

That night I offered to drive Elizabeth home. Knowing my BMW couldn't hold three passengers, Mary and Jennifer, who'd come together, offered to drop BJ off. Elizabeth looked exhausted and a bit overcome by all the excitement, but still stunningly beautiful nonetheless. As I drove into her quaint and quiet neighborhood, I thought about how normal it seemed. Nothing flashy, just rows of houses filled with hard working people inside. Opening the door for her was the easy part but helping her get out of the car without touching her back or the stitched up and bruised parts of her arms, was quite a challenge. BJ watched carefully, cringing with every move Elizabeth made.

I walked her to the door, using her frail disposition as an excuse to hold her hand. I noticed how soft it was, how small, and gentle it felt. I also couldn't help but think about how perfectly her hand fit inside mine. As a slight breeze passed, the scent of jasmine floated from her neck to just under my nose. She put the key in the lock to open her front door and then turned toward me. I wanted so badly to reach up and cradle her head in my hands, to kiss her good night.

I stared at her for a moment, intoxicated by her emerald eyes. "Thank you. It means so much to me that you were there tonight."

"I wouldn't have missed it," she said, not breaking away from the lock our eyes had become entangled in.

"Can I do anything before I go?" I asked, secretly wanting her to reply with a request.

"No," she replied slowly. "I'm fine." Then, breaking our stare to look down for a moment she said, "Oh, I almost forgot." Reaching in her small silver clutch she pulled out a white knight and placed it in my hand. My mouth opened as I looked at her wordlessly.

"Checkmate," she said, her lips curving into a small smile as she walked inside, her seductive emerald eyes beckoning me to follow.

KNOW YOUR MOVES

 THE PAWN

 THE ROOK

 THE KNIGHT

 THE QUEEN

 THE BISHOP

 THE KING

ACKNOWLEDGEMENTS

A special thank you to the most amazing editor, Jennifer Banash. You believed in this project and this series and continue to give so much to its success. It was also a huge honor to stand inside the emergency room with Dr. Kevin Allen and flush out some of the most challenging scenes. No book is completed without a final proofer. Thank you Jennifer Burgess for catching all the things we missed. And last, but certainly not least, a huge thank you to Casey Fritz for such an eye-catching, story-appropriate cover design and Emily at Albatross Design for the layout of each page. You two are a force to be reckoned with and we look forward to many more years and books to come.

ABOUT THE AUTHOR

Judy G. Walters is a nom de plume for a married couple, one of whom is a board certified physician, and the other a CEO in the healthcare arena. They have taken their extensive medical experience, along with the love of chess and brought them together for your enjoyment.

A DOZEN QUESTIONS
FOR YOU AND YOUR BOOK CLUB
TO PONDER

1. Which character could you relate to the most?

2. Which medical case was the most memorable?

3. Did reading the book impact your mood? If yes, how so?

4. Did you sympathize with Jaqueline or despise her?

5. Did you like the chess game or find it distracting?

6. Which twist did you not see coming?

7. This book is filled with moral ambiguity. Did that make you feel uncomfortable?

8. Which characters do you hope to see developed in the series?

9. What did you think of the writing style?

10. Who do you most want to read this book?

11. Would you want to read another book by this author?

12. Could you see this being a television or on-demand series?